Nobody's *Prince* Charming

Aimee Nicole Walker

Nobody's Prince Charming (Road to Blissville, #3)
Copyright © 2018 Aimee Nicole Walker

aimeenicolewalker@blogspot.com

ISBN: 978-1-948273-04-6

Cover photograph © Wander Aguiar—www.wanderaguiar.com
Cover art © Jay Aheer of Simply Defined Art—www.simplydefinedart.com

Editing provided by Miranda Vescio of V8 Editing and Proofreading—www.facebook.com/V8Editing/

Proofreading provided by Judy Zweifel of Judy's Proofreading—www.judysproofreading.com

Interior Design and Formatting provided by Stacey Blake of Champagne Book Design—www.champagnebookdesign.com

Copyright and Trademark Acknowledgments

Dedication

To my Whitney,

Fierce, loving, and independent. I am so proud to be your mother.

Chapter One

Darren McCoy

ONCE UPON A TIME, A FABULOUS GAY PRINCE MOVED TO THE tiny castle town of Blissville to help care for the ailing king so that the older man could live in his castle for as long as his health permitted. The evil Duke and Duchess of Goodville were eager to shove the old king in a home for aging monarchs, but the dashing young prince joined forces with the king to thwart their attempt to take the crown.

"Dare, maybe you should stay home today. It looks pretty slick out there," my grandpa, Ralph, said shakily. "I don't want my best boy to get hurt."

I briefly closed my eyes and wished I could spend the day with him. I thought of all the snowy days I stayed at his house when school was canceled due to severe snow or ice storms. We played card games or board games and drank hot chocolate. Grandpa made grilled cheese and tomato soup for lunch because it was my favorite then we watched The Price is Right and soap operas or cartoons until my mom or dad came to pick me up. I'd give anything to turn the clock back to simpler times when Grandpa was vibrant and healthy, and I was oblivious to the fact that our time with the people we loved was limited.

Okay, you've figured out by now this isn't really a fairy tale, but if it were, I would be the dashing gay prince and my grandpa would be the king. That meant that my parents were the evil, callous duke and duchess ready to throw my grandpa into Shady Acres, or whatever "the home" was called. I'd toured that place with Grandpa and saw the light leave his eyes. Knowing he wouldn't live long inside those walls, I moved in to look after him. Of course, I made it seem like I needed his help and not the other way around.

Grandpa thought I was working two jobs to pay off my college debt, which was partially true, instead of using the money to pay for his companions and private nurses that stopped in several times a week to help him bathe and check over his vitals. Medicare and his supplemental policy only paid for so much, very little to be honest, and I picked up the leftover balances, including his life-saving medicine.

"I wish I could stay home with you, Grandpa, but Josh needs me today. It's going to be busy at the salon with everyone using the gift certificates they received for Christmas. There's no better way to kick off the year than with a new hairstyle, manicure, pedicure, or a massage."

"If you say so." I could hear the frown in his voice.

Grandpa slumped a little further in his recliner by the big picture window where he watched the activity on our street in comfort. I looked forward to spring and summer when he could sit in our rocking chairs on the front porch, but his recliner would do until then.

"Don't pout," I said teasingly. "Maren will be here in a little bit to hang out with you. Wendy or Jill will be stopping by for bath time." I waggled my eyebrows at him suggestively, but he waved me off. It was better for him to be irritated with me than upset for his loss of dignity. "Jamal from Meals on Wheels is coming at noon to deliver lunch. You'll have a lot of company until I get home this evening. I'm not working at O'Dell's tonight."

I'd grown to hate working at the furniture store as one of their in-house interior designers, but it was the only place I could use my degree. I just never felt like I fit in there and knew that I never would.

"I'd rather spend time with you."

God, it was like a dagger to the heart. Why couldn't I just win the lottery so that I didn't have to work so many jobs? How much longer did I even have with him? He looked more frail every day. Hell, he even stopped pretending he could take care of himself. I wasn't ready to let him go.

I left the kitchen and squatted down beside his recliner in the small living room. "I'd much rather spend the day with you too, Grandpa. Playing cards with you would be an awesome way to spend a snowy day."

"But you've got obligations." Did he mean himself? Was he more aware of what was going on than I realized?

"I do," I agreed. "I wouldn't change a single thing about my life." Not regarding him, anyway. "I'm going to walk the few blocks to the salon rather than drive. I think it would be safer."

"Bundle up, Dare. Don't skip on the hat just because you don't want to mess up your hair."

"Yes, sir."

The walk to Curl Up and Dye wasn't too treacherous since a layer of snow had fallen to cover the slick, icy sidewalks. It was so cold that

I only saw a few kids playing in the snow to celebrate their extra day of freedom. I figured inside the houses, parents wept for the loss of freedom they'd expected to have that day.

The sidewalk in front of the salon was the only clear one I encountered because Josh Roman-Wyatt knew damn well that people didn't give up their hair appointments in his salon for anything less than the death of an immediate family member. He, or his husband, must've arrived at least an hour early to clean off the sidewalks and steps leading up to both entrances to Curl Up and Dye. It was possible they hired a company to handle snow removal, but I doubted it since Josh was such a control freak.

"Good morning," I said to Josh when I came through the rear entrance that led into a small kitchenette. My boss had both hands wrapped around a coffee cup to warm them. His red cheeks and nose told me that he was the one shoveling snow and salting the pavements around the salon. The grand old home used to act as Josh's private residence and his business. He and Gabe bought a new house and dedicated the second floor of this one to expanding the massage services.

"Who goes there?" Josh asked dramatically, squinting to see beneath all the layers of outdoor gear I wore. I had dressed in one of those puffy down coats that dwarfed my body, a fucking knit hat, and wrapped a scarf around my head so that only my eyes were visible.

"It is I, the court jester," I replied, keeping with my fairy-tale-kingdom theme from earlier in the day. "At your service." I dipped into a flamboyant bow.

"Oh, Dare!" Josh said excitedly. "I'm happy you're here before everyone else. I'd like to talk—"

His words cut off when the back door opened again. I knew without looking who had arrived because every hair follicle on my body came to life and goose bumps pebbled my skin.

"Good morning, Wren," Josh said cheerily. "Coffee?"

Wren grunted in response as he walked by both of us on his way to the coat closet.

Josh just shrugged and refocused his attention on me. "As I was saying, I'd like to talk to you about your future here at Curl Up and Dye."

"Are you firing me? If so, please do it now before I peel myself out of these winter clothes."

"Of course not," Josh said, dismissing the thought with a wave of his hand. "I wanted to promote you to salon manager. You're a real asset to the team and capable of doing more than reception-ist duties. It would mean more hours and longer days, but maybe it would be enough for you to get away from O'Dell's. I know that you're not happy there, but I understand if you'd rather focus on pursuing design work so you can establish your own design compa-ny someday."

"Oh wow!" I said, thrilled that Josh was happy with the work I did for him. "I'm truly flattered."

"It would come with a pay raise, but I'm not sure it would be enough to replace your secondary income," Josh told me. "Are you willing to consider it?"

"Secondary income?" Wren asked when he returned to the kitchen. Josh pulled Wren's favorite mug off the rack next to the cof-fee pot. "Thanks."

I could tell Josh was waiting for Wren to take his butch coffee to his station so that we could finish our conversation in private. Instead of leaving us alone, Wren turned around and leaned his hot ass against the counter and settled in like he was part of the conver-sation. The mysterious, broody man avoided conversation like the plague, so you can imagine my confusion right about then.

"Go take that stuff off," Wren said after he sipped the hot, strong brew. "I can't take you seriously when you're dressed like the little brother in *A Christmas Story*. Andy or something."

"Randy," Josh and I said at once.

"Whoever," Wren said dismissively.

"You're such an ass," I told him but stomped to the closet anyway.

When I returned to the kitchen, Wren was making my coffee for me. I should've been happy that he was doing something so thoughtful, but it only made me mad.

"What are you doing?" I asked bitterly. *Why pretend he cares about my happiness now?*

"Making you a cup of coffee," Wren replied in a voice that questioned if I was too dumb to live. At least he hadn't added, "What does it look like?" I would've launched myself onto his back and grabbed two fistfuls of his long, luxurious dark hair and...kissed him until he begged me to forgive him for being such an asshole.

My bitterness faded until all I felt was self-loathing that I continued to let the man affect me so strongly. I opened my mouth to respond, but no words came out. I snapped my lips closed again.

"That's a first," Wren said, grinning crookedly.

See, he didn't mean to sound like a dickhead, and he was telling the truth. I was the kind of person who started talking the minute I hit the salon and didn't stop until I left. But you know what? It was my happy place where people accepted and loved me for who I was. Yes, my grandpa loved me unconditionally, but seeing his continued failing health broke my heart. I needed my job at Curl Up and Dye to remember that life is more than gut-wrenching heartbreak. No one would know my deep sorrow by the way I acted at work. They saw a vivacious man who laughed, joked, and smiled like he didn't have a care in the world. That's exactly the way I wanted it.

"My brain is still half-frozen," I said, choosing not to engage Wren in a battle of wits that morning.

"What's this about a second job?" he asked like he had the right.

"I'm a go-go boy at Drinks and Twinks," I stated calmly. Okay, all systems were a go for battle.

Josh turned and spat his coffee into the sink. When he looked at me, his eyes were bulging out of his head. He once gave me some pointers about earning Wren's affection. He'd recognized some of Wren's standoffish behavior since he used to act the same way with the man he later married. It was something like: be honest, be patient, and don't play games. I had taken Josh's advice, I had vowed to stop trying to make Wren jealous, and even confronted the man about it. People would have varying opinions on whether I was successful, but to me, it was an epic failure never to be repeated. I had nothing to lose by poking the hornet's nest because I already knew I could survive the sting.

"Drinks and Twinks?" Oh dear God, the deep, scratchy timbre of his voice made my dick instantly hard. I'd heard that same voice the one and only time I'd been brave enough to try to tame the beast.

"It's a new club," I said nonchalantly. "It's all the rage, and I enjoy working there. I get to dance in a cage wearing sexy, little, barely-there underwear."

"Cages?" Wren asked. "Barely-there underwear?"

"Oh fuck," Josh muttered, looking back and forth between us like he needed to intervene.

"Oh yeah," I said, stretching the words out long and sexy. "The see-through ones are a real crowd pleaser, so I need to keep things—"

"I'm out of here," Josh said holding up a hand to stop me long enough for him to escape. "You're on your own now. I have two babies at home that need both their fathers. I can't be caught up in this." He gestured between Wren and me. "If you survive this little conversation, then we'll chat more about your promotion."

Neither of us acknowledged him. Wren was breathing hard like a bull, and I knew fucking well he was busy imagining what I looked like in skimpy underwear, or maybe nothing at all. My heart pounded hard in my chest as I waited to see what happened next. I should've stopped while I could, but I was too revved up to just go to my desk and power up my computer to start the day.

"Where were we?" Wren said once we were alone again.

"I was telling you about how I keep my boys smooth as a baby's butt so that they look amazing in mesh undies," I said.

"Cut the crap," Wren snarled.

"You doubt that I keep my balls smooth?" Did he want to see? Fuck, I wanted to show him.

"That I don't doubt at all. It's the go-go dancer part. I just don't see you shaking your ass in a giant, gilded birdcage."

"Birdcage?" I scoffed. "Honey, these are industrial metal. Fierce and sexy." I lowered my voice and leaned closer. "I don't just shake my ass."

Wren narrowed his eyes and crossed one leg in front of the other. *That's right, try and hide how you respond to the images.* "What does that mean?"

It was cruel and unkind, but I couldn't seem to stop myself from goading him. It was like I wanted to see what happened once I pushed him past his breaking point. I came close once, and I wanted to do it again, but instead of stopping at the precipice, I wanted to shove us both right over the edge.

"I give private dances too," I said, loving the way his eyes widened in shock. "Those out-of-town, closeted businessmen pay extremely well and—"

"Not another fucking word out of you unless it's the truth," Wren gritted out. "Quit trying to push me, Dare. It's not going to work."

"Your hard-on says differently."

"My dick isn't in charge," he refuted. "Tell me the truth about why you work two jobs." His voice sounded gruff, but his eyes showed concern.

I tried to find another witty comeback, but my snark eluded me. I'd carried this staggering weight on my shoulders for more than a year, and here was someone who seemed worried about me, when I was usually the one doing all the worrying. I cracked beneath

Wren's intense stare. One minute I'm trying to seduce him, the next I'm crying against his massive chest, pouring my heart out about my grandfather. Wren stiffened in shock at first. He wasn't sure what to do with his hands and patted my shoulder awkwardly. Wren must've suspended his determination to hold me at bay, even if temporarily, because his strong arms held me tight against his chest.

"Just breathe, Dare. It's going to be okay."

"I'm damned if I do and damned if I don't, Wren."

"What do you mean?"

"He used to supplement his retirement and social security by renting out the apartment over the garage, but he couldn't physically maintain the property. It needs a lot of repairs before I can rent it out again," I explained. "Those repairs cost a lot of money that I don't have. If I could afford to fix up the apartment, I could just work one job and spend more time with Grandpa. I have two jobs to try and save money for those repairs, but then I end up spending a big chunk of the extra money making sure Grandpa has a companion to keep an eye on him while I work the extra hours."

"Your parents aren't willing to help you?" Wren asked softly. "Not even sit with him in the evenings?"

"Their solution is for him to move into a nursing home. They don't care that he'd be miserable and would lose his will to live. Grandpa means everything to me, Wren. I can't do that to him."

"I understand," Wren said, wiping the tears from my face. For a big guy, he sure had a gentle touch. "Tell me what kind of repairs the apartment needs? Does it have heat, electricity, and running water?"

"Yes, but—"

"It's just cosmetic issues then. How much would you charge for rent?"

"I have no idea how much to charge for a studio apartment that never advanced beyond the seventies."

"How's five hundred a month sound? Would that help?"

"Do you know someone who'd be interested?" I asked hopefully.

"It just so happens that I know a guy who's looking to rent a one-bedroom apartment closer to work. What about the garage? How big is it and does the tenant get to use it?"

I narrowed my eyes. Wren surely didn't mean himself, did he? "It's a three-car garage and is mostly empty except for my grandpa's tools. He used to own a repair garage here in town but retired back in the nineties. He sold a lot of tools and equipment to the new owner and only kept the ones that had sentimental value. Grandpa even has a story to go with each one of them."

"I bet," Wren said, smiling gently. "Can I come by tonight and look at the apartment?"

"Wren, you don't have to do this."

"I know that I don't *have* to, but I want to. I really would like to live closer, especially on mornings like this, and I don't care if the wallpaper is outdated or the carpet needs replaced. I need a roof over my head, heat, water that also heats, and a place to stash my baby."

"Your baby?"

"If this works out you'll get to see her."

"*Her?*"

"Can you just answer my question?" Wren asked. "Are you free to show me the apartment tonight?"

I felt lighter than I had in months, and I should've shown my appreciation by giving Wren a straight answer. Instead, I tipped my head to the side and said, "Well, I need to give a few lap dances first, then I—" My voice hit a high-pitched note and squeaked to a stop when Wren grabbed both my ass cheeks with his big, strong hands. "Yes!" I moaned, not so much in answer, but because his manhandling brought me tighter against his erection.

"Oh no," Wren said, grabbing my hips and gently pushing me back so that our hard-ons were no longer pressed against each other. "Not here."

"Not ever," I finished for him dryly. I saw and felt how much

Wren wanted me, but he was still fighting it. I'd blown a few of Josh's rules already, but just maybe I could give patience a try. "You can come by after work if you want."

"It's a plan," Wren said then walked away without another word.

I stood in the kitchenette for a few more minutes to get my composure together. As I walked by Josh's station on my way to the front of the salon, I said, "I accept your generous offer." It didn't matter what he had in mind; I was truly grateful. For the first time in a long time, I had hope that things were finally looking up for Grandpa and me.

Chapter Two

Wren Davison

THE FIRST WORKDAY OF THE YEAR WAS EVERYTHING I expected it would be—busy, fun, and frustrating. The busy and fun parts helped distract me from the person who had frustrated me since my first day working at the salon.

Dare and I started working at Curl Up and Dye on the same day a little over a year ago. Since then, I've been on a never-ending roller-coaster ride. The first thing that caught my eye about Dare was his looks. I wanted to pretend that I was some enlightened, modern man but that would be a bullshit lie. I took one look at his pouty lips and pert ass and immediately started having ideas about what I could do with them. I've found many sets of lips and ass cheeks attractive before and could easily walk away from them without a backward glance, but his physical beauty wasn't what drew me to him time and time again like a moth to a flame.

Dare's inner beauty shone through his eyes and joy burst from him through his laughter. His desire to make everyone happy spoke volumes about his character. Those were the reasons I could hardly look away from him. He was everything I wasn't—charismatic, friendly, and good. Things went to hell when I touched them, people got hurt, and I couldn't live with myself if I dragged Dare down into the gutter with me, so I did my best to ignore his flirting and blatant attempts at making me jealous. I somehow found the strength to call a halt to his sweet seduction before things went too far, but his heartbroken sobs against my chest moved me in ways I never thought possible.

I didn't believe in love. I didn't believe in fairy tales. I didn't believe that two people could commit themselves to each other for the rest of their lives, so why pretend? I lived by simple rules, the first three being: fast cars, freedom, and hard fucking. That sounded like the opposite of what a person would say about themselves on a dating site, but I wasn't looking for dates. I didn't want a boyfriend. If I did, I wouldn't waste my time on one of those sites. I'd claim what Dare wanted so badly to give me. At first, he was probably captivated by my bad boy looks. I was used to it and would normally take advantage of the situation, but that would've been a violation of rule number four: never eat where you work. Oh, I wanted to gobble Dare up from head to toe then do it all over again, but he wasn't for me.

Dare needed way more than I could give him, and I wasn't talking about common decency either. He was the hearts and flowers, movie-date-nights, and take-home-to-your-mama kind of guy. I wasn't interested in two of those things, and the other one could never happen. *Damn, she would've loved him though.* I'd learned the hard way that loving someone could lead to utter devastation when they left you behind. The best way to avoid that was by never allowing someone close enough to hurt you. I had never met anyone who made me question my choices until Dare. That angered me almost as much as my obsession with him did.

For his own good, I needed to push Dare away, not pull him closer. So why then did I insist on knowing the truth that morning in the kitchenette? Why not just let him spin his wild tales about dancing in cages and giving lap dances to horny, closeted men. Fuck, I was equal parts fascinated and horrified at the thought. I was no prude, I'd seen my fair share of dancing go-go boys, and I'd even let a few take a ride on my lap, but Dare was different. I just didn't want to think about why that was. I also couldn't figure out why solving his problems had become my number one priority, but it was hard to feel mad when I saw how much happier Dare seemed.

Sexy, kindhearted, and fuckable were traits that were already hard to resist, but the kind of devotion Dare had for his grandfather was breathtakingly beautiful. It was like I was seeing him in a new light, one that was almost too beautiful to view with the naked eye, but I couldn't seem to look away. Where was my brain when I volunteered to practically move in his backyard? It was one thing to resist him at work, but knowing he was within walking distance was going to be brutal.

I had just about talked myself out of it until I saw him wrapping himself up like a mummy at the end of his shift. I wasn't paying attention when I arrived that morning, but I realized at noon that his car wasn't at the salon. That explained why he'd wrapped his scarf around his head and neck until only his eyes peeked through the knitted layers.

Before I could stop myself, I said, "Why don't you just hang here for a few minutes and I'll drive you home. We're heading to the same place."

"Oh, um…" I could tell he was eager to get home to check on his grandpa.

"I won't be much longer. I just need to clean up my station." I remote started my truck then left him in the kitchenette while I cleaned my station. I reminded myself to behave and keep my hands to myself and demanded that I not kiss his pouty lips as I swept up the last bit of hair beneath my chair.

When I returned to the kitchenette, Dare looked as if he were afraid to believe in me. I wondered if maybe our backgrounds weren't that different after all.

"I just want you to know that I will not be upset if you change your mind, Wren." It was cute the way he tried to put me at ease.

"Dare, there's something you need to know about me." He nodded eagerly, biting his lip nervously as he waited. "Rule number five: I never say things I don't mean, and I don't do things I don't want to do."

"That's two different things," Dare said. "That should be rules five and six."

"They mean similar things, so they share a rule."

"Saying and doing aren't even close to the same thing," Dare argued. "It would make sense if it was: say what you mean and mean what you say. They could share a rule."

"They're my rules, and I'll categorize them as I see fit."

"Well," Dare said huffily. Then he tipped his head to the side and studied me speculatively. "I'll let it drop if you tell me your first four rules. Not gonna lie, I kind of want to see if I can make you break them."

"Not a chance," I declared. His look said *we'll just see about that.* "Are we doing this or not?" Dare responded by waggling his brows. "Are we looking at the apartment or not?" I clarified.

"Rule number five: you say what you mean," Dare reminded me in a tone that made me want to turn him over my knee and spank his ass until it was cherry red. "Oh, I think I know that look."

"Stop talking and get in the truck." Damn, I sounded like an asshole. *Good, maybe he'll give up.* I walked out the back door and Dare could either come with me or not. Of course, the little shit followed me because he never gives up.

"Chester from Nevada City wore that same expression last week when he asked if I would lie across his lap so that he could paddle my naughty booty. I never thought of my butt as a naughty booty. Do you?"

I didn't answer him until we were both inside the warm cab of my truck. "It's the naughtiest kind of booty," I said between gritted teeth. Why bother lying when we both knew just how fascinated I was with his ass. I'd grabbed two handfuls of it on three occasions, and each incident was burned into my brain and relived when I stroked my cock to relieve the pressure in my sac.

Dare must've expected me to deny it because he stared at me for a few seconds without saying anything. That was two times now that I'd rendered him speechless. I liked it.

"But I know you didn't meet Chester from Nevada City at a place called Drinks and Twinks because it doesn't exist," I said smugly.

"Checking up on me, huh?" Dare asked, sounding mighty pleased with himself. "I think I got the name wrong."

"You got the name wrong?"

"I've only worked there a few weeks. I think it's Drunks and Twunks."

At this point, I could only shake my head. "You're not a go-go boy." Thank fuck because I couldn't stand the idea of anyone touching him.

"This is a big truck," Dare said, changing the subject. Where was he going with this? "I guess bigger bodies require bigger vehicles. Big hands," he said, nodding to my hands white-knuckling the steering wheel. "Big feet too."

"Yeah, Dare, I also have a big dick." I wanted to beat him to the punch.

"I was going to say heart, but I have to agree with your assessment also. I've never seen it or directly touched your dick, but I've felt it pressed against my stomach a few times."

"You have a big mouth," I said, shifting my truck in reverse.

"Mmmm. It works well on big dicks."

I nearly choked on my saliva. I'd set myself up for it, but Dare's boldness still somehow shocked me.

"Where to?" I asked, ignoring his remark and trying to keep my brain on navigating icy roads instead of wondering how hot and wet his mouth would feel working my cock.

Dare let it go, but I doubted my reprieve would last long. He gave directions to a tidy, two-story house a few blocks away from the salon. I understood why he chose to walk instead of drive that morning. It would've taken him longer to clean his car off than walk to work. I parked behind his light-blue car and shut the truck off.

From what I could see of the garage, it appeared to be in good structural shape. Of course, I couldn't see the condition of the shingles with six inches of snow covering the roof.

"The roof on the garage is metal like the one on the house," Dare said. "They're both in decent shape."

"Let's look inside," I told him.

"I have to run in and check on Grandpa and grab the keys. Do you want to stay here or come inside and meet him?"

"I'll say hello to your grandpa."

It's hard to say who was more surprised by my answer. I think Dare was just being polite and didn't expect me to accept his offer. I had every intention of saying that I'd wait in the truck. Once the words were out, I couldn't take them back without sounding like a dick.

A heatwave rolled out when Dare opened a door that led into a laundry room. "Grandpa likes it warm," he said, grinning sheepishly.

Warm? It was so hot that I couldn't breathe. How could Dare stand to live like that? I understood why after I followed him through the laundry room and kitchen to get to the living room. His grandfather dozed in his recliner while the evening news blared from the television. Dare tiptoed over to him and rearranged his blanket to cover his chest. I wished I had stayed in the truck when Dare placed a gentle kiss on his grandfather's forehead because I thought I might possibly choke on the lump of emotion lodged in my throat.

"He's sleeping pretty soundly, so we have enough time to explore the apartment before I need to make his dinner," Dare said when he returned to my side. He wouldn't look me in the eye. I wasn't sure if it was from embarrassment over the little scene I witnessed or if he felt as uncertain as I did about us living so close together.

I could tell by the way my heart raced that it was only a matter of time before I stopped fighting his cosmic pull and allowed myself to get sucked into his universe.

"Let me grab the key, and we'll check it out," he said. "Oh, maybe you want to look at it without me seeing your reactions."

"It can't be that bad," I told him. "Come on, Go-Go, show me the apartment."

"Okaaaaaay," Dare said.

I was grateful to step outside in the freezing cold to follow him to the detached garage. "Damn, I don't know how you handle the heat."

"I don't wear much," Dare said, but not in a provocative way. "I wear shorts and T-shirts right up until I have to leave the house. At night—"

"Yeah, I can figure that one out for myself."

"I was going to say that I turn on my ceiling fan, but I like the way your mind works better," Dare said mischievously. "Would you like me to confirm or deny if I wear my birthday suit to bed?"

"No." Some fantasies I wanted to keep to myself.

"Back to business," Dare said when we stepped up to the exterior garage door. I noticed that a bright light came on when we stepped within ten feet of the structure. At least I'd know if the little demon tried to sneak up on me at night. "One key unlocks both doors," Dare told me. "That could be a problem if we rented out the two spaces to different people, but..."

I tuned him out as soon as we stepped into the garage. It was a perfect space to store and work on my classic car and motorcycle. It was obvious that Dare's grandpa put a lot of love into the space.

"You should see your face right now," Dare said, snapping me back to the present. "I've only seen you look this stunned when you shoved me up against the door in the little mixing room and kissed me."

"You kissed me," I countered.

"Uh huh, keep telling yourself that, big guy. Follow me upstairs."

I trailed behind him wishing he'd taken off that ridiculous coat so I could at least ogle his ass. "You have a real selective memory, Go-Go."

"I have a perfect memory," Dare said. "You breezed into town making all the gals and guys quake with your broody mysteriousness. I was like that bouncy Chihuahua dog who just wanted to be your friend, but you slapped me down." Dare halted halfway up the stairs and turned suddenly to face me. I kept walking until we were at eye level. "Your words said that you weren't interested in me, but your eyes and actions said differently. Remember Trent?"

I groaned. How the hell could I forget the pompous doctor who moved to Blissville? The jackass showed up at the salon for a haircut, but only had eyes for Dare. Of course, none of us knew that the doctor used to date our boss until Dare took him to Thanksgiving dinner at Josh's house as his plus one. Trent thought it was funny to get a rise out of Josh's husband, but I didn't like that he used Dare to do it. I thought Dare really liked the guy, but it turned out he only dialed up the charm to make me jealous. It fucking worked too.

"If I recall correctly, I sought you out after work while you were cleaning the dye bowls out in the sink. I apologized for my behavior and said that I was done playing games and didn't want that doctor. I confessed that I only wanted you. Do you remember what happened next?" Dare asked.

"Of course," I said, but didn't expand.

"I do too. You scooped me up, pinned me against the door with my legs around your waist and kissed me until I nearly came in my pants. I also remember leaving a little love bite on your neck."

I wanted to refute him, but he was right. It was more than Dare taking Trent to Josh's for dinner that riled me up. The doctor sent him apology flowers then took him out to dinner to make up for his crass treatment. I also saw them together at the Christmas parade. Hearing that I was the one he wanted made both my ego and dick swell. I didn't think; I reacted. Like Dare, I almost *reacted* in my pants, but I crashed back down to reality before that happened. I'd set Dare back on his feet and apologized for manhandling him. I saw the hopefulness in his eyes for things to change between us and didn't have the heart to squash his fantasy right then, or even the next day when he touched the mark on my neck tenderly after he arrived at work. I had to fight the urge to touch the spot on my neck where I wore his mark for almost a week, just as I had to resist the desire for him to do it again.

"Dare, I told you..." My words drifted off when I saw the light dim in his eyes. I knew he was thinking about the morning I finally set him straight. I told him that I would never be the guy for him. I admitted my attraction but told him it could never go beyond that. Dare deserved a guy who could give him more than I could. It sounded cliché to say that it hurt me as much as it hurt him, but it did.

"I know, Wren. You don't have to tell me again about how 'it's not me; it's you.' I've replayed the whole 'you deserve better' spiel. We don't have to do it again. You're doing me a really big favor, and I don't want to repay that by making you feel uncomfortable."

Fuck! I could resist overtly sexual Dare, but not vulnerable Dare. I just wanted to tuck him up against my chest and protect him from the ugliness in the world, but I'd tried that before with horrific results. I couldn't let Dare get sucked into the vortex of fuckery that followed me everywhere. I'd much rather have him hate me than become another one of my casualties. I resisted the urge to cup his chin and rub my thumb over his pouty bottom lip.

"It's the best for both of us." *Believe it or not, Go-Go.*

Dare gave me a friendly smile, but the devilish twinkle was gone from his eyes. He turned back around and walked up the remaining steps until he reached the little landing in front of the door.

"Prepare yourself," Dare warned while unlocking the door.

"You're so dramatic," I said, moving around him to open the door. I reached inside the door and flipped the light switch. "Holy fuck!"

"I know," Dare said, fidgeting beside me. "Oh my God. I can't let you do this, Wren. It's too much to ask of anyone."

I looked around at the shaggy green carpet that matched the avocado-green appliances but clashed poorly with the orange Formica countertop. The walls were covered in fake wood paneling the same color as the kitchen cabinets, making it look dark and dingy. "Bedroom? Bathroom?" I asked.

"Through that door," Dare said, pointing his finger.

He didn't follow me, which was a good thing, because I didn't want him to see my reaction to the hideous bathroom. The entire space was covered in white tile with big orange flowers and green leaves stamped in the center of each one. The water turned on and heated fast, quicker than my current apartment in Cincinnati. The bedroom was more of the same paneling and shaggy green carpet, but it was a decent size that could easily fit my bed and dresser.

Dare didn't meet my gaze when I returned to the living room. I checked the thermostat and heard the heat rattle on. The apartment was the ugliest thing I ever saw, but it was air tight, warm, and had good water.

"I'll take it."

That ugly room became the most beautiful space when Dare turned that megawatt smile on me. If I didn't watch it, I'd be the one creeping across the yard to get to him. Hopefully his grandpa had a shotgun and could keep us both in check.

Chapter Three

Dave

I WAS NEVER SO HAPPY TO GIVE A TWO-WEEK NOTICE AS I was to Betty O'Dell the night after Wren gave me his first month's rent. Betty wasn't my problem, neither was her husband or daughter, Aaron and Claire. The three of them had always been good to me, but her two sons, David and Ethan, were not my biggest fans. Then again, I started to believe that one, or maybe both, were bigger fans than they would like to be. It was my experience that the more homophobic someone was, the more likely they were a closet case. I would not be sticking around to urge either of them out into the light of day. They could stay nestled in the safety of their alphabet family. Get it? Aaron, Betty, Claire, David, and Ethan. Yes, they did it on purpose.

Betty was kind when I gave her the news and even seemed sad

that I was leaving them. Aaron and Claire were mostly indifferent, but it made David and Ethan feel bolder about humiliating me in front of customers or the other employees. I told myself that I could buck it up long enough to work out my notice so that I didn't give them another reason to belittle me, but I was ready to commit murder just a few days into the two-week notice.

"He's light in the loafers but a good designer," Ethan had told a customer the previous night. *Light in the loafers?* Um, the fifties are calling, and they want their homophobic phrases back. He didn't even bother to lower his voice so that I wouldn't hear him like he'd done the other times. When I turned to face him, he and the male client were giving me the once-over. I recognized what I saw in their eyes, and it wasn't disgust. Of course, later they'd be disgusted that they weren't disgusted, if you know what I mean. That wasn't the only occasion that David or Ethan insulted me. They tried to find any opportunity to work the words fairy or fruit into a conversation. They disgusted me.

I was too stunned to say anything after the latest insult, but I stewed over it all night long, tossing and turning while I thought about what to do. It was clear that I would need to rescind my notice and quit on the spot, but I worried about how to handle it. While I thought Aaron and Betty would be horrified over their sons' actions, I knew that blood was thicker than water. Still, they were setting themselves up for a civil lawsuit if they didn't get their sons under control. I suspected that they said inappropriate things to the female designers too, but they never admitted as much to me. It was just a feeling I would get when I saw how uncomfortable the ladies were around them sometimes.

I didn't fall asleep until almost dawn, so I was looking haggard as fuck when I showed up at the salon for my shift. Wren did a double take and intercepted me before I could reach my desk.

"Hey, is everything okay?" His worried voice warmed the chill that had permeated my bones that not even Grandpa's sauna-like temperatures could chase away.

I briefly closed my eyes and released a long, shaky breath. I had vowed to stop flirting with him since he was helping me out and assured myself that my little crush would fade with time. If he kept it up, I'd fall head over heels in love with the man. It was obvious that he didn't *want* to want me, so I needed to cling to my resolve. "Don't do that, Wren."

"Do what? Be kind?" He looked truly confused.

Make me love you. I dug deep for a sassy comeback, but I was just too damned tired, and the truth would freak him out and send him running. I shook my head and smiled crookedly at him. "Ignore me. I'm just tired."

Wren scowled at me through narrowed eyes. "Are you sure? Is your grandpa okay?"

Do not fall in love with him. Do not fall in love with him.

"He's doing great. He was eating the oatmeal I made him and watching one of those shopping networks. Hopefully, Maren will arrive before he can buy another kitchen gadget that I'll never use." The thought made me smile and some of my sadness dissipated.

"If it's okay with you, I'd like to start moving some of my stuff tonight. I can do the bigger pieces this weekend, but I'd like to get a jumpstart so I can have a lazy day on Sunday." I always felt an undercurrent of energy radiating from Wren and doubted he knew the meaning of lazy.

"You can move in anytime," I assured him. "Can I help you with anything?" A few days ago, I would've offered to help set up his bed, or mess it up. I would've batted my eyelashes and pushed my lips out suggestively to make it clear that I was offering to release the pressure in his balls. This was a new year, and dare I say, a new me. *Ugh!*

The changes didn't go unnoticed by Wren either. "Are you sick?"

"No," I snorted. I could tell he wanted to know more, but he didn't push. I offered another smile before continuing to my desk.

Of course, it was too much to ask for a smooth day at the salon after a short night of sleep. It started off with massive cancellations due to a flu outbreak, but those empty slots were quickly filled by people with DIY hair disasters. I mean, I thought I'd seen it all, but I was so wrong.

By late afternoon, things seemed to calm down enough for me to grab a cup of coffee and a few minutes of quiet. Earlier, I'd taken a whopping five-minute lunch break to eat the pizza Josh had delivered for us.

"Was there a full moon last night?" Meredith asked when she joined me in the kitchenette. Meredith, Josh, and Wren each had two disasters to fix, while the rest of the stylists had one. Mere shook her head as she stirred a bit of honey into her chamomile tea. "I don't get it."

"I think it's all those videos people are watching on social media," I replied. "I've seen everything from people dying their hair with Nutella to cutting it with fire and knives. I think people are seeing these videos and thinking they can do it too."

"What they don't see is the years of experience it takes to pull it off, or the trial and error until the stylist can perfect the color technique," Meredith said. "Wait, did you say fire and knives?"

"Swords, really."

"What? Show me?"

"I don't know, Mere," I teased. "I don't think Josh will want you trying this out on salon clients."

"Oh, baby doll, I'd try it on Harley first," she said. I loved the look of joy on her face at just the mention of her husband's name.

I pulled up my history on YouTube and showed Meredith the video of the guy setting people's hair on fire before he sliced through it with a short sword. It was horrifying and fascinating at the same time.

"People are crazy," Mere said. "One false move and you're burned at best."

"Dead at worst," I added.

Heather poked her head into the kitchenette. "We got another walk-in disaster. Do you have time to fix it?"

"Yeah," Meredith said. "I'll be right there." She gave me a quick peck on the cheek and headed back into the wild.

I was too anxious to sit there and drink my coffee so I went into the supply room, which was little more than a large closet, to double-check the inventory of shampoos, conditioners, and styling products. I hadn't been in there long when I felt *his* presence. I closed my eyes and inhaled shallow breaths through my nose. *Resist, Dare.*

"Wanting to try this room on for size too?" I asked. *Damn!* That one just slipped out before I could stop it.

A low chuckle rumbled from Wren's chest. "That's a little better."

My heart raced when I looked at him over my shoulder and caught him checking out my ass. *Maybe we could fuck this out of our system and move on.* I was just about to suggest it when I recalled everything I had on the line. "Did you need something, Wren?" I started to reach for the shampoo and conditioner he preferred to use on his clients.

"I'm not here for supplies," he said.

I turned slowly to face him. "Then why did you come?" I swallowed hard when his nostrils flared. Neither of us had come yet—well, not together anyway. "I mean, um, what do you need?" That wasn't much better.

"I need to know who, or what, dimmed your sparkle today?" Wren stepped further inside the room and shut the door behind him. "I'm not leaving here until I get the truth out of you."

"What techniques will you use to make me talk?" *I couldn't help myself. I was bad, so very bad.*

Wren didn't stop moving forward until I was sandwiched between the shelves and his hard body. I could see, and feel, how much Wren liked my flirting, so why the fuck did he fight it so strongly? "You're going to tell me because you'll feel better afterward. Maybe I

26

can help you."

"I'm not helpless, Wren." I tipped my chin up defiantly. "There's no need for you to ride up on your steed to save me." It seemed I couldn't stop my fairy-tale references.

"I never said you were helpless or needed saving, Dare."

A million sassy replies flooded my brain, but I repressed them. "You've helped me enough already." I lowered my head because the concern and tenderness in his amber eyes weakened me and made me crave things I would never have with him.

Wren gently placed his hands on both sides of my neck and tipped my chin up with his thumbs. "Tell me."

For the second time that week, I unleashed my emotions on Wren. I didn't cry this time, because those assholes were not worth my tears. He stiffened when I told him about Ethan's remark. "I'm going to go in there tonight to rescind my notice. I don't even care about the money or the fact that they could trash my reputation to potential employers."

"That little fucker needs to be put in his place," Wren snarled. His body had gone completely rigid, and I found myself wanting to comfort him. I knew what would happen if I wrapped my arms around his shoulders and leaned into him, and it wouldn't matter to me that there was a salon full of people.

I patted his chest instead, not allowing my hands to linger and explore his hard pectoral muscles. "I'll tell Betty and Aaron tonight about it and walk out of there with my head held high." Wren wasn't appeased, so I tried a different tactic. "Thanks to you, I can come home and have a nice evening with my grandpa and turn in early to make up for the lack of sleep last night. Thank you, Wren."

Wren stared at my mouth like he was thinking of other ways I could show my appreciation, but he said, "You can stop thanking me."

"Not all saviors ride horses. Sometimes they ride on Harley motorcycles or drive pickup trucks," I said softly, running my hands over the bristles of his beard. It was so soft; I wanted to feel it every-where on my body.

Wren jerked away from my touch and took a few steps back. Was it my actions or words that ruined the beautiful moment? One minute, Wren was ready to kiss me, and the next, he looked like someone dumped a bucket of ice water on his head.

"I, uh, need to get back out there," Wren said gruffly. "Maybe I'll see you tonight."

I swallowed down my disappointment and said, "Okay." What else could I say?

I replayed the conversation over in my head for the rest of the afternoon. He was fine until I referred to him as a savior, but I couldn't understand why it upset him so much. I wanted to ask him, or apologize, but instead I used it as a reminder to leave the man alone. If that wasn't enough to get the point through my thick skull, Wren leaving after his final appointment without so much as a wave or goodbye was enough to do the trick.

It was my late night to work at the salon, so it was nearly eight o'clock by the time I arrived at O'Dell's to rescind my notice. I fig-ured at least Betty or Aaron would be there, but I was surprised to find them both in the office they shared in the back of the ware-house. They both sat rigid with tension, like they anticipated the conversation, but how? I hadn't discussed the situation with any of the sales staff yesterday. In fact, I'd told no one except... *No way.*

"Please have a seat," Betty said, motioning to an empty chair.

"It's come to our attention that you were subjected to a very un-pleasant encounter last night," Aaron said. "Betty and I would like to apologize on behalf of Ethan."

"We made it very clear to him that we won't accept that kind of talk around here, not even from our son," Betty said.

"Sons, Betty," I corrected. "They both do it, and I don't think they treat your female employees any better." Her mouth fell open in shock then she turned to look at her husband who seemed just as appalled. When they faced me again, they both seemed to age right before my eyes. I hated to hurt them, but I should've stood up for myself and the ladies sooner.

"I'm truly sorry, Dare. You've been a true asset to our company and we'll miss you." She slid an envelope across the desk. "After last night, I'm sure you'd prefer not to work out the rest of your notice, so we cut you a check for the hours you were scheduled to work. We're not trying to buy your silence or anything, we're just trying to do what's right."

"Wow," I said. "I have to admit I wasn't expecting this. Can I ask who told you about the incident?"

"That's not important, honey," Betty said. "It only matters that we make this right with you and make sure it never happens again."

"We wish you the best of luck, Dare," Aaron said. "Please don't hesitate to reach out if you ever need a referral."

"Um, thank you." I was still too stunned to say anything else, so I took my check and left.

I had to walk through the warehouse and the showroom to exit the building. I was hoping like hell to get out of there without running into Ethan or David, but luck wasn't on my side. Ethan stepped out from behind a display of bookshelves used in the home office display I set up.

"If you had a problem with something that I said then you should've told me yourself instead of sending your big boyfriend in here to fight your battles for you," Ethan said.

"I didn't send anyone in here to fight my battles for me, Ethan. Why the hell are you lurking around behind bookshelves? Closet getting too cramped?"

"W-w-what the fuck did you just say?" he stuttered. "Are you implying that I'm gay?"

"I'm not implying anything," I said. "I give it a year before you're arrested for soliciting a blow job in the men's bathroom at an airport just like all the other self-hating gays. Now kindly step away before I knee you in the balls."

Ethan's mouth fell open in shock, but he stepped away as I requested. I wanted to celebrate my little victory, but I was too fucking busy seething. Who the fuck did Wren Davison think he was? And why did he do it? He made no damn sense, which was probably the most infuriating part. We weren't friends. We weren't lovers. He made it clear to me that he didn't want any type of relationship with me. He pitied me and wanted to help. That was all.

I was so damn mad that I would've called him and ripped him a new one if I had his number. A wicked smile spread across my face when I saw his truck parked in the driveway in front of the garage and the lights on in the apartment windows above it.

"Even better."

I didn't stop to check on Grandpa first, I tromped across the driveway and up the stairs to find Wren before I could talk myself out of being mad at him.

Chapter Four

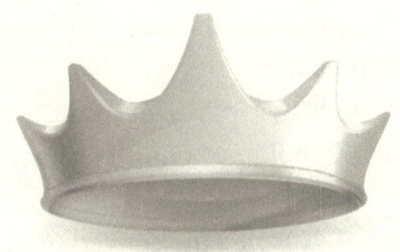

Wren

THE FLASH OF HEADLIGHTS THROUGH THE WINDOW alerted me that Dare had returned home. Hell, I'd only brought over a few boxes of stuff and should've been long gone, but I couldn't leave. Not until I knew that he was okay. I don't know what possessed me to stop at O'Dell's and demand to speak to the owners when I drove by the furniture store on my way to grab a few things from my downtown apartment. I hadn't even planned to stop; I just did it.

I knew Dare wouldn't let my actions slide without comment either. For the first time in many years, I was nervous. I didn't know what excuse I was going to give Dare for my behavior, and I didn't know how much longer I could resist him. Christ, I'd never met a guy I wanted more. What was it about him that drove me wild? My pulse was hammering in my neck by the time Dare pushed the door open so fast it hit the wall.

"Why?" Dare asked. "How did you even know where I worked? I never told you?"

"I've always known where you worked."

"You didn't learn about my second job until we talked about it at the salon," Dare argued, his long legs gobbling up the space between us. He kept coming until he was less than a foot from me.

"No, I asked *why* you worked a second job, not *where* you worked," I clarified. "You were the one who made up the bullshit about working as a go-go boy."

"I could totally pull that off," Dare said. His swift change of topic left me reeling. "I could put on little shorty shorts and dance around."

This was not how I expected the conversation to go. "Of course, you could."

"Don't patronize me, Wren Davison." Dare poked my chest with his index finger. "I need some answers and I want them now." He held up one finger. "How did you know where I worked?" A second finger went up. "Why did you take it upon yourself to approach the O'Dells?" A third finger joined the party. "Why do you do heroic things then get pissed when I acknowledge them?"

I snorted. "I'm nobody's hero."

"You don't get to decide how others define a hero, Wren." Dare placed his hand over my heart and I knew he could feel it racing for him. "Start talking."

"I saw you once at O'Dell's," I confessed.

"No way," Dare said, shaking his head. "I would've felt your presence." *Fuck, he needed to stop saying shit like that.*

"It was before we even met," I told him.

"Doesn't matter, I would've felt your pull." I could tell he would need proof before Dare believed me.

"Dare, you wore a pair of pressed gray slacks that emphasized the curve of your ass and a light-purple shirt with a tie in a darker color. You were so engrossed with your client that you didn't notice I entered the store. She was a tiny little thing and wore a big hat you'd expect to see on Queen Elizabeth."

"Mrs. Getty," Dare said softly, all traces of the anger that propelled him up the stairs was gone. "You like those gray slacks, huh?"

"I like what's beneath the slacks." My confession earned me the first genuine smile I'd seen on him all day. "To be honest, I don't know why I stopped there on my way to get my first load of stuff. I hadn't planned on it, and I think I'm as stunned as you are by my actions. I'm not sorry though."

Dare took the last step that separated us. Even through his coat, I could feel the heat radiating from him. "I should be mad at you for interfering, Wren. I meant what I said earlier. I'm not a helpless guy, but I do appreciate that you care."

"How'd it go?" I asked, pretending like I wasn't aware of the way his body reacted to mine and mine to his.

"They apologized for Ethan's behavior and handed me a check for the hours I would've worked over the next two weeks."

"That's the least they could do," I told him. "I have a real tough time believing they didn't know about his comments to you either. They turned a blind eye to his behavior rather than looking out for their employees. You mark my words, it's going to come back to bite them hard on the ass someday. A few weeks of wages will look like chump change if they ever find themselves on the wrong side of a lawsuit."

"Consider them marked." Dare's long index finger circled the place on my neck where he'd marked me. I knew where we were headed, and we wouldn't have a salon full of people to stop us. "I'm going to need you to answer one more question, Wren." He stared into my eyes while he continued to tease my neck.

"Yes."

"It wasn't a yes or no kind of question," Dare teased. "It makes a man want to take advantage of the situation."

"I was agreeing to answer one more question."

"Ah," Dare said. "In that case, tell me how you smell so fucking good? I've smelled every cologne at the mall, but nothing smells like you do."

I slid my hands around to cup his pert ass. "How do I smell, Dare?"

"Like sex and dark promises," he replied. "Neck-biting, back-clawing sex that goes on for hours until your body is limp, and your sheets are soaked. I want to smell you on my skin, my sheets… everywhere. I want to press my nose against your body and find out where the magnificent smell is the strongest." I clung to my control but acknowledged I was at the tipping point. "Although I'm pretty sure I know where." Dare slid his hand down and boldly cupped my cock and balls. "The juncture at your thigh. I want to smell you there. Let me, Wren. Just this and nothing more."

"Yes," I hissed between my teeth.

Dare never took his eyes off mine when he dropped to his knees and reached for my belt. He didn't look away until after he deftly had me unbuckled and unbuttoned. Dare swallowed hard when he saw the way my cock strained against my gray briefs. His tongue darted out to moisten his lips like he was preparing to suck me into his mouth.

Cupping his jaw, I pressed my thumb against his lips. Dare parted them and sucked my digit into his mouth down to the second knuckle. Then he pulled back and circled the tip with his tongue before drawing it back inside his hot mouth. My dick throbbed jealously, and my tenuous control slipped another notch until I was barely hanging on by a thread. I removed my thumb from his mouth and shoved my jeans down to expose my underwear and upper thighs.

Dare leaned closer, his nose not even an inch from my underwear, and inhaled deeply. I wasn't the only one fighting control either. I saw how badly he wanted to touch my dick, but that wasn't our agreement. Dare cupped the back of my thighs and pressed his nose to the juncture where my leg met my pelvis. His hot breath made me shiver as he ran his nose along the edge of my underwear at the crease of my thigh. I clenched my fists when the bridge of his nose bumped into my throbbing cock. Without thinking about the consequences, I cupped his head and pressed his mouth to my inner thigh.

Dare's fingers dug into the back of my legs as he parted his lips and sucked the sensitive skin into his mouth. He alternated between sucking and licking the flesh before stopping to check out his hand-iwork. Dare hummed in the back of his throat then put his mouth back on me. His tongue grew bolder and slipped beneath the leg of my briefs to tease my balls then licked a path until he found the head of my leaking cock.

"Dare," I said gutturally, my hands tightening in his hair.

He pulled his tongue out of my underwear and pressed his nose back to my thigh, breathing deep like he wanted to memorize the smell for eternity. One last kiss and he dropped his hands from my thighs and stood up.

"Thank you for that," Dare said softly. Lust had turned his blue eyes a darker hue, and his face was flushed with the raging desire we both felt. My thigh smarted from where he marked me, but I planned on reliving that moment with my cock in my fist as soon as possible. "Well, I must go masturbate now."

I wanted to stop him and suggest we do it together. I wanted to watch, hell I wanted to jerk us both off at the same time, but I hesitated too long to make a move, and Dare left without another word. *What the hell had I just let happen?* I stood in the apartment with my pants down around my knees and a dick hard enough to drill through ice. Why did I keep denying myself the pleasure he offered me?

I jerked my pants up and went after Dare, catching him before he made it out of the garage. He turned when he heard me running down the stairs. I slammed my mouth against his and removed his coat to get to his hot body. I broke our kiss long enough for us to whip our shirts over our head. The garage wasn't nearly as warm as my apartment, but I loved the way his nipples hardened into two sexy points I wanted to suck into my mouth.

Dare moaned and slid his hands over my abs, my pecs, and around my back to scrape my skin while I kissed him breathless. He nipped my bottom lip when I brushed the back of my hand over his erection.

Dare pulled his hands back to the front of my body and slid them down to the waistband of my underwear. "Can I touch you?" he asked.

"Fuck yes."

Dare slid both hands inside my underwear to cup my balls and learn my cock at the same time. *Fuck, I'm going to shoot fast. I needed to be inside him.* That's when I realized how out of practice I truly was. "I don't have anything on me, Dare."

"Me either," he admitted. "I don't get many opportunities." His greedy hands never stopped tormenting me.

"We'll have to improvise." I undid his pants and shoved them down to mid-thigh and then pushed my underwear and jeans down too.

I reclaimed his lips and kissed him hungrily as I knocked his hands away so that I could grip both our cocks in my hand. Our groans echoed through the space when our hot flesh met for the first time. Dare reached up and released my hair from the elastic band then tangled his hand in it, while his other hand circled and teased my hard nipple. As for me, I jacked us with one hand while teasing the crack of his ass with the other. Dare whimpered into my mouth every time the pad of my finger rubbed over his pucker.

Right then and there, I stopped fighting everything he made me feel and acknowledged that someday I was going to sink my dick as deep as it would go inside his tight ass. The friction of his cock against mine was out of this world and it only took a few tugs until I was ready to come. I needed him with me, so I slipped just the tip of my finger in his ass and we both shot all over my stomach.

I continued to kiss him until we both came down off our high. Pulling back, I looked into his sated eyes and wanted to drag him back up to that apartment and lay him down and… Never mind, that carpet was too sketchy for sex.

"There's the sparkle I've been missing today," I said gruffly.

"I don't think I have any *sparkle* left after that." Dare looked around the garage. "Let me find you something to clean up with."

"I see shop towels over there," I told him, nodding toward one of the tool benches.

Dare tugged up his pants and retrieved a handful of them. I tried to take one from him, but he seemed to enjoy cleaning me up. My muscles bunched and tensed beneath his simple touch. Dare dropped the dirty towels to the garage floor and gently pulled my pants and underwear up over my sensitive cock while sucking and nibbling on my pecs. Damn, I was already starting to respond again to his mouth on my body.

I pulled his head up to look into his eyes. "Next time there will be a soft surface and supplies so I can fuck you proper."

"Next time, huh?" he asked.

"Definitely."

"What if I want to fuck you proper too?"

Did he think to shock me? He would have to try harder. "Definitely."

"Wren, I'm not asking you for a commitment or any promises, okay?"

For the first time ever, I wanted someone to demand commitment and promises from me. It was enough to scare me shitless, but that didn't make it less true.

"We'll just see how this plays out, okay? No weirdness at work and no obligation for you to fuck me up in that apartment every single night after my grandpa falls asleep. Okay?"

"Sounds perfect," I told him. It sounded fucking horrible. "How about every other night?"

Dare whimpered in his throat then stepped back to retrieve his shirt and coat off the garage floor. "I won't hold you to it."

I pulled him to me for one last kiss after he was dressed again. "Go check on your grandpa. I'll clean up our mess."

"Okay," Dare said, sounding sleepy.

"See you tomorrow, Sparkles."

"*Sparkles?*"

"It's better than Go-Go."

"True. See you tomorrow."

I watched out the window until he was inside the house then picked up the shop towels and threw them in the trash can. I went back up to my new apartment and turned the lights off and locked up.

I hadn't come so hard in ages and was ready to grab a bite to eat and crash for the night. I felt a little more alert after hitting the McDonald's drive-thru in Goodville, so I got a little more packing done before I went to bed. Instead of taking a shower, I climbed between my sheets still smelling like Dare. I was just as obsessed with his smell as he was mine. Dare smelled like sunshine, hope, and happiness. I wanted—scratch that—I needed it in my life.

I just didn't want to take something good and beautiful and ruin it like I seemed to do with everything else I touched. I was good at styling hair and rebuilding cars and bikes, but neither of those skills came in handy with relationships. Darren McCoy deserved to be more than someone's fuck buddy, but I didn't have anything to offer him besides my cock and friendship.

The next morning, I reluctantly used the soap with the scent that he admired so much to wash him off my skin. I smiled as I held the bar of soap to my nose and inhaled. I wasn't the hearts and flowers kind of guy like Dr. Dipshit, but I could do something for him that I knew he would really like. I couldn't promise Dare anything beyond sex, but I could totally make his neck-biting, back-clawing, limp bodies, and sweaty-cum-sheet dreams a reality.

Until then, I had a little something that could tide him over. I whistled as I got dressed and made a cup of coffee for my commute. My first client wouldn't be there until ten o'clock, but I had an extra stop to make on my way.

Chapter Five

Dave

WOKE THE NEXT MORNING WITH AN EXTRA PEP IN MY step or sway to my hips. I almost expected birds and squirrels to help me dress and lead me downstairs to the coffee pot. It was kind of a letdown that it didn't happen, but I still whistled while I made my coffee and our breakfast. I didn't wake up expecting to find myself in an enchanted world where Wren was suddenly in love with me after one amazing hand job. If I closed my eyes and thought hard enough, I could still feel his calloused hand stroking our cocks together and taste his kisses on my tongue. Anyway, nothing had really changed, except it had. Every time I would look at him, I'd remember the way he sounded when he shot his load.

"I miss coffee," Grandpa groused when he shuffled into

the kitchen in the pajamas, robe, and slippers I bought him for Christmas. "Just this once?" he asked hopefully.

He startled me so bad I nearly dropped my cup. I really had to get my mind off Wren. "No, sir. The doctor said it makes your acid reflux worse." I realized then what a rude ass I'd been for drinking coffee in front of him. I started to pour it down the drain, but his harsh tone of voice stopped me.

"Don't you dare," Grandpa said, then giggled at his unintended pun. "Let me live vicariously through you."

"I don't know, Grandpa. It seems cruel." Then I tipped my head to the side. "I'm also concerned that you'll sneak a cup for yourself before Maren gets here."

"I wouldn't do such a thing," Grandpa blustered. "If that's the source of my misery lately then I need to give it up. You'll just have to be patient with me because it's only been a week and it takes a while to kick a habit."

That I knew too damned well. I'd known Wren for longer than a year, and I couldn't kick my addiction to him. It didn't matter if we were arguing, kissing, or coming; I just wanted to be near him. *Fuck me! I had it bad.* I shook off the thoughts and focused on the most important person in my life.

"Do you promise me, Grandpa?"

"Have I ever lied to you, Dare?"

"Other than the existence of Santa Claus, the Easter Bunny, unicorns, and the Tooth Fairy, you mean?"

"Hey, your parents told those lies. I just went along with it."

"Lies by omission," I told him ruefully.

"Have I lied to you about anything important?" Grandpa countered.

I thought back to all the serious conversations that I had with him on the front porch over the years. Grandpa was the first person I told about my crush on another boy. He wasn't surprised, no one was really, but it meant the world to me that he didn't look at me differently or love me less. He had been honest with me from the very beginning. He warned me that some people would have a problem with the fact that I liked boys, but it was *their* problem. They would get over it or they wouldn't, but I wasn't to take any crap from anyone. Ever. There was no doubt where my feistiness came from.

"No, sir."

Grandpa gave me a short nod. "Sit down then and let's eat breakfast before you rush off to work. Smells like you made my favorites." I filled a plate and set it in front of him. "Mmmm. Sausage links, scrambled eggs, and toast."

"I have a little something special too." I turned my body so he couldn't see what I poured into a bowl for him. I knew the other aromas overwhelmed the smell of his favorite food in the world.

Grandpa's eyes lit up when I set the bowl on the table. His brow creased into a deep V when he frowned. "Grits! Did I forget my birthday?" Grandpa chuckled nervously to cover his fear. It was true that he was starting to get a little forgetful.

"No, sir. I'm celebrating the fact that I got a promotion at the salon and quit my night job. Plus, it's nice to have found someone who wanted to rent the garage apartment from you. Maybe you can put that money toward a senior cruise or something fun." I smiled when he snorted. I couldn't very well tell him that the money he got from Wren would go toward his medication and his companion. I felt like I was the one being dishonest with him, but I only wanted to protect his pride and keep him in his home for as long as it was safe.

After breakfast, I helped Grandpa get dressed and situated in his recliner before I finished getting ready for work. I glanced out my bedroom window and realized that I would be able to look into Wren's bedroom window, which could either be a lot of fun or my greatest heartbreak. He wasn't my boyfriend and we didn't have any sort of arrangement, which meant he could bring anyone home he wanted and do whatever he pleased with them. It would gut me to see Wren with someone else, but there wouldn't be anything I could do about it except cry.

I pushed the morose thoughts aside and focused on the way I felt when I woke up that morning. I'd stretched lazily before I relived every second of the encounter in the shower. I held onto those euphoric feelings after I kissed my grandpa on his forehead and trekked to work in the blistering cold. I had my earbuds in, so I didn't realize a vehicle had approached until it pulled slightly in front of me and stopped.

Wren rolled down his window and gestured for me to take my earbuds out. "Get in."

"The wintry weather feels good," I lied. "You can start walking with me in the mornings from now on."

"Never going to happen," Wren replied, shaking his head. "I hate winter."

"Come on," I teased. "You'll save gas and reduce your carbon footprint."

"Those are both great things, and I'll happily do my part when it's not cold enough to get frostbite on my nuts. Seriously, get in. I have something I want to give you."

My face was so cold that I feared it would crack when I smiled, but my racing heart warmed the rest of me up. "Oh, and I desperately want to accept it. In your truck, though?"

Wren released a long-suffering sigh. "Dare, I won't pretend I don't want to fuck you six ways from Sunday, but not in my truck." An evil grin stretched across his face. "Well, not in broad daylight anyway."

A light bulb went off in my head and I had a sudden solution to our predicament. "There's plenty of room to pull this beast in the garage and…"

"Get the fuck in here now." Apparently, Wren didn't like going to work with a raging hard-on.

I jogged around to the passenger side and climbed in. Wren

dropped a brown bag unceremoniously on my lap. There were several things in the bag but none that I expected. Well, the lube and box of magnum-sized condoms were pretty much expected at this point, but I didn't think he'd hand them to me before work.

"What's this?" I asked pulling out a bar of handmade soap wrapped in cellophane. The ivory and amber bar was roughly cut in a rectangular shape. I looked at the rustic, brown paper label that was wrapped around the middle of the bar. "Wood Nymph," I read out loud. I held it up to my nose, and even through the plastic, I could tell it was the scent I associated with Wren. "Goat milk soap, huh?"

"It has a lot of vitamins and minerals, so it's good for the skin. It's also organic. No chemicals." Wren cleared his throat like he was a little embarrassed and refused to look over at me. Instead, he put his truck in drive. "They also make beard oil and balm."

"That's why your beard is so soft," I said. I closed my eyes and imagined him rubbing it all over my skin.

"Stop it," Wren growled. "I know what you're thinking."

"Only because you're thinking it too."

I glanced over at him and his blush was the only confirmation I needed. I also knew that he wouldn't want to act on any of these emotions at work. Wren was as buttoned-up and private as anyone I'd ever met. None of us knew a single thing about his personal life, and it would remain that way until he decided otherwise. I wanted him to trust me as much as I wanted to feel his dick inside me, so I vowed to behave at work and treat him as I did the rest of my colleagues.

"Do you mind if I leave this in your truck? I'll raise a lot of eyebrows if I get caught sniffing it all day long. Plus, people might peek in the bag and see the other supplies."

"Sure," Wren said gruffly.

"Thank you so much, Wren."

"Hey, it's no problem. We're going to the same place. I brought another load of stuff to take to the apartment after work." He pointed to the back seat with his thumb.

"Um, I was thanking you for this thoughtful gift."

"It's not that big of a deal." I could tell Wren wanted to downplay it, and I'd let him, but not until after I said one last thing.

"I said that I wanted to smell like you and you made it happen. That's a big deal." By this time, we had arrived at the salon so leaning over and kissing him was a big no-no. Instead, I folded the bag and placed it in the console between our seats. "I promise to behave today."

Wren looked over and I could tell he didn't believe me. "Should we make a bet?"

"That depends, Wren. What would your reward be or my punishment? If it in anyway would feel good or make me come, I'd most likely break my promise before we got inside the salon."

"Forget it then," he growled.

"That's what I thought." We got out of the truck together and headed toward the rear entrance. "I guess you could make me wear a cock ring all day or something to keep me in line."

Wren jerked to a halt and looked down at me. "Is that a possibility?"

"I'm a man who believes that all things are possible if you want them bad enough, Wren. Do you want it bad enough?"

The big man's nostrils flared, and a devious idea came to my mind. It looked like I had an extra stop to make during my weekend shopping. Until then, I'd be a very good boy. *Or very bad to make my punishment even better.* I saw how bad Wren wanted to kiss me and how hard he battled to hold onto his ironclad control.

"We'll continue this conversation in private later," I said sassily and continued up the steps in front of him.

"You can count on it," he growled in my ear when he caught up to me.

His dark promise melted my tension and caused lust to simmer in my belly. It was going to be a very long day, but I looked forward to my delayed gratification.

"Good morning," Josi said to both of us when we walked in. She most likely saw that we arrived together but refrained from commenting. Sort of. "Wow, the two of you look more relaxed than my clients after an hour-long massage. Are you cheating on me?" She narrowed her eyes as if she was really considering it.

I opened my mouth to remind her there were more ways to relieve tension than a massage, but I had promised to behave. "Never," I said then kissed her cheek. "Do you have another busy day?"

Wren stepped around us and left me alone with Josi in the kitchen. I grabbed a cup of coffee when Josi's first client showed up then headed to my desk. I looked over the master schedule for the day, hoping to head off any disasters that might crop up. Satisfied that I didn't see any potential for cataclysmic knockdown drag-outs, I began taking everyone's daily lunch order. It was something new I had started when I saw how often we were skipping meals or eating junk because of our busy schedules. Hungry stylists and sharp scissors aren't a good mix. I didn't mind calling in the order to the diner and picking it up. We didn't get to eat lunch at the same time, but the food from Edson and Emma's was easy to reheat and just as delicious as when it was fresh.

"I'm in the mood for broccoli and cheddar soup," I said. "What's everyone in the mood for?" I went to each station and took their order and tried my best not to lean in too close to Wren. "And what would you like?" He didn't answer right away so I jerked my eyes off the notepad to look at him. Had I somehow asked in a suggestive tone? I glanced around and no one else seemed to be looking at us intently, so I deduced that I had sounded as professional as I intended. The look in Wren's eyes said his mind had definitely headed straight to the gutter.

"Something salty," Wren said.

"Salty?" his client asked. "That's so unhealthy, Wren."

"Sometimes you must eat the things that make you the happiest, Mrs. Warren. Maybe I'll have something sweet too."

"If you say so, dear," Mrs. Warren replied.

"I do." Wren smiled when he saw how his words affected me. "I'll take a mushroom swiss burger and onion rings. Maybe I should go with fries to get my salty fix. I don't want to have onion breath for my clients all day." I suspected he wasn't so much worried about what his clients thought since he ate onion rings at least once a week. He was thinking about me and the kiss we'd share as soon as we were alone again.

"You can always chew gum," I suggested.

"Onion rings it is," Wren said.

The phones were pure chaos because the flu epidemic had struck Blissville and people were frantically rescheduling their appointments. I was relieved when it was time to pick up the food. "Take my SUV," Josh said to me when he handed me cash for his lunch.

"I don't mind walking," I told him.

"No need," Gabe, Josh's husband and our police captain, said as he came through the front door of the salon with two large carryout bags from the diner. "I got you covered."

"Slow day in Blissville, Captain?" Josh teased.

"Not really, but I'm never too busy to be nice," Gabe answered, but Josh still looked suspicious.

"Thanks, Gabe." I tried handing him the stack of money I'd collected from everyone, but he refused it.

"My treat," he said.

"That's kind of you," I told Gabe.

"Kindness is my middle name."

"And here I thought I vowed to love and cherish Gabriel Allen Wyatt for the rest of my life," Josh argued.

"Ha ha ha," Gabe said drolly.

"Bribing the locals," I heard Josh say after I took the bags of food from our police captain.

I knew those two could trade good-natured barbs for hours, but I was too hungry to stick around for the show. I had just dug into my bowl of soup when Wren entered the kitchen.

"I'm pretty sure that banter is their idea of foreplay," Wren told me after he found the container with his lunch order written on the top.

"Yeah," I agreed, "but it works for them."

When Wren sat down across from me, I realized it was the first time we'd eaten lunch together. I knew damn well it wasn't a coincidence. My heart sped up a little as I contemplated what it could mean. Instead of mentioning it, I leaned over and grabbed one of his big onion rings.

"Hey!"

"Now, we'll be on a level playing field." Okay, maybe I wasn't capable of being good. Wren's smile told me that it wasn't such a terrible thing. "Oh, and I ordered you a little something extra." I rummaged through the bags until I found what I was looking for. "Ah-ha." I slid it across the table to Wren. "To tide you over until you can have the treat you really want."

Wren smiled when he opened the container and saw his slice of black forest cake. He set his meal aside and tore into it, never even offering me a single bite.

Chapter Six

Wren

COULDN'T REMEMBER THE LAST TIME I SMILED AS MUCH as I did since meeting Dare. The people around me only saw my grimace-for-a-smile on rare occasions, but I was smiling a lot on the inside. Maybe I was the only one who knew, but it didn't make it less true.

My absolute favorite part was testing Dare's resolve every chance I got. Like licking the cherry sauce and chocolate off the fork the way I planned to devour his cock later. Of course, once he planted the idea in my mind, I couldn't help thinking about one of those devices that would restrain his cock. I'd heard of cages, but there was no way to hide one of those beneath the worlds skinniest jeans that he preferred to wear. I bet his boys sighed in relief each night when he took them off. Or would the blood rush to his cock, instantly filling it to hardness?

Dare's laughter floated to me from his desk, pulling my attention to him. My good mood faded when I saw who made him laugh. How the fuck had I forgotten that Dr. Cock Drizzle had an appointment for me to cut his hair.

"Don't do it," Josh said from behind me. I hadn't even heard him approach me. "I bailed you out last time, and I'm not doing it again." Josh was referring to the time that I got jealous when Trent brought Dare apology flowers. Apparently, Josh had promised his husband he wouldn't cut his ex-boyfriend's hair, and my immaturity caused him to take back his word. That didn't sit well with me, so I jerked my head in a brief nod so Josh would know that I was on board. "We can fantasize about shearing off his hair later."

"Now you're talking, boss." I planted a polite smile on my face as I approached Dare's desk. It must've looked more predatory than polite because both Dare and Dr. Dick Breath's eyes widened in alarm. "You ready, Doc?"

"For a haircut, right?" he asked hesitantly. "I'm not asking for a shave with a straight razor."

"I'm damned good with those," I assured him, "but you booked a haircut."

"We got off on the wrong foot," the doctor said. "I apologized to Dare before, but I'll do it again if it's necessary."

I figured he must own a pretty big pair if he was brave enough to schedule an appointment with me again. "It's not necessary." Dare and Trent both visibly relaxed, exchanging easy smiles. On second thought, Dare could use a taste of his own medicine. "Follow me to the shampoo room."

"Shampoo?" they both asked.

Dare narrowed his eyes suspiciously. "He gets a dry cut."

"Yeah, I get a dry cut."

"Not anymore," I told the doctor. I turned and walked toward the shampoo room. "You coming, Doc?" By the time I was done washing his hair, the man would be ready to come in his pants and Dare would know to never taunt me again.

"I'm thinking about trying something new," Trent told me when I wrapped the cape around his neck. "You know the style where it's shaved close to the sides and back."

"Like a fade?" I asked, studying the shape of his face. I ran my fingers through the longish strands at the top. He was sporting an asymmetrical cut that was cute, but not very professional.

"Yeah, but with length on top. Kind of…um…like Dare's style." It was cute how nervous he was just saying Dare's name in front of me. "I'm hoping you can teach me which stuff to use and how to style it right."

Even though I was the one who gave Dare the cut, I wanted to make sure it would work on Trent too. They did have the same angular jaw with the cute dimpled chin. I stepped to the door and looked toward the reception area of the salon and caught Dare looking in our direction. His eyes widened then narrowed when Trent joined me.

"Do you think that cut will work on me?"

"Yeah," I told him. "I can teach you how to style it and you can purchase the brush and products you'll need."

"Perfect," the doctor said, plopping down in the chair in front of the sink.

I'd changed my mind about giving Trent the same kind of scalp massages I gave Dare because it could send the wrong message to the doctor, but then Dare found a lame excuse to enter the shampoo room to keep an eye on things. He had his little inventory notepad in hand and acted like he was counting shampoos and conditioners, as if he hadn't already done it that week.

"I haven't tried a new st…. Oh! Oh my God!" Trent moaned when I dug my fingers into his scalp. I kept my eyes trained on Dare's reaction and nearly laughed when he dropped his notebook in shock. "Fuuuuuck," Trent moaned like a porn star when I really dug in. "I think I need to start coming here at least once a week. My God! Are you for hire?"

"He's not a whore, Trent," Dare snarled. "Wren, the illegal happy endings happen upstairs, not in the shampoo room." Then he angrily stomped out. I almost gave him a happy ending in the mixing room once, but I didn't point that out to him.

"Oh," Trent said sheepishly. "I didn't mean to imply you were a whore." His eyes were as wide and unblinking as an owl's.

"You didn't," I assured him. "Sorry, if I got a little carried away with my hands."

"Did you do that on purpose to get even with him for taking me to Thanksgiving dinner at Josh's house?" Trent asked when I rinsed the shampoo out of his hair. "You know that was all my fault, right?"

"Yeah," I admitted. "Sorry. Do I need to bring you flowers too?"

The doctor laughed good-naturedly. "You should've seen your face. If looks could've killed…."

"Yeah, you wouldn't be here right now."

"It's not my place to say—"

"You're right about that," I said, cutting him off. "We'll sort this out."

"Before some innocent bystander gets caught up in the middle of it," Trent suggested.

"Point taken."

I spent the next forty minutes cutting Trent's hair and teaching him how to style it with products, a rounded brush, and a blow dryer. I followed him over to the shelves that held our styling products and handed him the ones he needed to buy.

"The volumizer goes on wet," he said. "Then I dry it with the rounded brush and finish with the styling clay, right?"

"Yep. Make sure you work the clay really well with your hands first," Dare suggested. "Or else you'll end up looking like you have globs of cum in your hair."

"Good to know."

"Trial and error, Trent," Dare said sheepishly. "Do you want to go ahead and book your next appointment with Wren?" He was back to being professional and I didn't like it. Hell, I should like it, demand it even, but I missed his teasing looks and gestures.

"Sure," the doctor agreed. "How often should I come in to maintain this cut?"

"How fast does your hair grow?" I asked him. "Most people can go six weeks, but some people need trimmed every four weeks."

"I'll go with four weeks to keep it nice and tight." The doctor ran his hands over the super short sides as he looked at his reflection in the mirror behind Dare's desk. "I love it, Wren. Thank you."

"You're welcome, Doc. See you in a month."

I went to retrieve the broom from the closet next to the mixing room. When I turned around to go back into the salon, Dare stood in my way with arms crossed over his chest.

"You better kiss it and make it better. That was just mean." He wasn't playing either. His calm professional demeanor before was because I'd hurt his feelings. That I just couldn't abide.

"Dare," I said softly so only he could hear me. "If I kiss you, I won't stop. This isn't the time or place for the things I want to do to you."

"When will you be moving your bed into your apartment?" he asked boldly. He wasn't eager to roll around on that sketchy-looking carpet either. "How soon can we use the items you purchased?"

"I'm not moving my bed until this weekend," he said. "We'll improvise until then."

"There are plenty of surfaces in the garage or up in the apartment that we—"

I cut him off by placing my index finger over his lips. "I want you to be really comfortable for the things I'm going to do to you, Dare."

"Okay," he said shakily.

"I'll still take care of you tonight though."

"Okay." His trancelike responses made me smile, and I couldn't help kissing his forehead. That seemed to snap him back to reality.

"Back to work for both of us."

"Okay, Wren." I liked his submission more than I ever thought I could. I'd never experimented with power play, but he made me want to try it. *Jesus!* Cock rings, cages, and submission were never things I ever gave thought to before I met the little imp. Just what was he into?

Luckily, the rest of the day passed without incident or more flirting. As soon as Dare was back inside my truck, he reached for the soap I bought him like it was a treasure. He closed his eyes and inhaled the scent through the plastic.

"I'm going to make this last a very long time."

"Dare, I bought it from Marabel here in town. She has plenty of soap for sale. You don't have to use it sparingly." I nearly choked on my saliva when I thought about him lathering his hot, lean body with the soap. Would he linger on his cock and balls and pretend it was my hand instead of his own? I sure as hell would linger if I was the one washing his body with soapy hands.

"Yes, but this one is special because it's a gift from you." He sounded serious, but really? Had he received so few gifts that a bar of soap really wowed him? "At least I don't have to break into your apartment and steal a shirt to sleep in or something equally creepy."

Creepy? Nah, it was cute as fuck. *Jesus, what was happening to me?*

"Dare, I'll buy you a new one if you run out. There's no need to cut the bar into little slivers and dole them out slowly." He gasped like I talked about slicing off a finger instead of cutting into the soap. "Seriously, lather up and go to it." Dare blinked a few times then his lips curved into a wicked smile.

"You better get us out of here unless you want an audience, Wren. I'm a heartbeat away from climbing over that console and straddling your lap. I'd lure you into the back seat but it's full."

That was all I needed to get moving. The faster I unloaded the boxes, the faster we could do a different type of unloading. I wanted my mouth on his and wouldn't settle for anything else. My dick started to twitch to life when I pictured Dare on his knees.

"Stop it."

"What?" I asked.

"I can tell you're thinking sexy thoughts. Knock it off."

"How?"

"You're doing this little growly hum and your body is so tight it looks like it could shatter."

"Growly hum?" I asked.

"Yeah, like this." Dare gave me a growly little hum that made me want to pull my truck over. "Look at your knuckles." They were white from the death grip I had on the steering wheel. "What has you so revved up, Wren?"

"I was wondering if I should order Chinese or pizza for dinner," I said.

"No way, you're going to eat dinner with Grandpa and me."

My heart sped up even more and I thought I could be close to a panic attack. Meet his grandpa? That was a big fucking deal. He wasn't…we weren't…

"Wren, it's just food. I'm not introducing you as anything other than the new tenant. I want my grandpa to be comfortable around you is all."

"What if he doesn't like me?" What would I do? I didn't want Dare to choose between his grandpa and his…tenant. It sounded as ridiculous as I felt.

"Wren, he'll like you because I do." Dare reached over and touched my thigh to comfort me. "Maren made a lasagna today. Her grandmother came to the States from Italy, and I promise you that no one makes a better lasagna than Maren. I'm talking noodles made from scratch and robust meat sauce that simmered for hours."

"Okay."

"She makes this herb oil to dip the fresh Italian bread in. It's Grandpa's and my favorite, although I'll need to give him another pill to help prevent acid reflux."

"I think I just came in my pants."

"No, that was Trent earlier," Dare said dryly. "That was just mean, Wren."

I parked behind his car and turned the engine off. "You're right, and I apologize for that."

"Look, I want to get something straight before this goes any further." Dare blew out a long breath like he was buying time or trying to find the right words.

His hesitation made me nervous and I wasn't a person who gave in to nerves very often. "Hey, you can tell me anything."

"I just want you to know that I am not mistaking your gift today as a token for anything other than friendship. I promise that I won't get all clingy after we…you know," he gestured down to my dick, "do it."

"Use your adult words, Dare." Where had the bold, confident man from last night gone?

"Have mind-blowing, back-clawing sex that results in orgasms that could be confused as life-altering experiences. I promise that I won't confuse that with a commitment or something."

"Dare…" I wasn't sure what to say. Did I believe that neither of us would come out of this unscathed? No, but I wasn't willing to walk away either. "It's going to be okay."

It had to be because I couldn't stand the thought of hurting him. *What if you're the one who gets hurt, tough guy?* Could Dare be the knight to scale the high walls guarding my heart?

"Grandpa would've seen us pull in. I don't want him coming out here in the cold to check on us."

"Will he bring a shotgun?"

"Maybe back in the day, but not anymore."

"Good to know."

"He'd probably bring the ball bat from the hall closet." The porchlight on the side of the house came on. "Yep. That's our one-minute warning."

"I think I'm going to like your grandpa."

"You're going to love him."

Ralph McCoy was as adorable as his grandson, full of life and laughter. It was no wonder Dare fought so fucking hard to keep him home and happy. The lasagna was even better than Dare promised, and I ate two huge portions.

"I guess a guy as big as you can eat all that pasta and not gain weight," Ralph told me. "Must be nice."

"I work out a lot too," I told him. "That way I don't feel guilty when I get carried away on occasion."

"Smart man," Ralph told me.

"Dare told me that you used to own an auto body shop. What kind of work did you do?"

"I ran a full-service shop, so I did maintenance and mechanical work along with collision repairs. I loved every minute I spent in that shop and it never felt like work to me."

"You have some awesome tools in your garage," I said.

"You know a lot about cars?" Ralph asked me.

"I went to tech school for two years after graduating from high school, but I was more interested in classic cars instead of working on modern cars. There's really not much call for that in these parts. I used to cut my buddies' hair all the time and they told me I should become a barber. I didn't want to limit myself to just styles for men, so I really applied myself while at cosmetology school. I discovered that I really like it." I glanced over at Dare and he just blinked like he couldn't believe I had revealed so much about myself.

"What's your favorite classic car?" Ralph wanted to know.

"I have a sixty-nine Chevelle," I told him. "It's my dream car. She's a little rough around the edges but runs beautifully. Now I need to start working on her exterior."

Ralph let out a peppy whistle that made Dare smile. "That's my favorite year for American cars. All the big boys put out monster vehicles that year." Ralph set his napkin on the table and rose to his feet. "I have a photo album with some fine vehicles I've worked on or owned over the years. Let me go get it."

Once Ralph shuffled out of the room, Dare leaned forward and said, "Sixty-nine is my favorite blow job position. You want me to sneak you up to my room after my grandpa falls asleep?"

I closed my eyes briefly and groaned. I wanted to feel his mouth on my cock while he fucked my throat but knowing his grandpa could hear us was a real turn-off. I opened my mouth to remind him that we were just a few days away from privacy and a comfortable bed, but my vibrating phone distracted me. I regretted pulling it out of my pocket and looking at it. For one brief, shining moment, I actually thought I might have a chance at happiness. The caller represented the saddest time in my life and jerked me out of the fantasyland I'd been living in all day long.

"Dare, I'm so sorry to eat and run, but I need to go. This is important." I pointed to the phone. Even though I wouldn't answer the call or return the message, it totally ruined my mood and the evening for me. I needed to get as far away from Dare as fast as I could, because my mood was about to dive down into a raging darkness that I didn't want him to see. "Please give Ralph my apologies and tell him that I'll be back soon to look at his photos."

"Are you okay?"

"Dare, I can't…"

I got up, grabbed my coat, and left without another word. I didn't even remember to unload my truck. I was starting to think that moving into the apartment was the biggest mistake I could make, because the universe saw that I was starting to feel happy and that just wasn't allowed. If I cared about Dare, I'd leave town and never look back before he got hurt too.

Chapter Seven

Dave

"OH! OH! OH MY!"

I glanced away from putting Grandpa's sandwich together and saw my mom looking out the kitchen window at the flurry of activity going on in front of the garage. Her hand was on her neck and her mouth gaped open in shock. Mom's face was flushed pink, and I suspected it wasn't because Grandpa had the heat cranked up. It was move-in day and Wren had brought some buddies to help him move.

Apparently, my mom was impressed enough to have a spontaneous lady-gasm right on the spot. A lady-gasm is a phrase I associate with my mom and her lady friends when they see a guy who catches their attention. It's muted and more socially acceptable than an orgasm in public and tends to stimulate the brain more than any other part of the body. Then again, the brain *is* a sexual organ and where all the magic begins.

"Really, Mom," I said, rolling my eyes.

"Seriously, Mom," Kristy, my sixteen-year-old sister said dryly. "*Grease* is calling and they want their T-Birds back." You could hear the dramatic teen eye roll in her voice.

"Hey!" Mom and I said at the same time. I thought we might be offended for different reasons since *Grease* was my mom's favorite movie and musical.

"Wren's a good guy, Kris. Don't let the battered leather jacket fool you."

"Mmmhmmm," Mom contributed. Or perhaps Mom and I were on the same page after all.

"I'm telling Dad," Kristy and I both said at the same time.

Mom huffed and walked away from the window to join me at the counter. Kristy remained to supervise the activity. I suspected she found the three men more attractive than she let on.

"They're all wearing leather jackets," Kristy pointed out to me. "Which one is Wren?"

"The one with the long hair," I answered.

"Looks so soft," my mom said dreamily, earning a glare from me. "Oh, I see."

"No, you don't," I refuted. The last thing I needed was for my mom to start thinking Wren was her future son-in-law, nor did I want her to know about the carnal delights I planned to have with him up in that apartment. *Carnal delights?* I'd moved from fairy tales to bodice-ripper books. "We just work together."

"At the salon?" Kristy asked. "He doesn't look—"

"Kristy," my mom interrupted with a warning tone.

"Gay?" I asked her. "Kristy, you have so much to learn. First, don't base someone's sexuality on their job. Second, don't base their sexuality on the way they dress, talk, or even walk. Sometimes a person's orientation is a bit more obvious," I gestured to myself, "and sometimes it's not." I pointed at Wren through the window above the sink with the butter knife I used to spread mayo on Grandpa's sandwich. "It's best not to assume things about people. It's just rude and you make an ass of yourself."

Kristy gave me an apologetic smile. "I'm sorry."

"I appreciate that, but I'd like it more if you listened and learned."

"Duly noted."

"So what are your plans this afternoon?" Mom asked, changing the subject.

"I just need to do the usual grocery shopping and stuff."

By stuff, I meant that I needed to make a trip to a specialty store to buy a fun gift for Wren. He bought me the soap, and I came up with an idea of how he can keep me in line at work because I was failing miserably at it. Sadness washed over me when I realized that it might not even be necessary, because Wren had been very distant after he received that phone call earlier in the week. He avoided being alone with me and I was eager to get back to how things were between us. I'd given him as much space as I could, but I was going crazy on the inside. I had to try once more, and if that didn't work, I would back off and not make things awkward between us.

"Darren, I told you that Dad or I would be more than happy to do the grocery shopping for you and Grandpa," Mom said. "Why won't you let us help?"

Okay, I might've exaggerated a tiny bit about my parents being the villains in this not-so-fairy tale. Yes, they did recommend that Grandpa consider assisted living, but not because they were greedy to get his stuff or didn't love him. They just worried that he was going to hurt himself. They worried even more when I moved in and took over primary care because they felt it was too much responsibility for me to shoulder alone.

Both my parents worked full-time jobs and were busy in the evenings and on Saturdays with Kristy's sports and dancing. I couldn't afford to hire someone to sit with Grandpa seven days a week, so my parents helped out as much as they could on Sundays, so I could get a few hours to myself that didn't involve work. Unfortunately, grocery shopping was usually one of the things I did. Grandpa was very particular about the brands he liked, which meant that I sometimes had to go to a few different stores. I wouldn't ask that of my mom or dad.

"Mom, I don't mind. I appreciate you sitting with him and making him feel loved so that I can take a little breather."

"He *is* loved."

"I know," I replied quickly. I didn't want her to feel like she had to defend herself again, so I threw my arms around her. "We're making the best of it for as long as we can. I know I can't keep him home forever, but I want to do it for as long as I can."

"Go on and run your errands, Dare. Your dad will be here in a little bit and we'll have a nice family dinner like we do every Sunday." These gatherings were the highlight of Grandpa's week.

"What are you making this week?" I looked forward to seeing my family and eating my mom's home cooking.

"Pot roast, new potatoes, and baby carrots. I brought some of that Hawaiian bread you and Grandpa love so much." She kissed my cheek and made a shooing motion. "Get on out of here and get some fresh air."

I took Grandpa his lunch and left them to visit. I didn't want to bug Wren, but one of his buddies had parked behind me and blocked me in. Our driveway was wide enough for two vehicles until you pulled even with the house then it narrowed so that only one vehicle could drive back to the detached garage. Wren's truck was backed up to the building, but one of his buddies must have followed him over or met him here.

I was nervous as hell when I headed to the apartment. Classic rock and laughter was spilling out of the open door, but that all stopped when I knocked on the frame to make my presence known. The music and laughter both died an awkward death and three sets of eyes stared at me—two of them were surprised and one was anxious.

"Oh, hey," Wren said, sounding as nervous as he looked. Why? Did he think I would blab about what we got up to the previous week or did his friends not know he was into guys? Or maybe he just didn't want them to know he was attracted to me specifically. "Are we being too loud?"

"What? Loud?" Could it be that simple? "No, I'm blocked in and need to leave."

"Leave? Is everything okay? Is Ralph all right?"

"Oh yeah, he's fine. I just need to do some grocery shopping and run a few errands. My mom and sister are hanging out with him. They, um, usually do every Sunday so I can get away for a bit." I was babbling, and Wren's smile said he thought it was cute.

"I'm the one who blocked you in," a blond guy with ornery blue eyes said. He looked me up and down, but more out of curiosity than anything else. "Let me grab my keys, and I'll be right down."

"Thanks," I said, offering a friendly smile to him before I faced Wren again. "Do you need anything from the store, Wren?"

"Nope, I'm good. Thanks though." He was back to wearing his indifferent mask now that the surprise and worry were gone.

"See you later."

I turned and jogged back down the stairs. When I reached the bottom, the other friend spoke up and his words nearly made me trip over my two feet. "He's fucking adorable. No wonder you were so hell bent on moving into this…place."

"Shut up, Jimmy," Wren said then turned the music back on.

I wanted to creep back up the steps and listen in on the rest of the conversation, but the blond guy would be out any minute. I didn't want to get caught, so I just continued to my car to wait. When blondie came out, he stopped by my car and knocked on my window. I rolled it down and he smiled so wide the sun glinted off his teeth.

"I'm Danny by the way. It's nice to meet you." He extended his hand and I shook it, but Danny seemed reluctant to let it go.

"Darren, but my friends call me Dare." I tugged my hand back a little and he let it go with a laugh.

"I'm sure I'll see you around since you're Wren's neighbor." I wanted to be so much more than just his neighbor.

"See you around," I called after him.

Here was a guy who was blatantly interested in me but didn't stir up the tiniest bit of reaction. Why must I want a guy who clearly doesn't want me in the same way? I second-guessed myself the entire drive to the *specialty shop* out by the interstate. The last thing I wanted to do was make an even bigger fool of myself over Wren Davison, but I had to try once more. I knew he still wanted me no matter how hard he tried to hide it. *Said every creepy stalker who walked the earth.*

I'd been to Kim's Toys, but never by myself, so I was a bit intimidated. I expected protesters or religious zealots to be swarming around the parking lot to warn me I would go to hell for my wanton ways. *Wanton ways? Maybe I should try to write a book. That would be a snazzy title.* There were no protesters, religious or otherwise, and only two other cars besides mine in the parking lot when I pulled in. I casually ambled into the store like I did it on a regular basis and nearly ran back out when I saw a woman old enough to be my grandmother working the register.

She must've seen my panicked expression because she gave me the same gentle smile you'd expect if she was handing out chocolate chip cookies. "First time visiting, dear?"

"Uh... no."

"Let me know if I can help you find anything, although the store layout is pretty simple and items are sorted by category."

"Thank you," I said quickly to prevent her from rattling off the various categories. I appreciated her willingness to assist me, but some things a man wanted to find on his own, especially if I was going to be the one using it.

She was right about the store being laid out well. It didn't take me long to find what I was looking for and make my way to the register. I was surprised to find that several people were in line to check out. *Where had they come from? Did they carpool?* I lowered my eyes while I got in the back of the line. *You have no need to feel embarrassed. You have no need to feel embarrassed. We're all here for the same reason. Sex is a natural thing and people shouldn't be ashamed to enjoy it.* I kept repeating these things as the people in front of me checked out and left the store. At least there wouldn't be anyone behind me to witness my shame when the lady gave me the same spiel as everyone else as she tested the devices to make sure it worked before we left the store with the merchandise.

"For obvious reasons, we don't accept returns," the lady said to everyone in front of me as she scanned the items with a handheld device. *Beep.* "That would be pretty gross." Try outright disgusting. *Beep.*

Luckily, the sales clerk kept the remarks about the purchases vague. Instead of saying she needed to test the vibrating lifelike dildo the young woman in front of me bought, she simply referred to it as merchandise. I tried not to giggle when the dildo bounced all over the counter, because I wouldn't want someone laughing at me.

Beep. "Yep, that's our biggest seller," the woman said, repacking the dildo and its remote into the box. "It'll get you from 'oh, hello there' to 'who needs a man' in about fifteen seconds flat."

"Good to know," the woman said. I could hear the embarrassment in her voice and vowed that I would speak clearly and with pride when it was my turn to checkout.

I was doing good until I heard someone getting in line behind me. I could tell by the footfalls that it was a man, a rather large one, wearing work boots or something equally as heavy. It took everything in me not to turn around and look.

"I'm so happy you found what you were looking for," the clerk said when I finally arrived at the register. "I'm sure you heard by now that you can't return any merchandise."

"Yep," I said. I just wanted to get this over with so I could get the groceries bought and get back home.

"Oh! This is a nice choice too, although we don't sell many." She held the box up higher to check it out. *Beep.*

"You don't say."

"Have you seen the one that has an app instead of a remote?" she asked.

"Nope."

"I saw the ad on my favorite porn site." She paused and tilted her head to the side. "Now that I think about it, I'm pretty sure it was a scene from the site and not an actual item you can purchase. That would be something though, right?"

"Yeah, something."

"Your guy, or lady," she added quickly, "could pleasure you from miles away. I mean, if we can turn on our cars with an app from an airplane, we should be able to give our lover an orgasm."

"You wouldn't want that to fall into the wrong hands," the guy behind me said.

Fuck! I recognized that deep voice. I wished the ground would open and swallow me whole, but I wasn't that lucky.

"So true," the clerk agreed. I wanted to tell her that I changed my mind, but she fired up my new toy before I could say another word. "Perfect," she said. "Need any lube or condoms?"

"I'm good."

"I hope you'll come back and see us real soon."

"Um, thanks." I took my bag and made a beeline for the door. With any luck, I'd be gone before the guy behind me in line finished checking out. If I didn't have bad luck, I wouldn't have any because my car wouldn't start. I'd been meaning to buy a new battery, but I kept putting it off. It was money I could better use elsewhere, but I probably should've put that higher up on my list of priorities.

Fuck! I didn't want to call AAA and give them this address. Damn me and my stupid ideas. I looked over at the silver truck parked next to me and confirmed the identity of the man who stood behind me in the line. It wasn't that his truck was unique, it had his name plastered on the magnetic sign sticking to the door offering his carpentry skills. Andy Mason, aka Beefcake Andy.

I looked in my rearview mirror and saw that he was coming out of the store. *Bite the bullet and get out of the car, dumbass. This is a better alternative to having your mommy pick you up from the store.*

I opened the door and got out of the car. "Hey, Andy. Can I get your help a minute?"

"Uh, like help with what you just purchased in there?" He gestured to the store with his thumb.

"No!" Oh my God, I was going to stroke out and die right here in the parking lot of the sex shop in the middle of no-fucking-where. "My battery is dead!"

"Oh, so you want me to jump you, but in a different kind of way," he teased.

"Andy," I whined. "This is embarrassing enough as it is."

"No, embarrassing would be if you called AAA and they sent the guy who bought your grandpa's auto body shop. Me? I'm not going to give you a tough time about it. How about this? I'll jump *your car* and follow you to the auto parts store where you can buy a new battery. Or, we can leave your car here and I'll take you to buy the battery and bring it back and install it for you."

"Let's go with option one because I think that will be quicker for you. Thank you so much, Andy," I said in relief. "I am so glad you were here when this happened."

"You weren't five minutes ago," he said then burst into laughter. "I'm sorry I made the comment back there. I didn't mean to embarrass you." Andy gave me that big lopsided smile that turned almost every heart to mush. For me, I didn't even feel the tiniest tingle. I was hooked on a guy who preferred to grimace and grunt. *Damn you, Wren.* "Don't worry about me telling anyone about what I saw either."

"Thank you, Andy."

I was truly lucky he came to the rescue and had me back on track quickly. It was almost dark by the time I got home from the grocery store. I left my surprise for Wren in the glovebox of my car, knowing that I wouldn't easily sneak it past the prying eyes of my mom and sister. Unfortunately for me, I forgot about it until I woke up on Tuesday morning. I hadn't seen Wren since our brief chat on Sunday because the salon was closed on Mondays. I tried to talk myself out of retrieving the gift, but just the thought of teasing him and having him aroused all day was enough for me to brave the cold in my pajamas, robe, and slippers to get it.

Chapter Eight

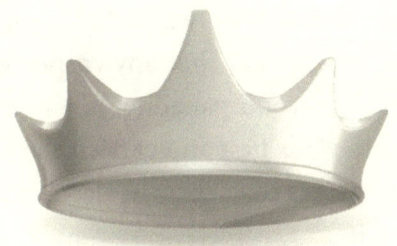

Wren

MY SELF-IMPOSED EXILE FROM DARE WAS MAKING ME cranky and question my sanity. Dare told me he had zero expectations, so why couldn't I just set my worries aside and enjoy what he was offering? I was so fucking hot for him that I couldn't see straight at times, and the only way I would get past it was to fuck it, or him, out of my system. If I could find a way to do that without hurting the guy, I was all for it, but I had serious doubts that either of us would come out unscathed. See, I didn't want to like how Dare lit up when I walked into a room, but I liked it a lot—too much. I'd also become addicted to his laughter and good-natured teasing. Those were the things that I didn't want to risk losing over a few orgasms.

It was easy to avoid him after we left the salon on Saturday, all day Sunday except when he popped in briefly, and even on Monday since the salon was closed. I would've rather spent it tangled up in my sheets with Dare instead of tearing down that hideous fake wood paneling that lined almost every wall in the apartment. I'd pulled back a small section first to make sure there was good drywall behind it. I worried that they'd gone the cheap route and just had plywood under the paneling, but it seemed like luck was on my side for once.

I should've asked permission instead of just ripping it off the walls, but Dare had said that he wanted to remodel the place but couldn't afford it. I was certain that any carpenter he hired would start with tearing off the wood paneling. Just in case Dare got mad, I cleared my bedroom walls first and carried the scraps down to the garage. I'd even pay to have the debris hauled away so Dare wouldn't have to worry about it.

By Monday night, I felt physically exhausted even though my mind didn't want to shut down. I took a long shower, jerked off, streamed shows on Hulu, and jerked off again, but sleep still eluded me. I wondered what Dare was doing. Was he jerking off too? Did he really sleep naked beneath the ceiling fan because his room got too hot? How much hotter could the two of us make it? I pictured his hair dripping sweat onto his back as I pounded him from behind. I was mesmerized by the path those droplets would take down his back and pictured myself leaning over to lick some of them.

I didn't fall asleep until nearly three o'clock in the morning and was a grouchy bastard when I woke up. Luckily, I had time to pull myself together since I didn't have to be at the salon until ten o'clock. Dare would leave at least an hour before me, so I didn't have to worry about feeling bad by not offering him a ride if he chose to walk to work again.

I took my time in the shower and let the hot water run down my back. My dick reared its thick head and demanded attention, as if I hadn't practically pulled the skin off the thing since I met Dare. I ignored it in favor of letting the heat seep into my sore muscles from the physical labor of the day before.

There was a knock on the door just as I got out. I knew damn well who was on the other side of the door and debated ignoring him for half of a second. Instead, I wrapped a towel around my waist and greeted him.

Dare's mouth fell open as his eyes raked over my bare chest. Did he remember how my chest hair felt against his smooth skin? Did it tickle his nipples and make them even harder? Fuck, there was no damn way I could resist him a second longer. I fisted his red sweater and pulled him into the apartment and slammed the door shut.

"Wait!" he gasped before I could crush my lips to his. "I came here to give you something."

"And I very much want it." I slid my hands down to cup his pert ass and pull him tighter against me. My towel wasn't much of a barrier and I knew he could feel how much I needed him.

"No, a different kind of *gift*."

"I have all I want right here." I nuzzled my beard against his neck.

"It's something to keep me in line at work. It's getting harder and harder to be good. I need help."

"I can feel how hard it is, Dare. Let me make you feel better."

"Wren, do you believe in delayed gratification?" he asked me, sounding so serious that I had to take a step back.

"You mean a longer delay than the year I've known you?" I tilted my head to the side and studied his pretty flushed cheeks. Dare was embarrassed. Why? "Do you mean edging?"

"Yeah, kind of. I hadn't given it a lot of thought until I teased you about a cock ring the other day. Then I realized that the idea of denying myself for hours really turned me on."

It had the same effect on me, but I wondered if we could really pull it off. "We both have a very long day ahead of us. Are you sure you want to try this on a work day?"

"Yes," he said breathlessly then pulled a tiny remote out of his pocket. "I'm giving this to you to keep me in line today."

I studied the wireless remote then looked back into his eyes. He was as serious as a heart attack. "Dare, what does this do?" I asked nervously.

"You won't hurt me, Wren."

There was nothing around his neck, but I didn't expect him to wear a fucking shock collar to the salon. It would be a more sensual form of punishment. "What have you done, Dare?" I placed my hands under the button-up shirt he wore untucked beneath the sweater and slid them up to touch his nipples. No vibrating nipple clamps. I shifted my hands to his cock and balls but couldn't feel the outline of anything against his hard-on, which left… "Oh, Dare."

He'd inserted a vibrating butt plug in his ass, which would stimulate his prostate when I hit a button on the remote he entrusted with me. I hit the lowest number on the remote and he swallowed hard but didn't make a sound. I smiled wickedly and tapped number two.

"Oh!" he said breathlessly. "Oh God!" I wanted to hold my finger on the button a little longer, but I had two more to test out.

I pressed his body against the door and lowered my mouth to his ear. "What does number three feel like?" I tapped it too.

"So good." He licked his lips to moisten them after breathing hard and fast had dried them out.

"One more number to test. Do you want to know now or wait until you push your luck at the salon?"

"Now!" I tapped the button and he let out a low, guttural moan that sounded like a mixture of pleasure and pain.

"Don't you come," I growled then nipped his bottom lip.

"I can have multiple orgasms," Dare panted.

I didn't want to think of anyone giving him multiple orgasms but had to know. I needed to know what mark I had to beat, so I could be the best he ever had, although I didn't want to think about why I felt that way. "How many?"

Dare just blinked at me like he was afraid to answer. I held my finger on the first button so that it sent multiple bursts straight to his prostate.

"Ohhhhhhhh, this was a really bad idea," Dare moaned but he was too coherent for the damn thing to be working properly.

I just couldn't have that. I held his gaze when I placed my thumb over the second button. *Zap. Zap. Zap.*

"TWICE! Dammit! I came twice on a few occasions."

I kissed Dare long and hard to reward him for his honesty. I pulled back and held up the remote where he could see it. I needed more answers from him. "Did you spurt cum both times? I'd heard of dry orgasms, but I've never had one."

"Yes, but not as much with the second orgasm," he whispered. "My prostate is very sensitive and reactive." He was too coherent for my liking.

"Yeah?" *Zap.* I hit number three for a short burst.

"Fuck! You'll make me come."

"Not yet," I said, shaking my head. "You don't get to come until tonight."

"T-t-tonight," he stuttered while nodding his head. "I'll be g-g-good."

I laughed then because I knew better. He wanted to push me to see how far I'd take things. I wanted to push him right up to the point where pleasure meets pain, but I'd be sure to do that once we're alone. "Dare, can you come without anyone touching your cock?"

"Yes."

"So, if I bring you back here tonight and hit this button enough times I will make you come without touching or licking your cock." Fuck, I was ready to come myself just thinking about it.

Dare swallowed hard but didn't look away from my eyes. I raised the remote where he could see it. "Yes, more than once probably."

"Dare, I want you to save at least one more orgasm for my cock.

I want your ass to strangle the orgasm right out of me."

"At least *one* more?" Dare licked his lips again and my mouth was close enough that the tip brushed against mine. "How many orgasms do you think I'll have?"

"More than any other man gave you." I brushed aside the strands of hair that came loose from his style during his almost-climax. "I won't stop until that happens."

"Oh God!"

"It will be like a religious experience." I leaned in for a final quick kiss then stepped back. "You better get to work or you'll be late. I need to take care of this," I gestured to the head of my cock that proudly poked out of the gap in the towel.

"You're going to jerk off?" Dare asked in disbelief. "Why do you get to come right now and I don't?"

"Because this is your little game not mine," I reminded him, holding up the remote. "You put me in charge of both your pleasure and your pain."

"Pain?"

"Ever heard of something hurting so good? That will be you tonight after I get ahold of that sweet ass, Dare." I grabbed him by the shoulders and turned him around to face the door. "Go to work, Dare. Oh, and leave that shirt untucked. We can't have you sporting wood at the salon all day."

"Okay." He sounded dazed and I worried that he'd fall down the steps, but he made it okay.

I had intended to jerk off, but it lost its appeal. I wanted Dare and nothing else. Besides, it was way sexier to let Dare think I'm stroking my cock while plotting all the things I wanted to do to him. I decided I would take a multi-faceted approach to his torment that day—physical, verbal, and visual.

The black leather pants were more about driving Dare wild, but they would make it harder for my dick to get the rise that it so easily did in his company. Thankfully, I would also wear an apron for the largest part of the day, which meant that Dare would get to see my ass in the tight leather and not much else.

I felt everyone's stare when I strolled into the salon wearing those pants and a charcoal-gray Henley. There was only one set of eyes that I cared about though. The small, square remote was in my front pocket, visible for everyone to see but impossible for them to know what it was. Dare knew, and just in case he wasn't sure, I pressed a finger against the remote through the leather.

His eyes widened, but he made no sound. He whipped his head back to his computer but he wiggled slightly in the chair. He was mostly good for the day, but I did think he smiled a little too long at the hunky carpenter when he stopped by for Josh to cut his hair. Dandy Andy or whatever they called him could train his eyes else-where, and just in case Dare needed a reminder, I pressed a number for a few seconds. *Zaaap.*

Everyone else in the salon thought he was choking, but I knew he was covering up a moan. "Wrong pipe," he told them before tak-ing another sip of water. If I was really mean, I would've hit him again, but he would've choked for real or spit water across his desk.

I backed off the little gadget until we were alone at lunchtime. Yeah, I purposefully started scheduling my lunchtime according to his, which wasn't hard since he ate at the same time every day.

"Any cake?" I asked, sitting across him.

"Not today."

"Oh, I'm going to need something extra sweet after the salty treat I'm planning tonight."

"I hate you," he snarled.

"You want to straddle my lap and ride my cock so bad you can't see straight."

"Is that an option?"

"Not here, Sparkles."

"I should hate that fucking nickname," he groused, poking his salad with a fork.

"But you don't because it's not intended as an insult," I told him. "Be sure to eat all the boiled eggs and grilled chicken. Protein is good for you."

"We both could've had extra protein if you hadn't been so mean."

"I had every intention of doing just that when I opened up the door, but you stopped me. Remember?"

"Oh yeah."

"Thank you for my gift, by the way. I can't recall a toy I enjoyed more."

"That's because you've only been on that side of the remote," he stated boldly.

"Good, huh?"

"So fucking good."

"Why do I have a feeling neither of you are talking about lunch?" Josh asked when he joined us at the table.

"What else could we be talking about?" Dare asked with a scoff.

"A myriad of things but let's pretend I'm wrong. How's the new chicken cranberry salad?"

"Delicious," Dare answered. "The best I ever had."

Josh quirked a brow but didn't say anything else before he tucked in to his meatloaf sandwich.

The rest of the day dragged on slowly, except for the one time I bent over to pick something up off the floor and the tight leather pocket accidentally pressed down a few buttons. Luckily, Dare wasn't in the salon area at the time. I heard a small squeak and found him in the supply closet, clutching his chest with one hand and pressing a hand against his cock with the other.

"Sparkles, I'm so sorry. It was an accident. Are you okay? Did you come?"

"Which are you most worried about?" he asked between pants. "It was close, but I didn't come."

"Are you in pain?" I asked. He sounded pulled tight enough to break. "Do you want to take it out?"

"Not that kind of pain, Wren. The good kind and I trust you to make it better soon. No phone calls to put you in a broody mood so that you forget I exist."

"I promise you." I gave him a quick kiss on his pouty lips. "I could never forget you exist, Sparkles. Not much longer, and I'll make you feel better."

It felt like an eternity though because Dare had to take care of his grandpa's dinner and get him settled in to watch some television before he could come over. I paced like a lunatic until I heard him knock on the door.

"You don't need to knock," I said, pulling him inside.

"You changed clothes," Dare said with a hint of poutiness in his voice. "I wanted to peel you out of those leather pants with my teeth."

"Next time. They were cutting the circulation off to my dick. We couldn't have that now, could we?" I gestured to his sweatpants. "You changed too. Dangerous choice though. What if I zapped you and you popped wood in those things?"

"I doubt it has that kind of range."

"Hmmmm." I had every intention of finding out. "Enough small talk. I need you to come." Dare followed me to my bedroom without me having to ask.

"I need to…. Oh!" Dare didn't see me pull the remote from my jeans pocket but he felt the quick pulse from me tapping a button. I sat on the edge of the bed and spread my legs to make room for him.

"Get your clothes off and come here." I patted my inner thighs invitingly. I hit the third button and saw Dare's cock bouncing against his sweatpants. He was free-balling it beneath the cotton.

"Get your shirt off, Wren. I'll make a huge mess." I placed the remote on my thigh and did as he suggested. I watched as he removed his clothes, but I didn't do it without tormenting him. *Zap. Zap. Zaaaaaaaap.* His cock bounced and pulsed with the need to

come. I knew he was close. "Turn around and let me see that ass."
Zap!

"Ohh fuuuuck." Dare turned and presented his bubble butt to me.

It was my turn to moan. "Spread your cheeks apart and let me see you better."

Zap. Zap. I watched as his hole tightened and quivered around the base of the plug protruding from his pucker. I reached out and teased my finger along his crack to give the plug a gentle push forward at the same time I pushed the button on the remote again. *Zap.* I felt the vibration up to my wrist and wondered how he'd taken the torment for so long. I hit it again, marveling at the way his body responded.

"Wren!" I heard the desperation and knew what it meant.

He spun back around, and I pulled him between my legs. I held my finger on the fourth button and watched his cock bob and throb a second longer before thick white cum spurted from his slit to splash against my chest and stomach.

"Wren!" My name had never sounded so good coming from someone else's lips.

Dare wobbled on his feet and collapsed against my chest.

"That's number one, Sparkles."

Chapter Nine

Dave

"I'M NOT SURE I CAN HANDLE ANOTHER ORGASM," I murmured against Wren's strong shoulder. I could think of no better place to rest my head after a shattering climax. "Maybe I just take care of you, and then we can nap." I reached down to undo his jeans, but he batted my hands away.

"We're not even close to being finished," Wren said, running his hands down my back to grip my ass cheeks. A gentle squeeze and bounce and the plug pushed against my prostate again.

"Oh!"

"That's right, Sparkles. You still have so much left to give me." Wren brought his hands up to my head and tilted it back so I could look into his eyes. Oh my, lust had darkened them to the color of a rich, expensive liquor. "I'm going to take it out now. Climb onto the bed and get on your hands and knees." In case I still had doubts, he slapped my ass once more and the vibration made me cry out. I saw how much Wren wanted me in his whiskey-colored eyes, and it felt so good to know the insane attraction wasn't one-sided.

Wren's desperation made me bolder; it reminded me that I was just as much his tormentor as he was mine. "Let me undress you the rest of the way first, Wren."

"This isn't a negotiation." Wren rose to his feet, picked me up, and set me roughly on his bed. "Hands and knees now." He retrieved the condoms and lube he purchased the other day from his bedside table and tossed them onto the comforter beside me.

I did as Wren directed but looked over my shoulder and watched as he revealed his body to me for the first time. I didn't miss the way his hands shook when he unfastened his button fly or how his body practically vibrated with need. Our mutual lust was a living, palpable thing that hung heavy in the air around us. I catalogued every inch of his gorgeous body so that I could replay this moment again in my mind over, and over, and over on lonely nights. Wren's long arms and legs were corded with muscle and smattered with the perfect amount of dark hair. I already knew how big and thick his cock was from the time he jerked us off together. A burst of energy spread through my body from knowing that his dick would soon be inside me. I would feel him for days and love every single minute of it.

He walked to me in confident, hungry strides that made me shake with anticipation. "On second thought," Wren said. He grabbed my ankles and pulled me flat onto the bed then rolled me over. "I'll save that position for after I've wrung all the cum from your hot body."

"Wren." I'd become a one-word wonder. Sometimes his name was a plea for more, sometimes it was an affirmation that he made me feel so damn good, and I had a feeling it would also be a plea for mercy. He'd ensnared me so much that the only thing I could think about was him—inside me, under me, and over me. *Wren.* He was all I wanted, craved, or needed.

It felt like a lifetime before he climbed onto the bed and situated himself between my spread thighs. "Arms above your head and keep them there." I did as he requested but smiled like the Cheshire Cat because I knew he was fighting for control. He didn't trust himself to hold out for two more orgasms if I touched him.

"What about my mouth?" I asked. "Can I suck your nipples while you fuck me?"

"No," he growled. Wren placed his hands on my knees then slowly slid them down the outside of my legs until he reached my hips. He gave them a firm grip then glided his hands back up and over my knees then down the inside of my legs, leaving goose bumps in his wake. "Perfection." I didn't agree, but it made my heart swell that he thought so.

"You've made us wait a very long time for this. Fuck me, Wren."

Wren grabbed the base of the plug then twisted and pushed it deeper inside me, smiling when my hips came up off the bed seeking more. "What was that you said about delayed gratification earlier?"

"I meant hours not months that stretched past a year." I raised my hips, trying to get that glorious push against my prostate again, but Wren stopped me by placing a firm hand on my left hip.

"Relax and give yourself fully to me," Wren said. "Let me take control of your pleasure."

I'd read about this in books before, but never tried it myself. Could I just lie there and take what Wren had to give me? Could I do what he asked without questions? Would I trust him to please me? The answer was yes. I wanted, trusted, and needed him. Period. I nodded, and he slowly released my hip as if he was unsure that *I* could be trusted.

I grabbed two fistfuls of Wren's bedspread above my head to keep from touching him when he rolled the condom down the length of his cock. Wren moaned as he smeared the lube on his eager flesh, making it nice and wet for a hard fucking. Christ, it was the sexiest thing, watching him prepare himself to please me. Especially with my cum still coating his stomach and chest.

When he was satisfied that he was slick enough, Wren reached between my cheeks and gently pulled the plug from my ass. Feeling empty after so many hours of being stretched elicited a displeasured moan from me. My skin was sensitive and tender, but his teasing touch around the rim of my puckered hole made me cry out in need.

"Wren!" There it was; my plea for more.

My whimpers of need triggered an answering growl from him. Wren gripped his cock and circled the opening, tapping the tip against it a few times.

"Wren!" That time it was a demand. The next sound I made was a strangled gasp slash cry as he pushed the head of his cock inside me. Fuck, he felt even bigger than he looked.

"Breathe, Dare. You can take me." He leaned down and kissed me until I relaxed again then rose back up to watch his slow penetration. I wished I could see it too. "You're just extra sensitive from being stretched for so many hours. I'll go easy on you tonight."

I saw stars when his cockhead nudged my prostate. Jesus, it would happen fast. He hadn't fully penetrated me yet, and my cock was already jerking like it was about to spurt.

"Fuck, that's sexy," Wren said, seeing my reaction to him too. Instead of sinking all the way inside me, he made short jabs to peg my prostate over and over.

"Wren!" My voice pitched higher and squeakier.

"That's right. Give me all your pleasure."

"Greedy bastard," I said between gritted teeth. Why was I fighting my release so hard?

Wren lifted my ass off the bed, balancing it on his strong thighs while hoisting my calves over his shoulders. He drew his cock back to the tip then punched his hips forward until he was buried to the hilt.

"Give it to me."

Wren pistoned his hips in and out of me hard and fast, making my cock and balls bounce. He loomed over me and stared into my eyes the entire time watching me for signs that I was about to come. The tendons in his neck strained against his skin and his hands dug into my thighs in a bruising grip. Sweat dampened his hair, making it darker and I wanted to run my hands through it, but couldn't until he let me.

I wasn't sure I was going to come again until he slowed the tempo and made shallow strokes inside me just deep enough to peg my prostate. My mouth opened in a silent scream and my balls retracted painfully.

"That's it," Wren said looking down at my cock. "Give. It. All. To. Me."

"Wren!" I yelled his name as I came a second time for him. There wasn't nearly as much cum, but it splattered hot against my skin.

"That's two," Wren said, then pulled out of me. "We're not done. On your hands and knees."

"Wren!" That time it was a whispered plea for mercy at the same time I complied.

Wren ghosted his fingers from the curve of my ass down to the sensitive area behind my knees before gliding them back up again.

"I know you can. I've never seen anyone as responsive as you." Wren wrapped his hand firmly but gently around my neck and held my upper body against the mattress as he slowly re-entered me.

God, the stretch, the burn, and the fullness was so fucking amazing. "Wren!" More pleading. I'd gone from *no more* to *give it to me* in a blink of an eye, or perhaps the long stroke of a cock.

"Keep your hands over your head," he reminded me. Wren moved his hand from my neck down to grip my hips with both hands as he rocked his cock in and out of me. "One more orgasm, Sparkles. I know you can do it."

"I never…"

"You were waiting on me." Wren alternated his tempo between long deep strokes and short punches, keeping me on constant edge.

"I can't. I'm too strung out."

Wren lowered his upper body to blanket my smaller frame. He wrapped one arm around my chest and dropped the other to my abdomen just above my cock. "Come for me again. I can feel you have one more in you."

I thought there was no conceivable way, but after only a few long strokes I started to feel another orgasm coming on. "Wren!" It was the affirmation he needed. Wren began hammering in and out of me, and the sound of our skin slapping together echoed through the room. "Wren!"

"I'm about to blow. Come now, or we'll start all over again."

My balls tightened and retracted as my orgasm started in my spine and spread throughout my body. "Wren! Oh God!" My cock throbbed like it always did but I didn't release any cum. It stretched on for several seconds longer than a normal orgasm and felt so good that it hurt. I was done, completely spent. "Wren!" I cried brokenly, knowing I couldn't take any more.

Wren pulled his cock out of me suddenly. I heard him strip the condom off his cock followed by the sound of his hand working his hard flesh. I wanted to watch but my head was too heavy to lift from the bed. Seconds later, he grunted loudly and his load splattered against my ass that was still suspended in the air. It must have been a hell of a load too because it was all over my lower back and ass cheeks; I even felt it dripping down my balls.

"Three," Wren said breathlessly as he rubbed his still semi-erect penis through his spunk all over my flesh. Then he cleaned me off with his shirt from the floor before he dropped to the bed beside me and pulled me into his arms. "You're so fucking amazing, Dare." He kissed the top of my sweaty head then rested his cheek against it.

I needed to get dressed and go back home, but my eyes were too heavy. "Home," I managed to say before I drifted to sleep.

I woke sometime later, stretching languidly after the amazing sex dream I'd had of Wren. My tight leg muscles and tender ass jerked me fully awake, and I realized that I was still in Wren's bed. I hadn't dreamed the three-orgasm encounter; it had really happened. Why was I still in his room? Alone.

"Wren?" I called out but received no reply.

I looked at the clock on Wren's bedside table and saw that it was eight o'clock. I'd been asleep for a few hours. *Fuck!* I jumped up then winced because I was smarting pretty good after that bout of awesome sex. I got dressed as fast and as gingerly as I could then went out into the living room. Wren was nowhere in sight. Where the hell had he gone? I felt Wren's possession with every step I took down the stairs to the garage. He wasn't there either, but his truck was still parked outside. Had he walked somewhere? I didn't mean to run him out of his own apartment. The thought of it made my heart hurt worse than my overused ass, so I pushed it aside. Grandpa was my main concern right then. It was almost time for him to go to bed, and surely he was wondering where the hell I'd gone. What if he'd fallen?

Relief washed over me when I saw that he was safe and sound at the kitchen table, and I was surprised that he wasn't alone. "Um, hey, guys," I said, rubbing my hand over the back of my neck nervously.

Wren's eyes raked over my body then snapped back up to meet my gaze. "I told your grandpa that you weren't feeling well and had fallen asleep while helping me unpack."

"That's mighty nice of you, Dare," Grandpa said, but he kept his eyes on the photo album in front of him. "Here's the one I was talking about, Wren." He pointed to a photo of a purple car. "Check out this nineteen-seventy Dodge Charger in Plumb Crazy. She was owned by a fella who lived here a few years between sixty-eight and seventy-two. Nice guy."

Wren looked at the picture Grandpa kept pointing at to get his attention. "She's a beauty, all right."

"Well, I think I've had enough excitement for the night, boys," Grandpa said then slowly rose to his feet. "Think I'll turn in."

"Let me help you get settled, Grandpa." I slowed as I neared Wren. "Wait for me?" I asked. Wren said nothing but nodded his head.

Once I had Grandpa in his room, I helped him change into his pajamas and get settled between the sheets. "Do you need anything? Want me to bring in a glass of water or juice?"

"Nah, go out there and spend time with your guy."

"He's not my guy, Grandpa."

"I might have poor vision, but I see the way the two of you look at each other. It's the same way I looked at your grandmother. I know love when I see it."

"Grandpa…" I let my words trail off because there was no point in arguing with him.

"If you wanted to convince me nothing was going on then you shouldn't have put your sweatpants on inside out before you came back home." Grandpa cackled when my face turned red. "Now get out of here so this old man can get some sleep. I need a sharp mind so I can beat Maren at *The Price is Right* tomorrow."

"Goodnight." I kissed his forehead and turned out the light. I left the door open a crack, so I could hear him if he needed me in the night. I would rather put some kind of monitor in his room, but I'd only found ones made for babies, which would rob him of his dignity. "I love you."

"Love you too, Dare. Now go spend time with your guy."

When I returned to the kitchen, Wren was no longer sitting

down. "Come here." His voice was husky and full of promise, and I didn't hesitate going into his arms. "I should've left you a note so that you didn't panic when you woke up."

"Why'd you let me sleep so long?"

"Guilt?" he asked. "I really wrung it out of you, so the least I could do was let you rest." Wren ran a finger across my cheekbone, caressing me with more tenderness than I knew he possessed. "Maybe then you would've noticed your clothes were inside out."

"My shirt too?" I looked down and sure enough, all my clothes were fucked up.

"Are you feeling okay?" Wren asked, changing the subject. "Did I hurt you?"

"Tender but amazing, although I do have one regret?"

"There wasn't a number four?"

"God no!" I chuckled. "I didn't get to touch you at all or put your dick in my mouth."

Wren took a shaky breath and released it. "I'll submit my body to you next time."

"How soon is next time?"

"When you can walk without a hitch," Wren replied.

"I don't need my ass to blow your cock. There's nothing wrong with my mouth." I pressed my nose against his neck and breathed in his scent. "Mmm, you showered."

"I couldn't show up at your grandpa's door with your dried cum all over me." Wren pressed his lips to my forehead for a sweet kiss. "Tomorrow night you can have your way with me. I'll be good and let you do whatever you want."

"I'll hold you to it." I walked him to the door where he kissed me one more time. "Wren, thank you so much for spending time with my grandpa. He looked so happy when I came through the door."

"He's fun to be around, so it was my pleasure." His lips tilted up in a wicked smile. "Sweet dreams, Sparkles."

I watched as Wren jogged across the driveway and disappeared into the garage. My world suddenly felt like it had shifted from its axis. I felt dizzy and giddy and ridiculously happy. Oh fuck! Grandpa was right. I was in love with Wren. I couldn't let on though, or I'd lose him for good.

Chapter Ten

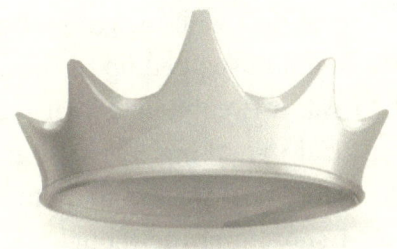

Wren

THE WEEK THAT FOLLOWED WAS ONE OF THE MOST incredible in my life. Things were going great at the salon, and I spent my evenings either naked with Dare at my place or fully clothed at his house hanging out with him and Ralph. On the few nights we were apart, I spent time stripping more wood paneling off the walls after Ralph and Dare gave their approval.

"You'll have to let us knock some money off the rent," Ralph had said. "It doesn't seem right for you to pay to live there and remodel it for free."

"It keeps me busy and out of trouble," I had replied. "I don't know a lot about remodeling and construction, but I do know how to patch and mud drywall. I'm thinking a fresh coat of paint will really liven the place up."

"You mean bring it to the current decade," Dare had teased.

I knew Dare was embarrassed by the condition of the apartment, but with new flooring and fresh paint, it would look like a brand-new place. Dare could worry about overhauling the kitchen cabinets and bathroom sometime down the road. I hadn't given much thought to how long I planned to live in the apartment; I just wanted to make things a little easier on Dare.

The only dark spots during the week were the daily calls from a man I didn't want anything to do with. After years of having his monthly attempts to reconnect with me ignored, my father had apparently grown tired of it and stepped up his game. What could he do about it though? I was a twenty-eight-year-old man who didn't need his permission to do anything. Every time he called, I sent him straight to voicemail. What was he going to do about it? Show up here in Blissville? I snorted at the thought. He had a new wife and a shiny new baby son. What could he possibly want with me? Furthermore, what could he possibly think I wanted with him?

When Sunday rolled around, Jimmy and Danny came over to eat pizza and watch football. Jimmy had even bought me a lava lamp and had it delivered to me midweek as another joke about how old-looking my new digs were. My friends could laugh it up all they wanted, but I was happier in that small apartment than I'd ever been in my entire adult life. I knew the source of my happiness had nothing to do with the walls that surrounded me and everything to do with the guy whose moans bounced off them.

"Hey, the place looks better already," Jimmy said, looking around the living room. "Oh man, you even plugged in the lamp." There was no way in hell I was going to tell him that staring at that dumb lamp eased the tension that rose inside me each time my sperm donor called. I could've changed my number, but what fun was that? I liked to be reminded of pain and betrayal because it kept me from making the same foolish mistakes that my mom had when she was younger.

Not doing such a fantastic job at it though, pal. You spend more time with Dare than you do without him. What kind of mixed signals are you giving the guy?

"Shut the fuck up," I whispered out loud.

"Bro, I was teasing about the lamp," Jimmy said, holding his hands up in surrender.

"I think there's something else bothering our boy," Danny said as he looked at me through narrowed eyes. "You look different, Wren. Whatever, or whomever, you're doing looks good on you."

"Don't start," I said, pointing my finger at him.

"Come on," Jimmy teased. "You don't seriously think we missed your reaction to the cutie pie who owns the place."

"His grandpa owns it," I corrected.

"Yeah, but I bet his grandson is the one collecting the rent. Am I right?"

"Oh, does he knock a little extra each month if you—"

"Not another motherfucking word about him," I warned them. I'd never known either of them to be so crude before, and I... *Fuck!* They'd set a trap to catch me, and it snagged me good. "Just shut up, Jim Bob and Danny Zuko."

"Low blow," Jimmy said. He hated his first and middle name pairing. "Who names their kid James Robert unless they want him to get beat up at school?"

"I don't look a thing like Danny Zuko from *Grease*," Danny argued.

"You kind of do but with blond hair," Jimmy told our friend. "It doesn't help that your last name is Zucker."

"Shut up and eat your greasy pizza. I bet lover boy wants us to get the hell out of here as soon as possible. I bet he has big plans with his new friend." Danny waggled his brows suggestively. "Can't blame you. He's fine as hell."

"Guys, I've known Dare for over a year now. He's not a *new* friend."

"Okaaaay," Jimmy said. "New boyfriend then."

"He's not my boyfriend either," I growled in frustration. "Since when have we ever chatted about our feelings and shit?"

"We've always talked to each other about what was going on in our lives," Danny countered. "None of us have ever met a person that we were serious about though." Danny said "person" because he and I were gay and Jimmy was bi.

"That hasn't changed," I told Danny.

"If you say so, Sparrow." I guess it was only fair that he invoked the nickname I hated after I used theirs.

"I say so."

Jimmy and Danny shrugged at each other and turned their attention back to the game. They soon got caught up in yelling at the Bengals and didn't notice how quiet I'd become. I stared at the television, but I wasn't really seeing it. I was reliving the week I'd just had and the happiness I'd enjoyed. I recalled the numerous ways that Dare and I made each other come, the laughs we shared playing rummy with Ralph, who cheated something fierce, and all the stolen sweet moments at the salon. I'd found every opportunity to kiss him or smell my soap on his skin.

Fuck me! I had my very first boyfriend. That was never my intention and wasn't what I wanted either. I wasn't made for relationships. Infidelity and selfishness were built into my DNA, and I could not subject someone as special as Dare to the hurt I was sure to bring into his life. I had to find a way to back us away from the edge before it was too late. Hurting him was the last thing I wanted, but it was better to do it before things went too far. Once I made that resolve, I tuned back into the game in enough time to watch the Bengals pull off a fourth quarter, miracle comeback.

After it was over, Danny and Jimmy went home. I walked them down to the garage then got busy working on my Chevelle that Jimmy hauled over in his box trailer along with my Harley. It was too salty and nasty to drive my classic car and too cold to ride a motorcycle. Pizza and a few beers was the least I could offer them for helping me out.

Working with my hands always helped me check out from bothersome thoughts, so I cranked up the classic rock and lifted the hood of my beauty to give her a tune-up that she probably didn't even need. I lost track of time and forgot about my worries until I sensed that I wasn't alone anymore. It scared me that I knew Dare was there without looking. It also bolstered my resolve to end whatever was going on between us. That was until I closed the hood and saw him.

"What are you wearing?" I asked, as if I didn't recognize the dark-blue mechanic's coveralls. "Steal those from Ralph?"

"Nope. Gotta love Amazon Prime's two-day shipping." Everything about Dare from the way he spoke and walked to the way he'd unbuttoned his coveralls down to his sternum spoke of seduction. "I didn't have time to have a customized name patch sewn on though."

"What would you have chosen?"

"Sparkles, of course." He didn't stop moving until he pressed his lithe body against mine.

"My hands are filthy, Dare." It was my last-ditch effort to put some distance between us.

"Make me filthy too." He pointed to the Harley behind him. "Preferably while bending me over that wicked beast." He reached inside his pocket and pulled out a condom and lube packet. His eyes sparkled with happiness and lust, and my resolve vanished into thin air.

"I can do better than that," I said boldly.

My first instinct was to wipe my hands off on a shop towel, but I changed my mind when Dare started unsnapping his coveralls, revealing more of his fair skin. I wanted to leave my handprints on his hot body, marking him. Needing to be the one to reveal every inch of his skin, I knocked his hands away.

"It's warmer in here than I thought it was going to be," Dare said when I simultaneously kissed his neck and pulled the coveralls from his arms and shoved them down to his hips.

"Torpedo heater," I explained. I reached beneath the fabric to cup his bare ass cheeks. Fuck, I couldn't wait to see the marks I left behind. I pulled back from him and quickly removed my clothes and shoes before I finished undressing him. "The motorcycle will feel cold against your bare skin. Do you want me to get a blanket from upstairs?"

"You'll warm me up."

Who was I to argue? I straddled the Harley and scooted back so there'd be plenty of room for Dare to lie in front of me. The only question was: facedown or faceup? The scene played out so vividly in my mind that I nearly moaned out loud. I crooked my finger for him to come to me.

"Roll the condom on me and make me good and slick."

Of course, Dare didn't just roll the condom on. He had to take his sweet time and torture me by licking my nipples and nibbling my neck, reminding me that he was the seducer in this scene. Once I was slick and ready, I patted the motorcycle seat in front of me.

"Straddle the bike and lie facedown with your head up by the handlebars."

For the first time since he entered the garage with the intent to fuck, Dare looked a little nervous.

"My legs will keep us from tipping over." I slapped the seat again. "Give me the best ride I've ever had, Dare."

He wasn't about to back away from that challenge. I bit my lip to keep from chuckling when he gasped at the first contact of cold leather and metal against his bare skin. Hey, I offered to get a blanket. My breath caught in my throat when Dare reached back and began stretching his hole with lubed fingers, prepping himself for my cock.

"Feel good?" I asked when Dare started to moan and grind

against the motorcycle seat. His sexy plump cheeks had never looked better than when wearing my mark on them.

"Not as good as you."

I gripped my cock around the base and lined up to his hole after he pulled his fingers free. Dare reached up and grabbed the base of the handlebars for leverage, and I thrust my cock as far as it would go on the first push.

"Yes!" Dare cried out, loving the bite of my penetration.

I gripped his hips tight and started a slow and easy ride, leaning back as far as I could to get a view of my cock gliding in and out. I pulled back until only the tip remained then slid back inside him until my balls slapped against his.

"Harder."

There was no way I was giving in to his demands or it would be over too soon. I wanted this ride to last a long time. My hands looked huge against Dare's narrow hips and his ass was stretched nice and tight around my cock. I lowered my right thumb and pressed it just above his pucker so I could feel the way he expanded as I moved in and out of him.

"Wren!" I loved how my name sounded so different each time he said it. I could tell by the raised pitch that he was ready to come. My guy was so damn responsive and sexy. There was never any guessing whether something felt good to him. That didn't mean I was going to immediately give in to him.

I continued working slow and steady, building us toward a climax. Dare's moans got louder as his need got greater, and I decided it was time to take pity on both of us. I raised up on my toes, leaned over Dare's back, and gripped the handlebars above him.

"You'll never be able to look at a motorcycle without remembering this night," I whispered in Dare's ear as I thrust fast and hard into him.

"Ohhh!"

"I'll never be able to straddle this bike without seeing you laid out before me with your plump ass cheeks spread apart to receive my cock. You look so fucking sexy like this."

"Wren!" His hole clenched around my dick and his body tightened beneath mine. I fucked him through his orgasm, and his spasming ass ripped mine from me.

I nuzzled his neck with my beard and loved the way he squirmed. "Keep that up and you'll get me hard again."

"We can break in the hot rod over there next," Dare suggested.

I doubted anything could ever top the motorcycle sex, but I was willing to give it my best shot. I held the bike steady while Dare climbed off and cleaned up. He tossed me a shop towel and I wiped his sexy release off the seat. I bit my lip to prevent a moan from escaping when he bent over to grab his coveralls off the garage floor. I fucking loved my handprints all over his flesh, especially the thumb print above his hole.

"Well, I hate to fuck and run, but I better get back to the house."

I should be glad that he wasn't sticking around, but I wanted to watch some television with him and just hang out like normal... *friends* do. Dammit, Jimmy and Danny were right. I'd let this develop beyond the fuck-buddy zone and knew I had to walk us back. Dare said he wouldn't make demands or ask for more than I could give him, and I was about to find out if he was being truthful.

Our kiss goodbye was awkward like maybe he already felt me pulling away from him. I was in no mood to finish the tune-up and went upstairs to remove the condom and shower off the grease and grime. I started with my hands so that I didn't get the shit everywhere. I stood beneath the hot spray and tried to ignore the acid burning my gut from guilt. I didn't want to be the reason Dare lost his sparkle. Any-fucking-thing but that. Just because I rarely expressed my emotions, didn't mean I was unfeeling and cold. It just meant I was cautious about who saw them. Dare made me feel comfortable in ways that no other living person ever had, including the mother that I had loved dearly.

I risked losing that connection, but I saw no other choice. Dare might feel hurt in the short term, but he'd be so much better without me in the long run.

Chapter
Eleven

Dave

A PERSON WOULD EXPECT ME TO WAKE UP FEELING PLEASED with myself the morning after successfully seducing Wren in the garage, but all I felt was dread. When he had first shut the hood on his car, I saw wariness and hesitation in his eyes. That faded fast as lust took over, but I couldn't get that look out of my head. I might've chalked it up to the lighting in the garage or my imagination if the look hadn't returned after we got dressed.

I could tell that he wanted to pull back from me but was worried about hurting me. I had no idea what made Wren so reticent to get close to anyone, but then again, I knew nothing about the man. It drove me crazy, but I wasn't willing to do anything about it. If I pushed too hard, I could lose all the ground I'd gained with him. I didn't want to go back to the days where he would grunt out responses rather than speak to me. I didn't want to give up shared lunches and soft kisses. I wasn't stupid enough to believe that I was working toward a real relationship with Wren, but we had *something* that I didn't want to lose.

After I returned home, I'd removed the coveralls in my bathroom to take a shower; that was when I caught a glimpse of two partial handprints on my hip bones where Wren held on as he fucked me. My heart raced with excitement when I turned my body in the mirror to see that I had a full handprint on both hips and ass cheeks. There was also a little smudge of grease peeking out of my ass crack. When I spread my cheeks to get a better look at the mark, I recalled the pressure of his thumb right there as Wren felt his cock moving in and out of me. My lust stirred all over again and I didn't want to be the only one feeling it. I retrieved my phone, turned my ass to the mirror, and snapped a picture over my shoulder. I wanted to capture the moment before I washed the evidence away.

I had planned on sending it to Wren but changed my mind the next morning. I'd made the last move and the next one would need to be his. I just hoped it wasn't an *it was fun while it lasted* speech. I knew we were headed toward that and wanted to delay it for as long as I could. Instead of sending it, I saved it for myself and put it to excellent use right away.

Mondays were my new favorite day of the week since the salon was closed and I no longer had to work at the furniture store to offset the loss of income. I could lounge around in pajama pants and watch television or put together jigsaw puzzles with my grandpa all day. I could even create new designs for my dream career that seemed to get further and further out of reach with every day that passed. The one bright side to working at O'Dell's was being able to use my education and talent to create pretty things. What fun was creating designs that only I would see?

Instead of moping about my uncertain future with the guy I wanted and the career I dreamed of, I pulled out my sketchpad and began drawing the first thing that came to mind. I had software programs for my laptop, and I always used them for the final presentation, but I liked to do it old school when an idea first presented itself. With no real plan in mind, I put my pencil to the paper and just started sketching like I'd always done, especially when I felt restless.

Within a few minutes, I realized I was creating designs for Wren's apartment above the garage. Gone was the hideous look of yesteryear, and in its place was a clean, modern apartment that anyone would be proud to call home. I took my time drawing out all the rooms how I envisioned them then transferred the specs to my software program to make them 3D.

By the time I was done, it was well past lunchtime. I felt terrible for making Grandpa wait so long to eat, but he was sleeping peacefully in his recliner. I set my drawings and laptop aside and made us grilled cheese and tomato soup for lunch. Grandpa only liked enough soup to dip his sandwich in and I could easily eat enough for two people. I wished I felt comfortable enough to offer Wren some lunch too, but I decided it wasn't a good idea.

As soon as Wren's name came to mind, I couldn't stop thinking about him. What did he do on his days off? The last two Sundays he spent with his buddies, but what did he do on Mondays? Grocery shopping? Laundry? *Laundry!* His apartment didn't have a hookup for a washer or dryer. I was sure he realized that when he checked the apartment over before he agreed to rent it, but I should've disclosed that. Lack of laundry facilities was one thing that drove Grandpa's previous tenant away a few years ago.

I kept that in the back of my mind as I woke Grandpa up from his nap and helped him get situated in the kitchen. Normally, I didn't bring my work to the kitchen table, but I had a sudden idea how I could upgrade the apartment beyond a fresh coat of paint, new cabinets, and flooring. The bathroom would require a lot more work, and to me, wasn't as pressing as the rest of the space. It was fucking hideous but fully functional. If only I could find a nifty place for a laundry closet large enough for a stackable washer and dryer. The apartment already had plumbing, so it would be a matter of adding a supply line and drain pipe for the washer. The dryer only required an electrical outlet.

I studied my 3D drawings while I ate my soup and sandwich until I came up with the perfect solution. The kitchen and living room were basically one large space broken up by kitchen cabinets, sink, stove, and refrigerator on the back wall. The flooring in the two spaces was also different, which helped separate the open space. I could easily reconfigure the cabinets to form an L-shape instead of taking up the entire back wall then I could add a pantry and laundry closet in the freed-up space. That's it!

"What has you smiling so happily, Dare? Are you reading a love letter from your guy?"

That almost made me snort tomato soup up my nose. "Grandpa, he's not my guy and Wren isn't the kind of man to send love letters." Maybe a text demanding I be naked and ready in his bed, but never a love letter.

"Nonsense," Grandpa stated loudly.

"Which part?" I asked.

"Both and don't sass me."

"Sorry, Grandpa," I said, but couldn't keep the smile off my face. I loved his fiery nature.

"Wren lights up when he looks at you."

Maybe when I'm naked. "Wren doesn't light up for anyone, Grandpa. He's very reserved and private. He shows very little emotion."

Grandpa snorted. "Keep telling yourself that, kid." He shook his head like he was disappointed. "Every man is the type to write love letters when he meets the right person." I opened my mouth to explain that I wasn't the right person for Wren, but Grandpa cut me off by holding up one finger. At least it wasn't his middle one, like he used when I took him to his doctor's appointment and some jackass

cut in front of us and stole the parking spot I had patiently waited for while a lady backed out. Grandpa had been none too happy
about it. I could tell by the distant look in Grandpa's eyes that his
mind was taking him back in time. He was going to share his wis-
dom with me, and I would patiently listen.

"I didn't start writing letters to your grandmother until I went
off to the war in Korea. Of course, we'd only been married for a
month before I was shipped off. People thought she was in the family way because we snuck off and got married as soon as I finished
basic training. That wasn't the case at all, because we weren't blessed
with your father for many years after that. No, I knew I was going
off to fight in the war. I'd seen the writing on the wall, and I wouldn't
take a chance that some other guy would come along and steal my
Norma from me. I did the only thing I could do. I made her mine.

"Looking back now, it was pretty selfish of me. I made her my
wife and then left her all alone within a few weeks. Oh, she tried to
sound cheerful in the letters she sent to me, but I read between the
lines. I did the only thing I could think to do to keep her interest,
Dare. I poured my heart out to her and hoped it would be enough.
By the grace of God, it worked. I returned home safe to her and she
welcomed me with open arms. I never regretted a single love word I
wrote to her, nor did I feel less of a man because of it. Norma knew
every day that I loved her above all others even through all the difficult years when we couldn't conceive a child. She was the greatest
love of my life and the other half of my soul. She made it so easy for
me to show her my love."

"Wow," I said, wiping the few tears that leaked from my eyes.
"You had an amazing life together."

"We did," he agreed, nodding his head. "I didn't see how I could
live without her when God called her home, but she made me promise that I would celebrate her life and not mourn her loss. I never go
back on my word, Dare. It's all that a man truly has to offer. People
can take your money, they can take your worldly possessions, they

can even steal your dignity, but they can't take your honor or integrity unless you let them. Remember that when times look bleak."

"I will, Grandpa."

"I know that you will, Dare. You're my best boy, after all." Grandpa looked at the clock on the wall with the big numbers so he could read it easier. "Oh boy! *The Young and the Restless* is about to start. You must've let me ramble on for a long time."

"No, I was late getting our lunch together. I'm sorry you missed the news."

"Not me," he said, rising to his feet. "It's a bunch of depressing bullshit. People have too much time on their hands if all they can do is cause strife for others. In my day, we listened to people talk and tried to find ways to compromise. Those days are long gone, Dare."

"You can say that again, Grandpa."

"Those days are long gone, Dare." Grandpa cackled as he shuffled to his recliner.

"You think Victor and Nikki are going to make it this time?" I asked.

"I won't hold my breath," he replied then turned up the volume as the opening song for the soap started to play.

I would've loved to get in my car and drive to IKEA to see some cabinets in person but couldn't leave Grandpa. I settled for doing a cost analysis for the materials based on my favorite cabinets I found online. I only needed to find a carpenter willing to take on the project, one who preferably worked at reasonable rates. My first thought was Andy, but he seemed so busy all the time. I was certain that I could put the cabinets together myself and would just need someone to hang them properly and do the plumbing and electrical work. To get a firm price on the material cost, I needed the exact measurements of the space I had to work with, which meant I needed inside the apartment.

My stomach tightened painfully at the thought of bugging Wren because I didn't want him to think it was another ploy to get inside his apartment *and* his pants. I really needed him to make the next move. It didn't hurt to ask if I could come up really quick. If he said no, I'd respect his wishes and get the measurements another time. If he said yes, I would take my laptop so I could measure and plug them into my program. "Here goes nothing," I whispered to myself as I pulled my phone contacts.

Hey, are you busy? I'd like to come up to get a few measurements. I'll be in and out in a hurry. I hit send.

Who you telling my size to? Will this appear in your Snapchat Story? Tumblr? Can't we just guess and say eight inches.

"What is he... Oh my God!"

"What's wrong?" Grandpa asked.

"Nothing, Grandpa. I just sent a message that wasn't very clear." *Shit!* "There's nothing to worry about."

Not your cock! The kitchen! I want to measure for the wall space for my new design plan. I didn't tell him that I thought his estimate was a little low. I'd say at least nine or ten, but I promised not to flirt or throw myself at his big cock.

Oh. It was impossible to know from a text, but I read disappointment in that single word. *Yeah, come on up. I'm a sweaty mess from working out though.*

I about broke my neck getting out of the house and nearly tripped up the steps to his apartment. Was he shirtless and sweaty? Was his hair down or did he tie it back? Man bun or ponytail? Either could make a nice handle if he... *No! Behave!*

Wren opened the door before I could knock. "Geez! It sounded like a herd of elephants trampling up these steps."

"Uhhhh." I had my answers. He was shirtless, sweaty, and his hair was pulled back into a man bun. I hated those things on anyone else but him, but of course, Wren made everything look sexy.

He looked at the laptop and measuring tape in my hands. "You were being serious," he stated, not asked. Wren stepped aside for me to enter.

"I'm almost always serious," I told him as I entered his apartment. I didn't bother hiding the fact that I was inhaling the air around him. He quirked his brow and I knew he was thinking about the many ways I'd flirted with him since we met. "I was serious then too." Wren's eyes darkened with lust, but I didn't linger. I was there to measure the kitchen and that was exactly what I'd do. "Don't let me stop you from your workout."

I headed straight to the kitchen without looking back. I set the laptop on Wren's small kitchen table and forced myself to focus on my task. I wouldn't get anything done except beg him to fuck me if I looked over and saw him doing sit-ups or push-ups or whatever the fuck he did to maintain that body. I became so involved in measuring and recording data that I didn't realize he had followed me until he cleared his throat. I looked up from my laptop and met his gaze. Why did he look so annoyed? He stood on the other side of the table with his arms crossed over his broad chest.

"Problem?" I asked innocently.

"Um, no."

I continued working in silence for a few more minutes until I had my last measurement. Wren walked around the table to join me as I plugged in my last bit of data. I hit enter and the kitchen image reconfigured on the screen.

"That's damn cool," Wren said, sounding impressed. "What's that large closet in the corner?"

"It's both a food pantry and laundry closet in one." I hit a button and the doors opened on the screen to show a stackable washer and dryer on one side with a food pantry on the other.

"Now that's really fucking handy."

"Yeah, I'm putting some estimates together for materials and labor," I told him while I saved the changes and made notes. "I can do a lot of it myself, but I will need to hire someone who can do the plumbing, electrical, and the bigger carpentry jobs. I can check out the home improvement store for scratch and dent appliances to save some money. If they unbox a perfectly good appliance by accident then they reduce the cost by a lot, sometimes half."

"You can do some of the work yourself?" Wren asked. I was used to people doubting my abilities, but it stung when he did.

"You'd be amazed what I can do."

"Oh, I'm sure," he said huskily, which meant it was time for me to go.

"I'm not sure when, or if, I can pull this off," I told him. "In the meantime, feel free to use our washer and dryer at the house. You don't have to stick around while you wait for your clothes to wash and dry. No trick, no obligation." I offered a friendly smile and a friendlier little wave as I strode past him. "See you tomorrow at work, Wren."

"Yeah, okay," he replied, sounding befuddled.

I gave myself a mental pat on the back for getting in and out of there like I'd promised myself. I could behave. I could resist him and not throw myself at him every time we were alone together. I felt pretty damn confident until he showed up at my door with a load of laundry and a wicked gleam in his eyes.

"Show me the laundry room, Sparkles," he said huskily.

I showed him so much more than that, but it was all his fault. He started it.

Chapter Twelve

Wren

REALIZED I WAS SENDING A FUCK-TON OF MIXED SIGNALS to Dare, which wasn't fair to either of us. One minute, I'm building a wall between us, and the next minute, I've carved out a gloryhole. That was just wrong on so many levels. I didn't want Dare to think I was just using him for sex, but what else was he supposed to think?

Dare had obviously picked up on my *stay back* vibes and honored my wishes, even though I didn't think that was the case when he sent me a text asking if he could take a few quick measurements. I couldn't resist teasing him, but he never took the bait. Not even when I opened the door sweaty and shirtless. Okay, he gaped a little bit and sniffed the air when he walked by me, but he didn't try to ogle me or flirt with me after that. He got straight to work measuring the kitchen for his design. And what a fine design it was too. I hated to say that he was wasting his time in the salon, because Curl Up and Dye was a wonderful place to work, but Dare had real talent that wasn't being realized booking appointments and keeping all of us in line.

I couldn't believe it when he just shut his laptop and left as soon as he was finished. He didn't attempt to seduce me one time, which revved me up even more than if he'd flashed his cock at me. Well, a close second maybe. I liked the idea of pursuing him, so I showed up at his back door with a laundry basket in my arms and slaking my lust on my mind.

Dare had been so adorable when he showed me to the laundry room and demonstrated how to start the old washing machine. "It's an oldie, but it still cleans the clothes really well. The detergent goes—Oh!" I loved the little sounds he made when I pressed my erection against him. He wasn't the only one who showed up prepared for a seduction. I had more than my laundry tucked inside that basket. I'd shut the door to give us some privacy then went about reminding Dare of the way we made each other feel. I don't know why it felt so important; it just did.

I placed my hand over his mouth when he started to moan loud enough to give us away. One minute he's pushing his ass against me begging for more and the next he bit me hard enough to break the skin when his orgasm crashed into him. The pain only made my pleasure that much sweeter when I flooded the condom.

I didn't just start my laundry and leave like Dare expected me to. I joined Ralph and Dare in the living room and tried to ignore the way Dare squirmed on occasion like he had a challenging time getting comfortable.

"How about I treat us to dinner," I suggested, surprising everyone.

"What can you cook?" Ralph wisely asked before agreeing.

"Oh, I had planned to place an order at the diner. I'm craving their cheddar broccoli soup."

"That does sound mighty good," Ralph said. "Would you mind if I ordered half of a Rueben sandwich too? Will that be too much?"

I had to swallow hard before I could speak. "You can have whatever you want, Ralph. Would you like a piece of pie too?"

"Is it my birthday?" he asked. I wasn't sure if he was being serious until I saw the twinkle in his eye. "I'd love a piece of the lemon meringue pie. Dare, do you think the lemon will be too hard on my reflux?"

I looked over at Dare and saw that he was holding back tears. He loved his grandpa so much that denying him anything would be painful. "Let me get you an extra pill to take so it can start working in your system before we eat."

Dare had tried to give me money for the dinner, but I wouldn't hear of it. We enjoyed a nice dinner and conversation while my clothes finished in the dryer. When they were done, Dare walked me to the back door and looked unsure of what he was supposed to do. Did he kiss me goodnight or just give me a cute little wave? He didn't have to voice his uncertainty because it was plain to see in the way he bit his lip. It made my heart ache to know that I confused him so much.

I leaned forward and gave him a soft kiss that lingered beyond a peck but didn't involve tongue. I wanted to slide my tongue between his soft lips, but that would've lead to other things that would've further complicated an already sticky situation.

So, I ended the kiss and went back up to my apartment and folded my clothes, noticing that they smelled like Dare. I brought a T-shirt up to my nose and sniffed it like a lovesick fool then tossed it back onto the bed in disgust. If I kept it up, I'd be passing him notes at the salon and asking him to go steady by the end of the week.

I don't know why something so silly soured my good mood, but it did. Even worse, I had weird dreams all night long that combined all the pain from my past with the happiness I glimpsed in my future if I just had a little faith. My sleep was fitful to non-existent, and I groaned when the sun streamed through my bedroom window. The first thing my sluggish brain registered was a sore middle finger on my right hand. I couldn't remember slamming it in a door or…. I held my hand up and sure enough there were faint bruises where Dare bit me the previous night. My finger wasn't swollen or stiff and there were no obvious teeth marks to give it away, but I would remember Dare coming for me every time it throbbed, or I looked down and saw the marks.

Without thinking it through, I snapped a closeup picture of the bruise and sent it to Dare with a message. *You marked me.*

I figured he was making Ralph breakfast because it took him awhile to reply. I'd already had my shower, drank my first cup of coffee, and ate my Corn Flakes and sliced bananas before he responded.

I guess we're even then.

How so? Did I bruise him?

Those big greasy handprints all over my ass, hips, and the thumbprint above my hole.

Fuck! How could I have forgotten about that? *Damn, I wish I'd taken a picture. That was so fucking hot.*

There was another long pause before he answered, and I wondered where he'd gone. *I will neither confirm nor deny right now, but I've heard a picture of the event you mentioned exists.*

No way. My dick started swelling. *Show me, Dare.*

Nope.

I'll make you. I knew damn well I could back up that threat.

Oh, this should be fun. He sent a laughing emoji then another text. *Gotta head to the salon. See you when you get to work.*

Was he joking? Did he snap a picture of his ass with my handprints marking him? I wanted that more than logic said I should. I mean, what would I do with it? *Jerk off.* It was the visual reminder of the most erotic sex I'd ever had. In fact, every sexual encounter with him far surpassed anything I'd ever experienced with anyone else.

I knew it had more to do with the person I shared the experiences with than the vibrating butt plug, power play, or garage seduction. It was the connection I felt to Dare that I'd never found with anyone else. It was enough to scare me spitless. I just didn't know what, if anything, I was prepared to do about it.

I arrived at the salon a little early so I could seek Dare out. It wasn't that I'd had some huge epiphany in the previous hours, but my desire to see that picture had grown. I did that smiling-on-the-inside thing as I hung up my coat and got my brain organized for my clients that day. I just wanted one little taste, one little tease from Dare, and perhaps a quick peek at the photo I knew damn well he had in his phone.

You know how it is when you feel something isn't right, but can't quite figure out what it is or even how you know it for a few heartbeats? I had that feeling after I made myself a cup of coffee and started walking toward the salon. Then it hit me. It was too quiet. There wasn't a single blow dryer going or conversation flowing between clients and stylists. The only sounds I heard were the heavy thud my biker boots made on the hardwood floor. Then I saw the reason for everyone's silence standing at Dare's desk.

Fuck. Me! I nearly dropped my coffee cup, but surprise was a reaction I refused to let him see. Anger boiled in my blood and propelled me across the floor faster. I could feel everyone shifting their attention from the rock legend standing at the front of the salon to me. Did they see the resemblance? As much as I hated to admit it, I couldn't deny he was my father no matter how hard I tried. I often wondered if it hurt my mother when she looked at me. After all, he was the source of her greatest misery and heartbreak.

"What are you doing here?" I asked in a deadly calm voice when I reached him.

"Hello to you too, Son."

"Son?" I heard several people ask at the same time. Dare wasn't one of them.

"Don't call me that, Alaric."

My sperm donor cringed and blew out a frustrated breath. "I've asked you not to call me that. It's Dad or Falcon."

"Neither is going to happen." I shook my head because Alaric "Falcon" Davison of the legendary band, Falcon's Descent, didn't care what anyone else wanted. He had decided that he wanted to be my father when I was seventeen years old, regardless of the fact I wanted nothing to do with him. I hated him more than I hated anything in the world.

"If you would've answered one of my calls you would know why I was here," he said. "This is where you work, huh?"

"You act as if it's a bad thing," Dare said defensively.

"Not at all," Alaric said, aiming a charming smile at Dare. "Is there somewhere we could talk privately, Wren?"

I had nothing to say to him, but I'd inform him of that in private rather than give the town of Blissville even more to talk about. Jesus, I was going to have to move after this. I looked at Dare who watched me through big eyes filled with concern. "Does Josi have a client upstairs right now?" I asked him.

"Um, no. Her first client isn't until noon. She's not even here yet, so go on upstairs."

I don't know what made me do it, perhaps I wanted to shock Alaric, but I suspected it had more to do with the way Dare looked like he wanted to shield me from pain. I reached over and lightly caressed the side of his face. Dare leaned into my palm and I forgot that the rest of the world even existed.

Alaric cleared his throat, yanking me out of my happy place with Dare. I turned and looked at him with as much animosity as I could muster. "Follow me. You have five minutes."

Alaric chuckled like it was no big deal I had disrespected him, but I knew it had to be a bug in his craw. He was used to people fawning all over him and stroking his ego. I had zero intention of doing either. The sooner he said his piece, the quicker I could get back on with my day.

Once we were alone upstairs, I turned to face him. I loved how uncertain he looked suddenly. "Was that little display with the cute receptionist your idea of shocking me, Wren? I've known you are gay for a long time. Terry told me. It doesn't matter to me, Son." Hearing him say my mom's name was like throwing gasoline on a fire. My rage burned inside me.

"What do you want?" I asked instead of answering his question or acknowledging his acceptance. "I can't possibly imagine what you have to say."

"I'm building a house in Indian Hill and moving back to the Cincinnati area. I've decided this rift between us is stupid. I'm not getting any younger and it's time you took your rightful place in my life."

"For fuck's sake, Alaric. You sound like some fucking king whose prince went astray. You might be the Rock King, but you're nothing to me." Hell, I couldn't even stand to listen to his fucking music without getting nauseous. "It doesn't matter that you want to make room for me in your life now that I'm twenty-eight years old. I don't have room for you in mine."

"Wren." My name left his lips in a long, exasperated sigh. "Will you at least meet me for dinner? You can rant and scream all you want for the mistakes I made with you and your mother." *Mistakes.* "All this resentment you're carrying around isn't good for you. It will rot your soul, Wren. One dinner and that's it. The ball will be in your court, and I'll respect your decision about the role I have in your life going forward." He would have no role in my life, of that I was certain. "I have reservations at Bobby Jack's steakhouse on the Ohio River. It's on the Newport, Kentucky side."

"I know where it is."

"Be there at seven."

"I said I know where the steakhouse is located. I didn't agree to have dinner with you."

"I understand," Alaric said before he turned and headed for the door. He stopped just before opening it and looked at me over his shoulder. "It will just be the two of us tonight. Samantha won't be there. I'd really like for you to meet her and your little brother, Tobias, but I won't push it."

"How big of you, Alaric," I snarled.

"I'm trying my best, Son."

"Your best won't ever be enough."

"I won't know unless I try. I hope to see you at dinner."

I said nothing else, just collapsed in a chair. I don't know how long I sat there wondering what the fuck had just happened or why. What could Alaric think he would change by forcing a face-to-face meeting with me after all this time? It had backfired spectacularly when my mom died and he tried to be the strong shoulder I needed. You would think he got the hint when I chose to go into foster care for my last year as a minor rather than move to LA to be with him. It turned out to be the best decision I ever made because that's where I met Jimmy and Danny.

There was a soft knock on the door, and I knew who it belonged to without asking. "Come in, Sparkles." As much as I wanted to be alone to lick my wounds, I needed his effervescence more than solitude right then.

"Hey," he said softly when he closed the door behind him. "Tell me how I can make this right, Wren."

I crooked my finger and Dare came to me without hesitation. I pulled him onto my lap, not caring about mixed signals or crossing lines, and lay my head against his chest. He wanted to comfort me, and I needed comfort. I knew he had a thousand questions running through his mind, but he didn't ask a single one of them. He just ran his hand through my hair and placed sweet kisses on top of my head.

"Do you want me to reschedule your appointments today? You look like you've had a terrible shock and by now everyone in this town knows that your, um, Falcon was here. The place will be crawling with busybodies."

I thought it was so freaking adorable that he wanted to protect me but hiding would only delay the inevitable. Besides, if I'd answered Alaric's calls last week, I could've prevented the entire disaster from occurring.

"Nah, I'll be okay." I held Dare a little tighter to show him how much his offer meant to me. "I can think of one thing that will make me feel a little better though."

Dare sucked in a quick breath, and I loved the way he reacted to me. "What's that?"

"Show me the picture."

Dare pulled out his phone and pulled the image up. It was every bit as sexy as I thought it would be, with my greasy handprints marking his fair skin. I needed to have it for myself. I didn't ask permission before I sent it to my phone. I smiled when I felt the vibration in my pocket that alerted me it had arrived.

"I have this dinner thing with Alaric, but I'd like to come over afterward." I hadn't even realized I was going until the words came tumbling out. "It could be ten or later before I get back to town. If that's too late…"

"Hush," Dare said then kissed my lips softly. "I'll be waiting for you."

It was exactly what I needed to hear to make it through the rest of the day.

Chapter Thirteen

Dave

AS ONE WOULD EXPECT IN A SMALL TOWN, WORD GOT around fast that a legendary rocker was spotted in Curl Up and Dye. I had hoped that no one besides me heard Falcon refer to Wren as his son, but I knew it was too good to be true. Wren might've been protected a bit more if the normal sounds of the salon drowned out the conversation, but it was so quiet that you could've heard a pin drop. The only noise was the thundering sound of Wren's steps as he angrily made his way to the front of the salon. The look on his face was darker than any storm cloud I'd ever seen. Even if I hadn't overheard Falcon refer to Wren as his son, I would've seen the resemblance with my own eyes.

The scowl that Wren wore to discourage the world from talking to him was the same one that Falcon used when playing a long guitar riff. Their wry grins were the same, as were the shape of their eyes and mouth. Of course, Wren's sly grins were reserved for me while Falcon's seemed contrived to sell records, T-shirts, and concert tickets. There were enough differences that I couldn't say Wren was Falcon's carbon copy, but it was plain to see that they were father and son.

The increase in salon traffic was maddening, but I kept a level head. I had two goals: keep the busybodies away from Wren and sell as many products as I could. Buying a haircare product, styling tool, or nail polish was the least they could do after so rudely prying into Wren's life.

One lady had leaned so far over the high counter of my desk that I thought she was going to fall over it. "Is it true? Was Falcon really here?"

There was absolutely no point in lying. "Yeah, he was here."

"Oh my God! I saw Falcon's Descent so many times in the eighties." I suspected her hairstyle back then was as unfortunate as the high-pitched squeal she let loose in front of me. "I had so many posters of them on the wall." She sighed dreamily, and I didn't even want to know where her mind had gone. "Is it true that Wren is his son?" The lady eyed my man up and down like he was her ticket to getting closer to the rock legend.

"That I can't confirm or deny."

I then wove a wild tale of how much Falcon loved the massage products upstairs. Josi didn't buy her oils and salts from a beauty supply outfit, she bought them from Marabel, the same lady who made Wren's, and now my, goat milk soap. Marabel offered a wide variety of skin, spa, and other amazing products using organic ingredients and high-quality essential oils. Both she and Josh would come out winners by the time I was done with the town.

At the end of the day, I was exhausted from the mental restraint it took to bite my tongue, my face hurt from forcing a smile all day, and my throat felt scratchy from the extra talking. The long, sweet kiss that Wren gave me before he left made it all worth it. I sighed happily as I went about my end of day routine. Wren freely showing me affection, no matter how big or small, was the shot in the arm I needed.

"Dare, you were incredible today," Josh said. I was so wrapped up in the sales data for the day that I hadn't noticed him approach. "Why don't you go on home and I'll finish the sales report and bank deposit. You've done more than your fair share around here today." He came around the desk and saw the sales figures. "Holy fuck!" Josh exclaimed then studied the figures some more.

"The downside is that I need to place an order for supplies first thing in the morning and pay to have an extra delivery," I told him. "We'll never make it to our normally scheduled delivery later in the month."

"It's a good problem to have," Josh teased then turned and looked at me. "I'm going to start paying you commission for the products you sell. You're one hell of a salesman."

I blushed slightly beneath his praise. "You don't have to do that, Josh. I really love working here and you pay me a good salary for the work I do."

"Dare, how often does a salon client leave without purchasing something when you check them out?" Josh asked.

"Um, not often. Mrs. Dowdner refuses to buy products and insists she can get the same quality for a fourth of the cost at the supermarket," I said.

"And that's why Mrs. Dowdner comes back every three weeks so I can tone her hair," Josh replied with a smile. "I'm serious though. How does ten percent commission sound in addition to your hourly wage?"

"Generous."

"Okay, we're starting your commission today," Josh said, gesturing to the data on my computer screen.

I did the quick math in my head and grinned broadly at him. I knew just where I would put the extra money. "Thank you so much, Josh."

"Thank *you*," Josh replied. "Now get out of here."

"See you tomorrow, Josh."

"You know what I appreciate the most from you today?" he asked when I'd gone a few steps.

"What?" I asked, turning to face him once more.

"The way you shielded Wren from the chaos without making it seem like you were slaying his dragons for him." I smiled at the terminology he used since it went along with my fairy-tale mindset. "I'm sure there were many times that you wanted to tell them how rude they were being, but you politely changed the topic away from Wren each time. That took a lot of skill."

"I care about him, Josh. I don't want people to pick at his pain like fucking vultures. He's a person with feelings, not roadkill on the side of the road."

"Gruesome visual," Josh said, making a face, "but it's true all the same. I've always known how you felt about Wren, and if he didn't know it before, he does now."

Did he? Was that why his lips lingered against mine before he left to get cleaned up for dinner? Did he know that my feelings went beyond *caring*? I was in love with him, there was no other explanation for the way he made me feel.

"Off you go," Josh said, making a shooing motion with his hands.

It was a long day, and I should've been exhausted, but knowing I would see Wren sent a jolt of adrenaline through my system. My pulse raced with the possibilities of what would happen in my small bedroom. I knew that sex was a possibility, but I was more curious if Wren would confide in me about his relationship with his fa-Falcon. I couldn't refer to the man as Wren's father until Wren did. My chest still felt tight from Wren reaching for me and asking to see me later. My heart might just explode if Wren really turned a corner and opened up to me freely. I thought it was worth the risk to my health to have those unguarded moments with Wren outside of a sexual situation.

When I got home, Grandpa was sitting up a little straighter in his chair. He was always happy to see me, but he was even more so than usual. *Not him too!*

"Grandpa, there's nothing much to tell. I wouldn't tell you even if I knew something."

"So, it's true. Wren's father is Falcon?"

"How do you even know who that is?" I asked instead of answering.

"Nice evasion technique," he said then smiled wryly. "I'm old, Dare, but not so old that I don't know who Falcon is, even if I think he is overrated. In my day, performers had talent. Record companies didn't have to hide their imperfections with technical mumbo jumbo. Singers stood on a stage and sang. Some of them danced, some of them even played instruments, but none of them busted their guitars into dozens of pieces, screeched into the microphone, or wore leather pants with the ass cheeks cut out of them."

Grandpa's comment reminded me of Wren's leather pants and the way they clung to his ass. He'd look fucking awesome in a pair of assless... "Hey, how do you know about assless leather pants?"

Grandpa rolled his eyes. "Your father and mother were crazy over that band. They'd come here for those music award shows and eat up every second that Falcon's Descent performed. They even went to a few concerts back in the day."

"I suppose most local people did since Falcon is originally from Cincinnati. We have the Hit King with Pete Rose and Rock King with Falcon."

"Well, Cincinnati is called the Queen City, so it stands to reason she gives birth to a few kings too," Grandpa said. "Is Wren okay?"

"Yeah, he's okay," I replied. Grandpa smiled wryly because he knew I pretty much confirmed that Wren's father is Falcon without coming out and saying it. Grandpa got his answer without me betraying a confidence. I pointed at the cagey man to let him know I was onto him. "That's all I'm able to say. This isn't my story to tell, Grandpa."

His wily smile morphed into a deliriously happy one. "I see how it is."

"You can't see anything without your magnifying glass," I told him. "You better dial down that grin or your dentures will fall out."

Grandpa hooted with delight. "Get in there and fix me dinner."

"Did nurse Wendy soak your teeth in OxiClean or something? They're looking extra white."

"Boy, you're not too old..."

"You'd have to catch me first," I replied sassily.

"Yeah, you got a point there. What's for dinner?"

"How do you feel about Salisbury steak and mashed potatoes?" The prepackaged frozen meat and gravy wouldn't be as good as my grandmother's, but Grandpa seemed to like it okay. "Maybe some peas to go with it?"

"I hate peas," he grumbled. "How about lima beans?"

"Who trades peas in for lima beans?" I asked as I made my way to the kitchen. "You're supposed to finagle and wheel and deal for cream corn or something good."

"Is that an option?" Grandpa asked.

"Well, I'm trying to keep your starches and carbs balanced, but I guess I can make an exception."

"Yes!" Grandpa said excitedly.

"It's going to cost you though," I teased.

"What's the price?" he asked suspiciously. God, how I loved that man.

"I want dirt on Mom and Dad. I'd prefer to see photographic evidence of the eighties. How big was Mom's hair?"

Grandpa held his hand several inches above his head. "Big! And curly like you wouldn't believe. And your dad!" Grandpa started to laugh in earnest. "Have you ever seen a picture from his mullet phase?"

"No! I must see it."

Grandpa gingerly rose to his feet and shuffled to his room to retrieve a photo album. I looked in the cabinet to see what other treats I could find for him. I found a box of sugar-free chocolate pudding that I could make with skim milk to cut calories, fat, and carbs. I could fold in some of the sugar-free whipped topping that I saw in the refrigerator into the pudding to jazz it up a bit, making it more like a whipped mousse.

After I put the tray of frozen Salisbury steaks in the oven, I joined Grandpa at the table to look through the album he found. It reminded me of the time I found Wren sitting here with Grandpa after I'd fallen asleep in his bed after he nearly fucked me to death. My heart fluttered in my chest and my greedy hole did a little fluttering of its own. It seemed that I would never get enough of Wren. In fact, instead of feeling sated, the craving grew stronger after each time we were together.

I had to acknowledge that it could all blow up spectacularly in my face if Wren never returned my affections. If I hadn't already acknowledged that my feelings extended beyond physical, I would've known it after today. My physical need to be with him was a distant second to making sure Wren had a soft place to land should he need one after meeting Falcon for dinner.

I challenged Grandpa to a game of Battleship after dinner, but he decided to turn in early. Grandpa didn't even eat his dessert, opting to save it for the next day, which was something that never happened. I worried that he wasn't feeling well, but I saw that the devilish twinkle had returned when I tucked him in.

"Tell Wren I said hello."

He turned in early so that I could visit with Wren. "Grandpa, Wren isn't home."

"He's going to want someone to talk to when he gets back."

Grandpa patted my hand. "You be that person for him. I'm a sound sleeper so don't you worry about me."

"Grandpa," I said, blushing bright red with embarrassment.

"I meant that I wouldn't overhear your *conversation*, but I know what you had in mind." He cackled again and pulled his blanket up beneath this chin. "Goodnight, Dare."

"Goodnight, Grandpa."

Once back in the living room, I pulled up my renovations for Wren's apartment and looked at the cost analysis. The commission bonus I would receive from Josh would be almost enough to cover the plumbing and electrical estimates I worked into my budget. I checked my savings account and looked at my bill budget for the upcoming month. If I packed lunch and did away with a few unnecessary luxuries, I could swing it. The first thing I'd need to do was get some solid figures from a licensed professional. I knew just who I was going to call the next day.

I decided to play around with a bathroom design also but ended up creating one far too big and luxurious to fit in that apartment. I realized I'd designed my dream master bathroom instead. I looked at the large shower enclosure and imagined how sexy it would be to watch Wren soap and wash himself through the glass. What else would I watch? If I came upon him pleasuring himself, would I stop so I could join in or just watch him stroke his cock? I started to feel my dick swell and tucked the fantasy away for another time. I might even share that one with Wren to see if he wanted to play along. Perhaps a sexy game of "what-if" via text message one night. We could let our imaginations run wild and play out some fantasies. *Not helping, Dare.*

I glanced up at the clock and noted it was past ten and Wren still hadn't made it back home. I hoped it was a good sign and he was working through his issues with Falcon. I knew next to nothing about the rocker, so I couldn't say if I wanted them to develop a deeper relationship. I only knew that I wanted Wren happy at all costs.

The exhaustion from the day caught up to me and my eyes kept getting heavier and heavier, no matter how hard I tried to fight off sleep. I hated the idea of missing Wren coming over to talk to me, but I knew it was a high probability with every minute that ticked by. Just when I thought I couldn't take it any longer, his headlights flashed across the room when he pulled into the driveway. The low rumble of his truck sent my pulse racing and my sleepiness vanished in a snap.

I hurried to the door at the side porch and turned on the light so he'd know I was awake and expecting him. He sat in his truck for a while, and I worried that he'd changed his mind and would rather be alone. I wanted Wren to come to me on his own volition and not feel obligated. That conviction faded as soon as he stepped out of the truck. Even in the dark, I could see that his body was tight with tension. I wanted to do anything and everything to make him feel better.

Wren jogged up the porch steps and I opened the door for him, unsure how in the hell I was supposed to greet him. Wren took the guesswork away and pulled me into a hug. I felt his tension ease when I wrapped my arms around his waist and leaned into him.

"There's my Sparkles," he whispered gruffly.

Then he kissed me like months, instead of hours, had passed since we parted ways at the salon. I wasn't complaining, but my intuition told me that Wren needed something more than kissing and fucking. As much as it pained me to do it, I pulled back from him. Wren didn't hesitate when I reached for his hand and led him up to my room, but it was probably because he thought I was going to suck or fuck him. I was more than willing to do those things, but he needed a different kind of release first.

Chapter
Fourteen

Wren

WE DIDN'T SAY ANYTHING ON OUR WAY UP TO DARE'S ROOM because neither of us wanted to risk waking Ralph. We were lucky that we didn't get caught when we pulled that stunt in the laundry room. *Okay, the stunt that I pulled.* I knew that Ralph liked me, and I even suspected he knew that his grandson had become very important to me, but that didn't give me the right to be disrespectful in his home. It wasn't because we were gay either. I would've felt the same if we were a straight couple sneaking up to… *Couple?* I rolled the word around in my head a few times, expecting a negative thought to refute its validity but none came. I discovered I liked the way the word felt, sounded, and even tasted on my tongue. Just because I didn't speak it out loud didn't mean it was less true.

When we got to Dare's room, we silently undressed each other in between soft kisses in the muted light from the lamp on the bedside table. The mood between us was different like we both had realized something important that day: what we shared was poignant and real. There was a confidence in Dare's hands when he touched me and in his eyes when he looked at me. Did he see and feel the same changes in me?

Even my arousal was different. Rather than the all-consuming fire, it was a slow-burning flame that never seemed to diminish or burn out. It vibrated through me like normal, but new emotions joined the passion: tenderness and a desire for something I didn't deserve and shouldn't want. I'd been stingy with my heart for my entire life, giving it only to my mom who had died and a boy who was nearly rejected by his family for loving me. My mom didn't choose to willingly leave me, but the boy did. I didn't blame him, but it still hurt, especially when our breakup was only a few months after my mom's death. I had no one in the world I could count on until I met Jimmy and Danny. I sure as hell couldn't count on Falcon. Just thinking about him brought on a fresh wave of exhaustion, which killed my arousal.

Dare didn't seem to mind. He pulled back the sheets and blankets then gestured for me to climb inside. He joined me after I got situated then turned off the light before he rolled over and lay his head on my chest. In the dark, it was easier to find the words that I couldn't speak to anyone else. Hell, Jimmy and Danny didn't even know that Falcon was my sperm donor, yet here I was about to tell Dare everything.

"Wren," he said softly in the darkness. "You don't have to tell me anything if you don't want to, okay? If you do want to talk, I promise you that nothing you say will leave this room."

"I know, Sparkles." I trailed my hands up and down his back, finding comfort in the rhythm and already familiar feel of my fingers bumping along his spine. "You'd never betray my trust." I knew it as certain as the sun would rise in the east. No matter what happened between us, Dare would keep my confidence. "Once upon a time," I began to lighten the mood. I expected Dare to snort, but he giggled. "What?"

"That's a phrase I use frequently in my head. I tend to work everyday events into fairy tales."

"Yeah? Who am I?" I asked.

"Prince Charming, duh. Only with longer hair, biker boots, and a beefier body. My prince rides a Harley instead of a horse."

"Sparkles, I'm nobody's Prince Charming."

"You don't get to decide that," he said in a singsong voice. "I decide who my Prince Charming is and no one else."

I ignored the fluttering in my stomach and dug deep for a gruff response. "Fine, but don't say that I didn't warn you."

"Once upon a time…" Dare prompted.

"There lived a beautiful maiden who made a mistake by giving her heart and everything else to a selfish king." Fuck! This did sound like a twisted fairy tale, but I somehow doubted that Disney would want to buy the rights to this story. "You see the king wasn't born into royalty, he was elevated to that status by his legions of fans. The king forgot all about his roots and the girl he promised to marry someday. He rode off to conquer the world and never looked back. Therefore, he didn't know that his maiden had given birth to his…"

"Prince!" Dare offered.

"Bastard son is more fitting." It sounded harsh, but it was true.

"Wren, please don't talk about yourself like that," Dare said, snuggling tighter into my side like he could ease the hurt somehow.

"The maiden never informed the king he had a child nor sought gold or jewels for support. She didn't want to be accused of using the prince to hold onto the reluctant king after he so clearly wanted to be free. So, she raised the…"

Dare grabbed my nipple and twisted hard.

"Ouch! Why the fuck did you do that?" So much for trying not to wake Ralph.

"You will not call yourself a bastard in my presence ever again, Wren Davison. Do you hear me?"

"Loud and clear, Sparkles. Fuck, that hurt!" I rubbed a hand over my aching nipple. "You're going to lick it and make it better after I'm done weaving my tale." It wasn't a question.

"I'll lick anything you want."

I thought my dick had fallen asleep, but apparently it was just taking a catnap. It started firing back to life, encouraging me to get the hard part over so that I could get to the good stuff with Dare. "Anyway, the maiden raised her beloved child on her own." It was true, my mother was crazy about me. "One day, the maiden got sick and kept getting sicker." My voice cracked and Dare stiffened against me. He lifted his head and pressed a kiss against my heart. "The beloved son had only recently obtained his driver's license, but he drove the maiden to the hospital one night after she collapsed in the bathroom. The doctors ran some tests and determined her blood counts were all wrong, dangerously so. After more tests, the maiden had a diagnosis. Cancer."

"I'm so sorry, Wren."

I kissed the top of his head to let him know he had nothing to be sorry about and then continued the story. "For all his life, the beloved boy wanted to know who his sire was, but the maiden wouldn't tell him. She kept saying it was just the two of them in their family and that was all they needed. The maiden's health continued to decline, and she frequently took heavy-duty pain pills to help ease her discomfort. The beloved boy knew he was losing his mother, even though she told him she'd get better. She said her faith was strong enough for the both of them, but the boy knew. He feared what would happen once his mother was gone. Who would love him? It didn't matter that he was nearly a man himself by this time, he was terrified of losing his mom and being all alone in the world.

"One night, the beloved boy waited until his mother was heavily medicated and asked about his father. He was shocked to say the least but had no reason to doubt the maiden. If his father was a king among men, then he could make her well again. He could pay for a better hospital or treatment. He could fix the maiden. The boy further betrayed his mother's trust by searching through her belongings until he found some contact information for the king's manager."

"Uh oh, I think I've read this fairy tale," Dare said softly. "The manager refused to pass the information along to the king that he had a prince and the prince's mother was ill."

"You *have* read this one," I said, trying to lighten the mood. "It gets worse, and I bet you don't know this part of the story. It might change the way you look at me."

Dare hummed in his throat like he doubted it but didn't say anything more.

"The beloved boy needed money to pay for his mother's treatment, so he started drag racing her pride and joy on the weekends to earn money for medicine and food."

"The car in the garage?" Dare asked, temporarily sidetracking me.

"Yes," I confirmed. "It was the only thing she had left that belonged to her father and she was no longer on speaking terms with her mother after she refused to have an abortion or give me up for adoption."

"The maiden was fierce," Dare said.

"Fearless," I added. "Anyway, I was arrested for drag racing and the maiden wasn't at all happy. She didn't have any money to bail her beloved son out of juvenile jail, so she called the only person who did."

"She had better luck with the evil manager?" Dare asked.

I smiled at the description because it was pretty accurate. "She never said how she accomplished it, but I suspect she threatened to go public with my existence. I mean, even I know that I look a lot like the guy. Just my picture would be enough to stir a lot of trouble, then add the fact that the evil manager neglected to inform the king that he already knew about me. All I knew was that one minute I was in juvenile detention, and the next I was looking into eyes the exact same color of mine. Not only that, the king called me a name that I never expected to hear from anyone else: son."

"What happened next? Unfortunately, I suspect there was no happily ever after."

"The king suspended his tour to spend time with the mother of his son, and he attempted to comfort the beloved son after the maiden lost her battle with cancer."

"Wren, I'm so sorry." I heard the tears in his voice and my breath caught in my throat. Had anyone ever been moved to tears on my behalf? Other than my mom? I didn't think so.

"If it's okay with you, I'm going to lose the fairy-tale talk now." Dare nodded against my chest. "Looking back now, I can see that I was really angry. I mean angry at the fucking world. For more reasons than just that the universe stole the only person who loved me."

"What do you mean?"

"Alaric made my mom so happy during those final months, and I saw what our family could've been like if he hadn't chosen booze, women, rock and roll, and world tours over us. If he'd fulfilled the promise he'd made her when he first formed the band…" I shook my head because it was old fucking news. I'd just rehashed it with Alaric again, and I still didn't feel any better. Why bring Dare down too? "Anyway, I was too young to know what I felt at the time, but it was sadness and bitterness that he could make her happy in ways that I couldn't. I don't mean anything gross or inappropriate by that," I was quick to explain.

"I know that, Wren."

"I tried so hard to make her smile and bring joy to her life those final weeks, but it was Alaric who lit up her world. A better person would've been grateful to him for putting his life on hold and trying to make my mom's life better, but I couldn't. When she passed away, he actually wanted me to live with him. I fought him. I told him I'd rather go into the foster care system or run away than move any-where with him."

"Tough crowd," Dare teased lightly. "I'm sure that didn't go over well."

"The court ordered a blood test, and they confirmed that I was indeed Alaric's son. By this time, I had been placed in a group home for boys. It wasn't easy, or even that nice, but I met two boys there that would become my best friends."

"Jimmy and Danny."

"The very same. I also had a boyfriend at the time, and I didn't want to leave him."

"I'm starting to get jealous."

"Don't, Sparkles. No one can hold a candle to you." It was the sappiest thing I'd ever said to him or any other human being. I blamed it on the emotionally draining day. "The boy's parents freaked out when they caught us kissing and that was the end of our romance. Trust me, it wasn't anything like the kisses we share."

"Good to know. Back to the story with your, um. Alaric." Dare patted my chest and nuzzled his nose in my chest hair.

"He was prepared to fight me, and I encouraged him to do so. I told him that I'd blab everything I knew to a sleazy tabloid. Maybe he felt I wasn't worth the battle or maybe he thought I'd change my mind. Either way, I finished out my senior year while living at the group home, and I never saw Alaric again until he stepped foot in the salon today."

"What a fucking loser," Dare said, propping himself up on his elbow and forearm so he could look down at me. Of course, it was black as pitch in his room, so he couldn't have seen much. "He never tried to contact you again? Wait, he mentioned you ignoring his calls."

"I said that I never saw him again; I never said he didn't try to contact me. He called me at least once a month over the last eleven years, and every day during the last week." I shrugged like it was no big deal. "He used to send money and gifts, but I returned them."

"That's a little better," Dare said.

"I will always be grateful to him for one thing, though," I said softly. "He made sure my mom got a proper burial with a beautiful casket and headstone. He let me pick them out and didn't question the cost. I just wanted her to have the very best."

"That was very thoughtful."

"I think he truly loved her at one time. I don't think I was ready to see that until tonight, but he gave me some photos he had of them together. I know that she never got over him, and so tonight…" My voice cracked. "I at least thanked him for making her so happy before she died. I guess he's not a total asshole."

I didn't want to let go of the anger, because it was so much easier to handle than the heartbreak. Lying in Dare's bed with him pressed against me, I realized that I never properly mourned after losing my mother. I went straight from devastated to angry and just stayed there. I never advanced beyond that stage of grief.

It washed over me then. So much pain, regret, and heartbreak welled up inside me that I thought I would burst. My body shook as I tried to repress it and shove it all into a box that I could examine later. Dare must've sensed that the dam was about to rupture because he rolled on top of me, getting as close to me as he could and offering me comfort. I wrapped my arms around him, holding him as tight as I could without hurting him. The bubble of grief finally burst, and a soft sob tore from my mouth as tears spilled from my eyes.

"I've got you, Wren. Let it all out." He spoke soothing words while I cried against his shoulder. Dare ran his hands through my hair and placed tender kisses all over my face as the tears started to recede. I'd never felt exhaustion so swift and so strong.

"So tired," I murmured.

Dare rolled off me, but I didn't let him get far. I turned over too so that we were facing one another and sharing the same pillow. I needed to feel his heart beating against my chest to ward against the sadness that could follow me into my dreams.

"Sleep well," Dare whispered right before I lost consciousness.

I did dream of my mom, but instead of sadness and sorrow, she smiled and waved at me like she did from the beach when I'd swim in the lake. "I've missed you, Wren," she shouted to me. "Don't stay away so long next time."

I woke with a start, and it took me a few seconds to realize that I was in Dare's bed instead of my own. At some point, Dare had turned his back to me, and I had wrapped myself around him. As sleep faded from my mind, I became aware of my body—namely my hard-on pressing against Dare's pert ass. I nudged forward a little bit and Dare pushed back against me. I gripped his hip and pressed my hard-on tighter against his ass.

"I don't have any supplies beyond lube," Dare moaned. In the shaft of moonlight coming through the window, I could see him arching his back. "I should've been more prepared."

"Lube will work." Dare rolled forward to open the drawer then handed the tube to me.

Then we both shoved our underwear down our legs and kicked them off. "I'm not going to penetrate you, Sparkles. I wouldn't betray your trust like that."

"Just do something, Wren. I'm going to die." He started to roll onto his back, but I stopped him.

"Stay right there and squeeze your thighs tight."

Dare moaned, anticipating what I was going to do. I slicked my cock then slid it between his upper thighs, rubbing along his taint and the underside of his balls. I pulled back and drove forward again and again, using his tight thighs to rub one out. My hips started rocking faster as I chased my climax. I reached over his hip to grip his cock with my lube-slicked hand and jerked it in time with my thrusts.

"Come with me, Dare. I need you."

We came together in the moonlight. Dare's cries were muffled like he was biting his pillow, and I grunted softly against the back of his neck. I grabbed his T-shirt off the floor and cleaned us both off. I wanted to fall right back to sleep with him, but it didn't feel right. Instead, I rolled Dare onto his back and kissed him long and slow to express how much I cared for him, how much I appreciated that he was there for me when I needed him. There was so much I wanted to say to Dare but didn't know how.

I went with something easy. "I can't wait to see you in a few hours, Sparkles."

"Me too," he said softly, sleep already re-claiming him.

I tiptoed downstairs, trying not to make any noise on the old wooden steps. My worry was justified too because Ralph opened his bedroom door just as I started to creep by.

"This is…um…"

"Exactly what it looks like," Ralph said wryly. "I used to be a young man too, Wren. I understand."

"I don't mean any disrespect, sir."

"Of course not. You're a good man," Ralph said. "But if you ever hurt my Dare…"

He let his words trail off, but I heard him perfectly. "I won't, sir," I promised.

"See that you don't." Ralph shuffled his way toward the bathroom mumbling something about an old man's bladder.

Dawn was only a few hours away when I let myself out the door and headed to my apartment. My promise to Ralph stunned me, but it was true. I'd rather cut off my right hand than hurt Dare. I just needed to find a way not to fuck things up with him like I was prone to do.

Chapter
Fifteen

Dave

HATED WAKING UP TO FIND WREN GONE. SPENDING THE night in his arms was something that I had fantasized about plenty of times, but I never expected it to become a reality. It was fucking heaven for the few hours that it lasted, surpassing my most vivid imagination, especially when Wren rutted between my thighs and jerked me off until we came together. There was a tenderness in his kiss before he left that I'd never experienced before, even after I consoled him at the salon after Falcon left.

Something had shifted between us after Wren confided his past to me and allowed himself to grieve over his mother's death. I'd never forget his broken sobs as long as I lived, but I was glad that I could comfort him and so grateful that he trusted me. I recognized it as the honor it truly was and vowed to never let Wren down. In one way or another, it seemed like someone always disappointed him. I would prove to him that I was different than everyone else, but I suspected he already knew. I was his Sparkles after all.

I grinned in the mirror as I brushed my teeth. That nickname would've been an insult from anyone else's lips but his. It wasn't the name itself but the tone of voice he used that let the affection shine through. I mattered to him.

Grandpa was already out of bed and sitting at the table reading the newspaper with his magnifying glass. "The Blissville Daily News has turned into a gossip rag. They need to mind their own damn business and allow a man some privacy," he mumbled when I entered the room. My heart swelled with pride when I realized he was defending Wren. What else would the BDN be gossiping about if not for a famous rocker landing in town? "I thought the National Enquirer was dropped on my front porch in error."

"I don't think the National Enquirer has home delivery options," I replied, but my lips curved up into a ridiculous smile.

"Don't get smart with me, Dare." Grandpa looked up from the paper and smiled ruefully. "Someone had a visitor last night." My happy little bubble threatened to burst until he laughed and shook his head. "That boy is much too big to be tiptoeing around here in the wee hours of the morning. He should've just stayed over and had breakfast with us."

"Uh..."

"Look, in my day people didn't have sleepovers before marriage, but times have changed. Back in my day, two men or two women couldn't openly show their affection with one another either. Everyone had to hide who they were and that's no way to live, Dare. Now, I want to say that I am more enlightened than the rest of my generation, but the simple truth is I put myself in your shoes when you came out. I cannot imagine what my life would've been like if I had to hide my love for your grandmother like a dirty secret. I wouldn't want that for you either. It took some time to reprogram the noggin," he tapped his head with a bony finger, "to remember to ask about boyfriends instead of girlfriends, but I did it. Anyone can. People who don't adjust their thinking, just choose not to. Plain and simple. Life isn't nearly as complicated as people make it out to be."

Grandpa went back to looking at his newspaper while I began making breakfast. "Oatmeal okay?"

"Can I have blueberries and bananas in it?"

"Sure."

"Will you split an English muffin with me?"

"Absolutely."

Grandpa didn't say anything else until after I set his breakfast in front of him. "You and Wren didn't wake me up if that's why you're so quiet this morning. My old bladder did. I went to bed earlier than usual, and it messed me all up." He looked at me pointedly. "That was my decision, not yours."

I appreciated that he wanted to ease the awkwardness and decided to take him at his word. "Eat your breakfast while it's still hot."

I finished getting ready for work after breakfast and hugged my grandpa goodbye after Maren showed up. I wanted to get to the salon early and place my special order before chaos resumed. Whoever hadn't heard about Falcon's appearance yesterday would've read about it in the paper. That meant we could anticipate more craziness for the rest of the week until the newness wore off. Instead of feeling discouraged, I was excited about the extra money I could make from people's poor taste. It would mean that I could start my remodeling project even faster.

As soon as I thought it, I saw Andy Mason's truck parked in front of Books and Brew. That didn't surprise me because the hunky carpenter stopped in there every morning, and it wasn't just for the amazing coffee and pastries. Andy had his eye on one of the owners and needed a daily dose of Milo Miracle as much as, or more than, a cup of java. On a whim, I pulled my car over and parked behind Andy's truck.

It was late enough in the morning that most people had already stopped in for coffee on their way to work, not that Andy was hard to spot. His size and looks made him stand out in most crowds. Andy sat at a small round table and had his eyes locked on the counter where Milo greeted customers with his twin sister, Maegan. I didn't know the story between Milo and Andy because I was from the neighboring town of Goodville and had only met the two men when I started working at Curl Up and Dye. Unlike most, I had no desire to poke and prod into people's lives, but I had to admit it was kind of fun observing the two men.

Andy would watch Milo's every move but look away in time so that Milo never caught him in the act. Milo ignored Andy except when he wanted to assure himself that he was still there. I wondered what would happen if the two guys locked eyes on one of those instances. Would they share a moment? Would they realize the longing they had inside was mirrored in the person they desired most? Would they... *What the fuck was I doing?* I really needed to stop weaving fairy tales out of everything.

Andy was too busy watching Milo talk to an older, sexy-as-fuck man to notice I was approaching his table. The carpenter's eyes narrowed suspiciously, and I decided to talk to him at a better time. Andy's gaze shifted to me just as I started to turn around.

"Dare!" he said excitedly. *Too excitedly.* "It's been so long since I've seen you." Andy jumped my dead battery and followed me to the auto parts store. We didn't share a *moment* or anything, but the casual observer wouldn't know that by his greeting. Andy rose and pulled out the extra seat at the table for me like we were on a date. His eyes flickered to the counter quickly, and I knew what he was up to.

I glanced at the counter too and saw that it was Milo's turn to raptly watch my exchange with Andy. Oh man, this wasn't a good idea.

"Sit down and let's chat. Would you like me to get you a coffee?"

I shook my head, but not just because of the coffee. "Maybe this isn't a good time," I said hesitantly.

"Nonsense." Andy patted the back of the chair to emphasize he wanted me to sit. Of course, I noticed that he would be able to gauge Milo's reaction while I would only feel his hot glare on my back. I didn't need to make an enemy of anyone in the town I now called home. "What's up?" Andy asked, returning to his seat.

"Well, I have this renovation project in mind, and I need to hire someone to help me."

Andy shifted his focus back to me, and I had his full attention. "What kind of renovation project?"

I gave a brief overview of what I hoped to accomplish since I was pressed for time. Andy nodded as I explained, like he was picturing the job in his head. "I have a sketch and a 3D rendering of the space at home. Is there a time we can meet to go over the project in more detail?" I asked.

"I'm actually free this evening. Will that work?"

"Let me check with Wren to make sure he doesn't have a problem with that. Do you have a card with your number on it? I'll let you know in just a bit." I wasn't going to wake Wren up. It was his morning to sleep in, and I figured he'd need it after the day he had.

"Wren? The guy from the salon?" Andy asked.

"He's renting the apartment space from me," I told Andy.

"Okay, sure." Andy pulled out a card from his wallet and slid it across the table. "Just leave me a message if I don't answer. I'm free after six."

"Thanks," I said. When I stood up, I caught Milo's speculative look and decided to nip this in the bud before things went too far. I had enough going on in my life without getting caught up in Milo and Andy's games.

I gave Milo my best disarming smile when I stepped up to the counter. "Please don't spit in my coffee," I said after I placed my order and paid for it.

Milo's eyes widened in shock and his face blushed a soft shade of pink. "I don't know what you mean."

"I was only talking to Andy about a rehab project and nothing more. Besides, I have a guy."

"It's not my business," Milo said then turned around to make my coffee. Maybe it wasn't his business, but he sure wanted it to be. When he finished, Milo returned to me and said, "One medium salted caramel mocha hold the spit." His smile assured me that we were in a good place.

"Who's the sexy daddy you were talking to anyway?"

"Oh, that's the new superintendent the district hired. His name is Romeo Bradley. Sexy, right?"

"Very." I noticed the time on the clock and needed to get going. "I better get to work. Take care, Milo." I waved at Andy as I left and sent up vibes that those two would quit wasting time circling each other.

The morning was every bit as chaotic as I thought it would be. I hoped that most of the busybodies came and went before Wren showed up, but I wouldn't hold my breath. I was used to people, especially the ladies, being disappointed if he wasn't in the salon during their visit, but the dissatisfaction was greater than usual.

"I think he's off for the rest of the week," I started to say at one point. The last thing I needed was these people to flock back into the salon later that afternoon or the next day. I was fast losing my ability to distance myself from the situation. I didn't want to anger our clients, but Wren had a right to his privacy. I regretted the lie immediately because it would be disproved in a few hours and it only ramped up the excitement.

"I bet he went to LA to be with his dad," one lady had said to her friend.

"That's the last we'll see of him. No way he'll return to Blissville after seeing what LA has to offer," the friend replied.

I knew that Wren was in his apartment sleeping off an orgasm instead of leaving on a plane for the west coast, but doubt started to creep into my mind. Falcon could give him the kind of life that most people dreamed of, and it was selfish of me to wish anything different for Wren.

"Nah," a third lady piped in. "I read in the paper this morning that Falcon's Descent has announced that they're taking some time off from touring. The guys have been doing it for almost three decades and need some time to relax with their families."

"And Falcon lives in LA," the first lady countered then rolled her eyes like the newcomer was dumb.

"Falcon is from Cincinnati and the article specifically said that he was returning to his roots. But a person would need to read to know that," the third lady fired back.

"Are you implying—"

"Ladies, please," I firmly said, cutting them off. "Please don't get into a cat fight in the salon over this. Wren's personal life really isn't anyone's business, nor is Falcon's. Being a celebrity doesn't mean that his private life should be up for discussion. Instead of focusing on things that won't impact your life in a positive way, let's talk about things that will." It might've sounded like a piss-poor sales pitch, but it worked when flattery was added. "This nail polish would really show off your slender fingers," I said to one. "Your hair looks lovely today. It would be a shame if the wind messed it up," I said to another. "An hour-long massage is just the thing you need to put a smile back on your face. Josi is the absolute best at making all your tension melt away. Would you like to look at her pamphlet to see what services she offers?" I asked the third lady. I sold the polish, the hairspray, and booked an appointment for Josi.

After that exchange, I needed a few minutes of quiet. Wren was due to arrive and I didn't want him to see how aggravated I'd become or he'd blame himself. He found me at the coffee pot in the kitchenette when he arrived.

"How's it been so far?" he asked.

When I was trying to win Wren's affection, I blurred the lines at work all the time. I wanted to continuously plant myself in his way and imprint myself on his brain. Earning his affection didn't change that, but it did make me realize that there's a time and place for everything. I wanted to throw my arms around Wren's neck and kiss him until we both forgot about the last twenty-four hours, or my newest fears, but I didn't. Instead, I poured him a cup of his butch coffee and smiled warmly at him. "It's fine."

"You're a terrible liar," Wren said, backing me up against the cabinet. "Is it the busybodies or something else that's troubling you?"

I wanted to say, "Don't leave me for LA. I can sparkle brighter than any overcrowded city." Instead, I replied, "It was a busy morning, but hopefully it will settle down a bit this afternoon."

"Hmmm."

I could tell he wasn't buying it, so I moved to distract him by changing the subject. "Listen, I ran into Andy at Books and..." My words trailed off when Wren made a sour face. "What?"

"Andy the carpenter that all the guys are hot for?" He tipped my head back so he could stare into my eyes.

"I'm not hot for Andy," I said honestly.

"I'm not hot for Andy either," Josh said as he breezed in. "Pay no attention to me. I just need to grab a glass of water, and I'll be on my way."

Wren kept his gaze locked on mine the entire time Josh poured himself a glass of water. Was he trying to peer into my brain to see if I was lying? Well, I wasn't. Andy was a good-looking guy, but he wasn't the man I wanted. Everything I desired was standing right in front of me.

"What were you saying about Andy?" Wren asked when we

were alone again.

"I told him about my remodeling ideas, and he would like to come over at six to look at the space. I told him that I'd needed to check with you first. You probably won't be home by then, but I can use my key to let him in if that's okay with you."

"It's your apartment," Wren said, but that wasn't much of an answer.

"That you're renting," I replied. "It would be very rude of me to traipse Andy through your apartment without giving you proper notice."

"This means a lot to you, doesn't it?"

"It does."

"Then it's fine with me but stay out of the bedroom."

"Oh, did you leave your Fleshjack out or something?"

"No, but there's a bed there, and I don't want Handy Andy to become Handsy Andy."

I snorted. "I'm not sure what that guy ever did to earn his reputation, but he's only been nice to me, never flirty. He could've made all kinds of jokes when he ran into me at the sex toy store, but—"

Wren's growl cut me off. "Sex toy store?"

I lowered my voice. "I ran into Andy the day that I bought the butt plug. I went out to my car, and the battery was dead. Andy jumped me—my battery—and followed me to the parts store so I could get a new battery. He even installed it for me."

"Is that so?" Wren didn't sound all that impressed.

"Hey, you were doing your damnedest to put some distance between us at the time. I wouldn't have felt comfortable calling you, and I sure as hell wasn't calling my mom to come pick me up."

"I can understand that," Wren conceded then let out a sigh. "Okay, so Andy is a nice guy."

"He is, and I think you'll like Andy if you give him a chance."

"For you, I'll try anything once."

I smiled wickedly as a dozen ideas popped into my head.

Wren groaned softly. "I'm going to regret this, aren't I?"

"Nothing ventured, nothing gained," I said then wiggled out from where he still had me pinned to the cabinet. I blew him a playful kiss before I left him alone in the kitchenette looking at me with smoldering eyes. Was he counting the minutes until we could be alone like I was?

Chapter
Sixteen

Wren

BEFORE I KNEW IT, FEBRUARY ARRIVED WITH MORE SNOW but thankfully less drama. The town stopped whispering as I walked by and quit referring to me as the Rock Prince. Hell fucking no. I meant what I said to Dare; I was nobody's prince of anything. My response to the ridiculousness was a silent sneer or glare to let them know my displeasure, and the townsfolk eventually left me alone. On the outside I was a grimacing, angry man, but on the inside... I was smiling, laughing, and loving my life for the first time in years, maybe ever. Only Dare got to see that side of me.

I'd never experienced any of the emotions that I shared with Dare. My insides never lit up like a Christmas tree when someone entered the room until he came into my life. My abs never felt sore from laughing so much until I was introduced to his sparkling wit.

And the passion... I never felt the driving need to physically connect to anyone the way I did with him. My sex drive didn't begin the day I met Dare, but it was forever altered. Sex was about more than chasing orgasms now. It was about long kisses that melted my frigid heart and tender touches that I felt to my battered soul.

I started putting Dare's wants and needs before my own such as accepting Andy's presence in our lives. Admittedly, we didn't spend a lot of time around him when he started renovating my apartment, but I still knew he was there. Which reminded me of another new emotion Dare brought to the surface—jealousy. I'm not talking about the mild annoyance that some people experienced, I mean the white-hot burning kind. I wasn't about to beat anyone up or commit a violent act, but I made sure to mark Dare as mine at every opportunity. I wanted his DNA to be altered to include me as surely as he changed mine.

One afternoon while eating lunch together at work, I glanced up at Dare and it hit me that I was in love with him. Me, hard-ass-never-let-anyone-too-close Wren Davison, was in love for the first time. Some guys would smile and reach across the table and take their sweetie's hand and confess their feelings; I choked on my bite of ham and swiss on rye. Not like a sesame seed almost went down the wrong pipe kind of choke either. This wasn't the type where you knew you'd be okay after making an ass of yourself and drinking half a gallon of water. No, this was a hunk of sandwich lodged in my throat and I couldn't breathe kind of choke.

Dare's eyes widened in alarm as he leapt from his chair and circled around to mine. "Stand up!" he shouted. "I know the Heimlich."

This bastard wasn't coming out without help, so I either stood up and let him help me or I risked death. If the latter happened, at least it would be with his arms around me. Fuck! I didn't think or talk like that. How long had my oxygen been cut off to my brain?

"I got you, Wren," Dare calmly said, placing his fist beneath my sternum then covering it with his other hand. "Here we go." After two sharp pushes against my diaphragm, the hunk of sandwich dislodged from my throat and shot out of my mouth to land on Dare's plate. Luckily it was empty.

"Gross," Dare said then poured me a glass of water.

I greedily chugged it down and wiped the droplets that clung to my mouth and beard with the back of my hand. "You saved me," I said, my voice as rusty as if he pulled me from the desert after days without water.

Dare shrugged like it was no big deal. "I took first aid classes before I moved in with Grandpa. I couldn't be the reason something bad happened to him."

I leaned forward over the chair in front of me to recover and Dare wrapped himself around my back, resting his forehead between my shoulder blades. "You're the man," I said, aiming to lighten the mood as I accepted the comfort he gave me. Of course, I never stopped to think about what the position might look like to anyone who entered the kitchenette.

"Oh, excuse me," Meredith said. "I didn't mean to interrupt. I just wanted some chamomile tea."

I stood up so fast that I nearly knocked Dare on his ass. "It's not what it looks like," I told Meredith.

"It never is, sweetie," Meredith replied then winked playfully.

"Why don't you sit down and rest your feet and let me make you a cup of tea," Dare said.

"Don't fuss," Meredith told him. "I'm pregnant, not suddenly incapable of doing things for myself." Mere had recently informed us that she and her husband, Harley, were expecting a baby in July. They'd waited until she reached the second trimester to make the announcement. We were all thrilled for the couple, even me who felt awkward as fuck around tiny little humans.

"This isn't about strength or capability, Mere," Dare said softly, as he guided her to the chair. "It's about you standing on your feet all day and taking a few minutes to rest in between clients."

"Yeah, okay. I appreciate—" She stopped suddenly. "What the hell is that?" She pointed to my partially chewed chunk of ham sandwich.

"Ham, swiss, and Dijon mustard on rye bread," Dare answered casually as he carried his plate to the trash can to dispose of the offensive glob. "It was lodged in Wren's throat and I was forced to give him the Heimlich. That's what you walked in on, not playtime."

"We keep that separate from work," I assured her. Well, mostly. I thought there might come a time when we took advantage of that little mixing room after hours if we were ever alone.

"Finish your lunch," Dare said to me, pointing at the few bites that remained of my sandwich.

"Bossy," I said, but picked up my sandwich and took another bite.

"You two are really cute together," Mere said. "It's good that you pulled your heads out of your asses to make room for other things."

I almost choked again.

"Meredith, you are wicked!" Dare said like she had truly shocked him, but his delighted smile said he was saving her line to use on me in the future.

"Wicked good," she countered as she stood up and accepted the cup of tea. "I'll let you guys finish your lunch together. Besides, my empty salon chair is more comfortable than these hard ones."

Dare made himself a cup of coffee and sat back down across from me. He sighed happily after the first sip which made me happy too. That reminded me of my earlier revelation, but I didn't choke or panic the second time around.

"What made you choke?" Dare asked then took another sip.

Another guy would probably make something up and save his declaration for a romantic moment. Not this guy. "I realized that I'm in love for the first time in my life."

Dare spat his coffee across the table then sputtered. I thought it might be a bad sign that we both nearly choked on the realization

148

that I was in love with him.

"Dude!" Dare said, wiping the table. "You need to warn me when you're about to get romantic." He glanced up suddenly as if a horrible thought occurred to him. "You were talking about me, right?" I nodded. "Wait! You realized that you're in love with me and it made you choke? Loving me is that bad?"

I couldn't resist him another second. Work, clients, and co-workers be damned, I hooked him under his arm and led him to the mixing room.

"We won't have long," Dare said breathlessly.

"I don't need long."

"A ringing endorsement if ever I heard one," he said sassily.

"Not for sex," I scoffed. "For this." I backed him against the door, cupped his face with both hands, and lowered my face until my lips hovered above his. "I love you, Dare. I didn't know I was capable of loving someone until you came into my life. You're the absolute best thing to ever happen to me."

Dare's breath rushed out of him in a soft, "Oh."

"Better?"

"Much." He smiled up at me with so much love.

"And?" I prompted.

"Um, and kiss me?" Dare guessed.

"That or you could tell me how you feel too." Panic started to race through my blood. Had I misread the signs? Fuck! What if he didn't feel the same way? Shit! "Not that I need you to say anything, especially if you don't feel it too." I started to drop my hands and take a step back, but Dare wrapped his hands around my wrists and stopped me.

"Wren, I've known for a while now that I'm in love with you."

"We've only been dating for a month. It's too soon for me to even know it."

"Yet, you do," Dare pointed out. "We didn't just meet a month ago. We've known each other for more than a year. This has been building up slowly like an amazing orgasm since the first time we locked eyes on one another. Falling in love with you was the ultimate delayed gratification."

"You're very wise for someone so young," I told him.

"I'm only three years younger than you."

"Still, most guys your age are still clubbing on weekends."

"That wasn't the life I wanted before I moved in with Grandpa, so don't worry that I feel like I'm missing out. I have the life I want, and more importantly, I have the man that I want."

There was a soft knock on the door. "I don't mean to interrupt your *choking* again, but Wren's next client is here."

"Be right there, Mere."

"He doesn't take long," Dare added, making Meredith giggle and earning a swat on his pert ass.

"You'll pay for that later," I warned.

"With flesh," Dare added eagerly. I figured the best punishment would be denying him my dick, but that wasn't about to happen.

"We'll just have to see about that." I gave him one long kiss that left him wanting more and returned to the salon. Dare wasn't the only person who received my genuine smiles, but he was the one who got most of them. The teenage boy sitting in my chair always pulled a grin from me. "Hey, Mark," I said, bumping his much smaller fist with mine. "Your hair is growing out nicely."

"Thanks! I can't wait until the top is long enough for you to give me an awesome cut."

"He has a photo album filled with a bunch of different styles on his phone," his father, Chaz, said.

"Both my dads agree that I can have any style I want as long as I get my math grade up," Mark said excitedly. "Anything will look better than the buzz cut I gave myself before I ran away from my old foster family."

Mark was born Marissa and his foster family refused to accept that their foster daughter was actually a transgender boy. I don't know the details of everything that Mark suffered, but I knew enough to get really angry when I thought about him looking for food in the dumpster behind Books and Brew before Christmas. The town was on high alert at the time looking for the group of people known locally as The Christmas Bandits who were stealing decorations and vandalizing properties. Someone had seen Mark enter the alley behind the store and called the cops.

Gabe was livid when he found out that Mark had run away from Goodville and his police department wasn't notified to be on the lookout. It turned out that Mark's foster parents hadn't even reported him as a runaway. They just went about their lives as if nothing were wrong. Chaz and Kyle had already started the process to become foster parents and Gabe knew that Mark would get the love he needed from two of his closest friends.

Mark had been coming to see me every three weeks to keep the sides trimmed while the top grew out. The buzzcut he'd given himself hadn't looked bad, but he would definitely look older if he had a more sophisticated style.

"How much longer do you think?" Mark asked excitedly.

"You're one of the lucky ones because your hair grows quicker than most."

"I think a lot of that has to deal with the testosterone he's taking," Chaz added.

"Your voice does sound deeper," I told Mark. "Dude, I hope you get to avoid the squeaking awkwardness that most of us experienced as we hit puberty."

"So far, so good." Then Mark started laughing. "Daniel can't say the same," he said of his boyfriend. "I think it's cute though." He looked up at his dad in the mirror with wide-eyed panic. "I need to get Daniel something for Valentine's Day."

Fuck! Valentine's Day was just around the corner. I hated that kind of bullshit holiday, but Dare deserved something special from me. Something nice and cheesy that made him blush and want to ride my cock.

Chaz cleared his throat, pulling my attention back to him. "You look as panicked as Mark."

"I don't know what to get Dare," I whispered. I didn't tell Chaz it was the first time I would celebrate the day with anyone. Hell, thirteen-year-old Mark had more game than I did.

"It doesn't have to be something extravagant, it just needs to come from your heart," Chaz replied.

"Says the romance writer," I grumbled. I bet he always knew the right things to say and never butchered declarations of emotions. It must be nice not to stick your foot in your mouth each time you opened it.

"Dude," Chaz said with a sneer. "Don't even look at me like I'm a smooth operator. One of these days I'll tell you the many ways I nearly blundered the best thing to ever happen to me."

"He's not smooth," Mark piped up. "Not at all."

"This isn't one of the times I want you to back me up," Chaz told his son. "Where were you when I argued with Daddy about what constitutes a Christmas movie?"

"A Christmas tree or music in the background makes it a Christmas movie," Mark said.

"No, no, no! Where have I gone wrong?" Chaz asked dramatically. "I just can't deal with the two of you sometimes." He ruffled his son's hair and left us alone to do our thing while he went and talked to Dare. If anyone knew how crazy Dare's job could be at times it was Chaz since he held the position before writing full time.

"He's a trip," I said to Mark.

"You have no idea," he replied. "I'm the luckiest boy in the world though."

"I think so too," I said, answering his smile in the mirror with one of my own. "Show me your favorite cut so we can start laying the groundwork." Mark showed me a picture of a guy with a fade cut. It was bisected by two shaved lines to emphasize the gradually shortened lengths. The first line was up near the top that allowed for longer bangs like Dare sported, the second line was a few inches shorter than that. "That's a cute cut." I held up the longer strands on top of his head. "Your hair isn't as long on top yet, but that cut will still look good on you. Is that the one you want?"

"Yeah, but let me ask Dad first."

Chaz came over and gave me the okay then left me to work my magic. Mark chatted away about school while I shaved the back and sides of his hair and scissor cut the top to give him shape and form as it grows. Most of my clients didn't say anything to me beyond what they wanted to accomplish during their appointment, which I usually preferred. Mark was the rare exception because I loved his banter.

When I finished, Mark just stared at his reflection for a few seconds. I worried it fell short of his expectations until he jumped up from the chair and hugged me. "I love it, Wren. Thank you so much."

"My pleasure, my man," I said, patting his thin shoulder. "See you in a few weeks, yeah?"

"You bet. Good luck with finding a present for Dare. Dad wasn't bullshitting you though. Just give him something from the heart. Everyone appreciates that, even other dudes."

After Mark left, I didn't even second-guess that I took dating advice from a thirteen-year-old because everyone had more dating experience than me. Besides, I knew that he was right. Even if Dare didn't mind cheesy gifts, he deserved something special. The idea of the perfect gift came to me later that afternoon, but I wouldn't be able to pull it off without some help.

Chapter
Seventeen

Dave

REN DAVISON LOVES ME. WREN DAVISON LOVES ME. IT played in my head on an endless loop for days. It never got old, and I never wanted it to stop. I especially never wanted to stop hearing him whisper those words in my ear when he made love to me. I was one drawn heart away from a lovesick teenage girl. I didn't give a fuck because, wait for it… Wren Davison loves me!

As Valentine's Day drew nearer, I started to panic. Wren wasn't the kind of guy to celebrate card company holidays, so I wasn't sure what to do. I didn't want the occasion to pass without celebrating, but I didn't want to make him feel bad if he didn't give me anything. I thought about driving back to Kim's Toys, but I wasn't sure a vibrating plug that matched mine or a new cock ring was the tone I was going for with his first Valentine's Day gift from me.

I ended up putting a basket together with his favorite soap, beard oil, snacks, and a hot rod calendar to hang up in the garage. It was harder than hell to find one that didn't include scantily clad ladies. That wouldn't do anything for Wren, but it gave me an idea for a future gift if I could find a way to pull it off. Wren wouldn't like just anyone taking pictures of me striking sexy poses in various states of undress or completely naked. I'd have to think long and hard about how to pull that one off.

Valentine's Day fell in the middle of the week. Maren had plans and couldn't stay, so going out with Wren on a real date wasn't a possibility. I wouldn't risk leaving Grandpa home alone for long because he was battling a cold, and I wanted to keep an eye on him without him knowing I was doing it. Instead of a date on the town, which would've consisted of the diner, I made a nice dinner for three. I didn't restrict Grandpa's diet either since it was a special occasion.

"Filet mignon, shrimp, herbed potatoes, and asparagus," Grandpa repeated excitedly after I answered his nightly question of what's for dinner. "Is it my birthday?"

"Not today," I replied. "Soon though."

"Is it Wren's birthday?" he followed. Wren joined us every night for dinner, so his presence was expected.

"No," I said then realized I didn't know when Wren's birthday was. I had a strong suspicion that he wouldn't give up that information freely either. I would have to resort to trickery or sensual torture to get the information out of him, but I'd do whatever it took to ensure his next birthday was one he'd never forget.

"What's for dessert? Are those little heart-shaped chocolate cakes?"

"Brownies," I replied. "I just need to dust them with powdered sugar." I thought about using some festive Valentine-themed sprinkles but changed my mind. Simple and understated would be best. Besides, I didn't want Wren thinking I went to a lot of trouble if he blew the holiday off. I even hid his gift in my room for that reason. I would find other reasons to give him his goodies, even if I had to do it a little at a time.

When Wren showed up, I was shocked that he held a large vase of roses in pink, ivory, and red. *Don't cry. Don't cry.* "They are so beautiful, and I love them so much." I gave him a kiss and took them from him so I could smell and fuss over them.

"Dare, is it your birthday?" Grandpa asked with wide eyes.

"No," I said. "It's Valentine's Day."

"Mercy! I should go to my room and let you boys have the night to yourselves."

"No way," Wren said. "I have something for you too, Ralph." He held up his other hand. I'd been so excited about my flowers that I hadn't noticed the bag in Wren's other hand. "I rented a movie that I thought we could all watch together." I noticed that he looked a little uncertain, but I understood why when he pulled the movie out of the bag.

"*Casablanca,*" Grandpa said, holding it against his heart like a treasure. "My Norma loved this movie so much, Dare." Grandpa had told us that the previous week, which was how Wren knew about it. "I used to tease her about it just to get a rise out of her." Grandpa's chin wobbled, and I had to turn to the counter to keep from reacting. My grandmother had passed away twenty years ago when I was just five years old. I barely remembered her, but Grandpa found ways to keep her alive for all of us. What must it be like to love someone that much? I was pretty sure I was on my way to finding out.

"This was one of my mom's favorite movies too," Wren said. "She watched it a lot during her last days. I always associated sadness with the movie, but I think I'd rather watch it and remember fondly. What do you say, Ralph?"

"I think that's a wonderful idea."

"I have a gift for you too," I told Wren then jogged up to my room to retrieve it.

My gift wasn't as pretty as his, but he seemed to enjoy pulling out each little item. "Thank you, Sparkles. These are some of my favorite things from my favorite person." Oh lord, I was either going to melt on the spot or send Grandpa to his bedroom after all.

We kept things light during dinner and dessert. I decided to warm up the little brownies and serve them with ice cream and caramel and chocolate drizzles.

"I haven't eaten anything that delicious for a long time," Grandpa said. "Everything was cooked perfectly. Would you boys think ill of me if I licked my dessert plate clean. I know darn well the warden," he pointed at me with his fork, "will return to serving me bland food tomorrow."

"I got fresh peaches for your oatmeal," I told him.

"Hey, now we're talking," Grandpa said. "Maybe you're not so bad."

After dinner, we went out to the living room to watch *Casablanca*. To be honest, I loved the old black-and-white films, so it wasn't a hardship for me to watch. I curled up next to Wren and offered the warmth of my body in case he found it emotionally hard to watch the movie again. When I saw him smile in random parts, I knew he was embracing the memories instead of trying to hide from them.

I didn't think I could love him anymore than I already did, but I was wrong. After the movie ended, I helped Grandpa to bed. Wren waited on the couch for me to return like usual. I hoped for a long make out session before we went our separate ways. I figured I'd go to bed hard and hungry because Wren understandably didn't want to go up to my room, and I didn't want to leave Grandpa alone to go to his apartment for an overnight stay. We always found time for sex, but it was usually more hurried than either of us preferred and I craved a night in Wren's arms.

"I have one more gift for you."

"What?" I asked. "You've already given me flowers."

"Those are just to tide you over until you can have your real present." Wren got up and retrieved a card out of his coat that he'd laid over the back of his kitchen chair. "This is my real gift."

I opened the envelope and pulled out a card, but it wasn't the commercial type that I expected. It looked homemade. There was a drawing of cupid and his bow, but it wasn't the curly-haired cherub I associated with the name. It was a sketch of me wearing a white cloth tied around my waist and huge golden wings. I held a gilded bow in my hands and had just released an arrow that struck a character that looked just like Wren in the heart. The look on cartoon Wren's face was one of disbelief while cartoon Dare looked pretty pleased with himself.

"This took incredible skill, Wren. I'm so impressed. Why are you only wearing leather pants in this picture?" I asked.

"I know how much you like them, and I wanted you to see that your arrow pierced my cold heart."

"Your heart was never cold," I told him. I pointed to the gold and red object on cartoon Wren's head. "Is that a crown?"

"It is," he replied. "I'm your Prince-Not-So-Fucking-Charming."

I snorted at his description. "I have kissed plenty of frogs to get you."

"That's enough of that talk," Wren groused jealously. "Open your card."

I opened the card and had to bite my lips to keep from crying when I read the words he wrote to me. He didn't speak of roses and violets and the colors that matched them, he promised me the one thing I wanted most in the world.

This card entitles you to one entire night in my arms.

"How?" I asked.

"The reason Maren couldn't stay with Ralph this evening is because she's staying over on Saturday night so I can take you on a real date. I made dinner reservations and booked a hotel room. If you're a real good boy, I'll take you to Drinks and Twinks for—"

I cut off his words when I straddled his lap and kissed him. My body went up in flames and my cock hardened at just the thought of spending the night with him. Not just a few stolen hours, but a full night with his arms wrapped around me. I would get to hear him breathe while he sleeps, kiss him awake, and show him with more than words just how much I loved him.

"Wren, it's perfect. Thank you so much. I love it, and I love you."

"I love you too, Sparkles."

We kissed and made out like teenagers, but as I predicted, Wren left before things went too far. I couldn't let the night end like that, and had no desire to relieve the pressure with my own hand, unless…

I sent Wren a text. *Look out your bedroom window. The night's not over yet.*

It was surprising that I hadn't taken advantage of the fact that our bedroom windows faced each other before then. There was a park behind our house so no one could look into my window unless they were taking a late-night stroll on the walking path in twenty-degree weather. Wren had more risk than me, but the only house that could see into his window was vacant. Andy bought it to renovate and flip, but he wasn't there this time of night.

Wren appeared in his window fully dressed like I was. He quirked a brow, but his grin said he knew exactly what I was up to. I held up my phone and dialed his number.

"What are you up to, Sparkles?"

"As if you don't know." I put the phone on speaker and set it on the ledge. Wren did the same. "I thought of a perfect ending to a perfect night."

"Yeah?" Wren asked, whipping his shirt over his head and tossing it to the floor.

"I have to see and hear you come, Wren. I can wait a few more days to feel your body unravel for me as long as you give me this much."

"I'll give you anything you want, Dare." Wren lost my nickname when he was really turned on. I liked it a lot.

I took off my shirt too then reached for my pants.

"Wait," Wren said. "Get out your little vibrating toy."

"Wren." His name was a whimper on my lips.

"Do it."

I got the vibrating plug, remote, and lube from the drawer.

"Slick it up and turn around so I can watch you insert it in your ass."

I did as he asked, leaning forward a little so he could really get a view. I heard him unzipping his jeans through the phone.

"Nice and slow," he said.

I looked over my shoulder and watched him slide his hand beneath the waistband of his underwear to stroke his cock. I wanted to see his thick hard-on but watching his hand work beneath the fabric was sexy.

I whimpered in delight once the plug was fully inserted and pressing against my prostate. "Wren!"

"Don't come yet," he growled. "Turn around and pick up the remote off the windowsill."

I moaned because I knew he was going to make me feel so fucking good, even if he wasn't in the same room with me. I was mesmerized by the motion of his hand and didn't hear him the first time he gave me a number for the remote.

"Dare," Wren said firmly. "I won't go easy on you since you weren't paying attention. Press the number three and hold it until I tell you to let up."

"One," I said, attempting to negotiate.

"Nope, that barely makes your dick twitch. I was going to be nice and let you lightly tap the two, but not anymore."

"I'll be good."

"You'll hold down the three until I say otherwise, or I'll pull the curtains closed and finish myself off in the shower."

"Wren," I whined. "You're so mean." He started to close the curtain with his free hand. "Wait!" I held up the remote and held down the number three. *Zaaaaaaaaap.* "Ohhhh. Ohhh my God."

"You can call me by my first name," he said sexily. Fuck, he was the Prince of Prostate Torture. My cock twitched and jerked and my boys tucked up high and tight. "Let go."

It was both painful and pleasant to stop. Painful because I was on the edge of coming that quickly, but pleasant because I wanted to last longer and give him a great show.

"My turn," I said. "Pull your dick out and let me see it."

"Nope, this is my show."

"It was my idea," I countered. When Wren didn't make a move to comply I reached for the shade above my head. "If you're nice, I won't hang up the call and you can hear me moan your name when I come. You just won't be able to see it."

"Little evil—"

"Get your cock out," I repeated. I shook the shade a little to emphasize that my hand was still on it.

Wren did as I asked, and my mouth salivated. He was too far away for me to see if he was leaking, but I knew he was. I could almost smell his arousal and feel his need for me. He braced one hand on the window and worked his cock with the other.

"So fucking sexy," I growled, wanting to be with him more and more every day.

"Tap the four twice," Wren said. "Don't try to trick me by hitting the one or two or I'll know."

Zap. Zap. "Yes! Yes!" I semi-shouted with each tap.

"That's my guy," Wren purred. "So sexy and responsive. I can't wait to have you all night long. Think you can come more than three times?"

"No," I gasped. There was no way.

"We'll see about that." Wren's dark promise almost sounded like a threat. "I bet you can."

"Tease your nipples," I told him.

Wren straightened up from the window and grabbed his nipple. "Your mouth feels better."

"Pinch and roll it, Wren. Pretend it's my teeth and imagine you're fucking my ass instead of your fist." Hell, my dirty talk to him amped me up even more.

"Four," he said breathlessly. I knew his orgasm was close. "Hold it until you come. Don't you dare stroke your cock either."

My heart raced with the pleasure I knew I was going to feel—physically from the plug and emotionally from seeing Wren come undone. I held down the four and my body tensed all over. *Zaaaaaaap.* My abs tensed harder than during any stomach crunches and my thighs shook.

"Mmmm, I love the way your cock throbs and jerks when you're about to come," Wren growled. "Come for me, baby. Hard and long. Let me hear it."

"Ahhhhhhhhh," I said when the first spurt of cum jettisoned from my cock and splattered against the window. "Wren!" It wasn't the same as his dick pounding me, but it helped to know he was watching and growling with pleasure as he stroked his dick in fast, jerky motions.

"Right there with you," Wren growled seconds before his release hit his chest and stomach.

"I want to be there with you when you fall asleep," I said.

Wren pressed his hand against the window and I did the same. We weren't holding hands, or even touching, but I felt the connection in my heart as if we were. "Only a few more days, Sparkles. I love you."

"I love you too." I didn't want my sadness to ruin our beautiful night, so I blew him a kiss. "Goodnight, Wren."

He reached up and snagged the kiss from the air. "Goodnight, Dare." We were complete dorks in that moment, but I didn't care. *Three more days,* I chanted to myself as I cleaned up my mess on the window, got ready for bed, and waited to fall asleep. *Two more days*, I chanted to myself the next day at work to help the time pass. *One more day*, I reminded myself on Friday as if I could forget. I followed that up with, *Only a few more hours,* in the morning and afternoon at the salon on Saturday.

After work, I took a shower and packed my overnight bag then spent time with Grandpa while I waited for Maren to arrive. I was nervous about leaving him, but he would be in capable hands.

"You have a great time, Dare. Bring me back a souvenir."

"We're just going to Cincinnati," I reminded him.

"Doesn't matter," he said.

"I'll get you something great," I promised him.

When Maren arrived, I kissed Grandpa's forehead and hugged her tight. "Thank you," I whispered gratefully.

Maren followed me to the door. "You go have yourself a wonderful time, young man. No one deserves a night out with his sweetie like you do."

"Thanks, Maren. Don't hesitate to call if you need me."

"You know I will, sugar. Now get on out there. Wren is looking worried like you might stand him up or something."

I looked out the door and he did look nervous. That was no way to start off our weekend. I kissed Maren's cheek and opened the door. The slow smile that spread across Wren's face was filled with dark promise.

Chapter
Eighteen

Wren

THE FIRST STOP ON OUR DATE WAS THE NEWPORT Aquarium. Both of us had always wanted to visit, but neither made the time. Dare was the perfect person to share the experience with, and I was glad I waited. The aquarium's acrylic tunnels made you feel like you were a part of the ocean life as you walked through them. Having sharks swimming above you and beside you was surreal. It was dark, peaceful, and even felt romantic for our first official date. Dare loved the penguins and their shenanigans the most, but I was enthralled by the majesty of the jellyfish. Dare and I stopped by the gift shop to buy Ralph a stingray coffee cup as a souvenir before we headed to dinner.

Since we were already in Newport, I decided to take Dare to Bobby Jack's. Their food was delicious and the river views were beautiful. I never thought the staff would remember me from the dinner I had with Alaric a few weeks prior.

"Welcome back to Bobby Jack's, Mr. Davison," the hostess cheerfully said when we entered the restaurant. She seemed disappointed that my father wasn't my plus one and curious about Dare's role in my life. "Will it just be the two of you tonight?"

I placed my hand on Dare's lower back like a lover would do. "Yes, it's just the two of us."

Her eyes widened slightly but the smile never fell from her face. "Follow me, please. We reserved our best table for you."

The hostess led us to a table that overlooked the Ohio River as the sun was starting to set. "Oh, this is beautiful," Dare said then turned to the hostess. "Thank you." Even if she was disappointed that I was there on a date, she couldn't help returning Dare's megawatt smile with one of her own. He had that effect on people. My Sparkles.

"You're very welcome. Enjoy your evening."

"Aw, I think she had a little crush on you," Dare said when we were alone. "I can't blame her. You look so handsome tonight."

I just grunted at his compliment and diverted the conversation. "*You* look delicious." I planned to take full advantage of our night away and gorge myself on Dare later. Who knew when we'd get our next opportunity for an overnight date.

"Charmer," Dare said, blushing adorably pink. He knew exactly where my thoughts had gone.

"Only for you, Sparkles. Everyone else gets a snarl."

"Including me," said a voice I wasn't ready to hear again so soon. Why would fate continue to piss on my plans? So caught up in Dare, I didn't even notice that someone else had entered the little cove. We were hidden from most of the restaurant, which meant the hostess must've told him I was here and where he could find me.

Alaric stopped at our table and smiled tentatively at me. At least he was smart enough to be wary. He'd stuck to his word and stopped calling me. He'd left the ball in my court, and I hadn't done anything with it yet. I'd thought about it a lot after our dinner together, but I hadn't made my next move.

"It's good to see you, Wren." Then Alaric turned his focus on Dare.

My body tightened with tension because I wasn't sure how he would treat my boyfriend. If Alaric ever hoped to have a relationship with me, he would mind his step with Dare. It seemed that I had nothing to worry about because Alaric gave Dare one of his genuine smiles and extended his hand. I'd seen enough of his fake smiles to know it was the real thing.

"I didn't get a chance to formally introduce myself the first time we met. I'm Alaric Davison." Not Falcon, not Wren's dad, just Alaric. I liked it.

"I'm Darren, but my friends call me Dare."

"Dare suits you," Alaric said. "You have an orneriness about you that challenges people."

"You could say that again," I agreed. "I'm surprised the hostess didn't tell me you had reservations also."

Alaric turned his attention to me. "I used a fake name, so she didn't know until I arrived. I really don't want to be lavished with false affection, I just want to take my wife to dinner."

"She's here?" I asked, suddenly curious about the woman he married a few years after my mom died.

"Yes, Samantha is here. She didn't want to impose on your dinner." More like she was afraid of her reception. I wasn't such a dick that I would've snarled or been mean to her, but how would she know that. All Samantha Davison knew about me was that I kept rejecting Alaric's attempts to be in my life.

"Where's your table? I'd like to say hello." Just like that, I lobbed the ball back into his court. It was a huge step, and everyone at the table knew it. Alaric's eyes widened with hope and Dare smiled at me like I'd handed him the crown jewels.

"Stay, I'll bring Samantha to your table so she can meet Dare too." Alaric started to walk away but jerked to a stop. "If that's okay with you."

I nodded.

"I'm so proud of you, Wren," Dare said when we were alone again.

"I don't want him to get his hopes up, but I want to try." At least to honor the memory of the woman we both loved.

"A chance was all he asked for and you're giving it to him. Take it as slow as you need, babe." His little endearment made me smile.

"Wow, that's two smiles in one night," Alaric said as he approached the table for the second time. This time he was joined by his wife, my stepmother.

I'd seen Samantha Davison's picture many times, but I never would've recognized her on the street. Of course, it was doubtful she dressed like she was attending a music award show or movie premier every day of her life. I felt like I was seeing the real person without the makeup, glamorous gowns, and Hollywood hair. Samantha Davison was a natural beauty who didn't need any of that extra stuff to steal everyone's attention in the room.

Even though I tried to avoid seeing or reading anything about Alaric, it was big news when Alaric married an African-American woman. Pictures of them were splashed all over the tabloid rags and entertainment magazines at the checkout lane in grocery stores. Should the color of Samantha's skin have mattered? Hell no, but that never stopped ignorant ass people from spewing hate. It was obvious that Alaric was head over heels for her and that's all that people needed to know. It was equally obvious that Alaric didn't give a fuck what anyone thought about his marriage.

Dare and I both stood up when she arrived.

"Hi, Samantha. It's good to finally meet you," I said warmly. Instead of shaking my hand, she gave me a hug.

"I must look terrible, but I was so excited to get out for a little bit that I didn't stop to put on makeup. If I'd have known…"

"You look beautiful the way you are," I assured her. "I'd like you to meet my boyfriend, Dare."

"Hello," she said, greeting Dare with a hug. "It's good to meet you."

"You too," he returned, looking a little shell-shocked. "This is you without makeup, huh? Wow."

"Alaric is lucky I didn't just wear my sweats and raggedy T-shirt out the door," she told us.

"It would've been a slight improvement over pajamas," he teased then kissed her temple. "I'll take any moment I can steal with you."

"Smooth, Alaric," she said but smiled up at him.

"Did I read that you joined a law practice here in Cincinnati?" Dare asked.

"Kemp, Knolfield, and Barnes," she replied. "I joined their team of civil lawyers. I'm really looking forward to getting involved in the community." Samantha Davison was so much more than a pretty face. How an ivy league educated woman such as herself ended up with someone as rough as Alaric was beyond me. Maybe he showed a side to her that he didn't share with anyone else. Kind of how I saved all my good parts for Dare.

"Wife, mom, and a kick-ass lawyer," Alaric said proudly. "I'm a lucky man."

"You're really pouring on the charm tonight," Samantha said then narrowed her eyes. "This isn't the part where you tell me you're coming out of retirement already, is it?"

"Nope, I'm done with the road."

"For good?" I asked in disbelief. I'd heard on the radio that they were taking a year off; they said nothing about retiring.

"That part is a secret for now. Only our families know, which you," he pointed to Dare and me, "are family. We'll break the news to everyone else later."

"Alaric is now a stay-at-home dad," Samantha informed us.

"You are?" Dare and I both asked.

"I'm truly insulted that the two of you don't think I can be content changing diapers and spending time with my youngest son."

Youngest son. It had flowed too naturally to be contrived. No matter how many times I rejected him, I was still his firstborn son.

"Oh, I didn't say that," Dare said, rushing to soothe any ruffled feathers. "It must be a huge change though."

"Yes, but the absolute best."

Our waiter approached us then with a puzzled look on his face. "Would you prefer to dine together? I can move you to a larger table?"

"Oh no!" Samantha said. "We're not infringing on your date night, but hopefully the two of you could have dinner with us soon. Perhaps meet Tobias?"

"That would be great, Samantha. I would love to meet my little brother." I looked at Alaric then and said, "I'll call you soon."

"I look forward to it. I hope the two of you have a great night." Samantha hugged us both again before she headed back to their table, leaving us alone with Alaric.

An awkwardness descended over me because I wasn't sure how to end our conversation. A handshake was too formal, and I wasn't ready for a hug yet. Alaric didn't seem to have the same reservation because he pulled me in for a tight hug. The hug he gave Dare was a little gentler, but still sincere.

"I hope to talk to you soon," Alaric said then reluctantly walked away.

"Well, that was a pleasant surprise," Dare said once we were alone again. He picked up his menu and began looking it over. "I'm in the mood for surf and turf, but we just had that the other night."

"The dinner you made was delicious," I told him. "In fact, I think it would rival anything on this menu."

"Wren, you're already getting laid tonight, so you don't need to lay it on so thick."

"Oh, Sparkles. What am I going to do with you?"

"I can think of many things," he said sassily. "Can we order our meals to go?"

"No," I told him. "We'll have plenty of time for that later. This date is about more than sex. I want to show you off around town for everyone to see how lucky I am."

"Wren," Dare said, setting his menu down on the table. "We're around people all the time. I would be happy with spending every second of our time away in that hotel room."

"I thought you might like to see a movie or go to a club after dinner."

"Nope and nope." Dare shook his head. "We can stream a movie in between bouts of sex. I can give you that lap dance you've been imagining since the day I first brought it up. The only person I want to see is you." He glanced up at the waiter who was walking toward our table. "And him. I am good and hungry."

Dare took advantage of our secluded, candlelit cove and spent the entire meal seducing me with his smiles and teasing touches beneath the table. He slipped off his shoe and ran his foot up the inside of my calf, my inner thigh, and didn't stop until he reached my crotch. There, he curled his toes around my cock and sent bolts of pleasure straight to my balls.

"Dare," I said softly, warning him that I'd make him pay.

"If I could get by with it, I'd crawl beneath the table and suck you off right now."

Even the way he ate his food was sinful. He kept me hard and on the edge until we got back to my truck. By then it was completely dark, so I didn't try to stop him when he leaned over the console and released my aching dick from my jeans.

"You play lookout," Dare said before he took my stiff cock all the way to the back of his throat. I tried to keep an eye on our surroundings, but it was impossible to look away from his beautiful face pleasuring me in the thin shaft of moonlight coming through the windshield. As my orgasm built, my head felt too heavy for my shoulders. I let it fall back against the headrest and closed my eyes, not worrying if anyone watched Dare suck my dick right then.

"So good, Dare," I grunted as he continued to work me to the edge and back me off. Just as I was about to shoot in his mouth, he pulled off and sat up.

"I think we're ready for the hotel room now," he said, wiping the saliva from his lips.

"I think you need to finish what you started." I gestured to my wet, throbbing dick that he hadn't bothered to even tuck away. Of course, if he touched it right then, I might shoot my load. Dare smiled evilly because he knew it too.

"I will back in our room. I have big plans for you." He reached over to tease my cock by sliding one finger along its rigid length. "*Big* plans." Dare pulled my briefs over my erection and zipped my jeans back up. "Take me back to our room, Wren. I *dare* you."

Traffic was a bitch crossing the bridge and getting back to our hotel. Once in the parking garage, Dare leaned into me with a teasing open-mouth kiss that was so hot that I nearly burst into flames. He tugged my bottom lip with his teeth then licked it to make it better. Dare flitted the tip of his tongue inside my mouth to tease mine then darted back out.

I vibrated with a need so strong that it bordered on violence. I pulled back from him and opened the door, leaving Dare to choose between staying or going. I needed the chilly air in the parking garage to cool me down. I heard the passenger door open and shut followed by Dare's footsteps as he followed behind me. His laughter echoed throughout the garage, and I vowed to get the last laugh that night.

I kept my cool as we walked through the lobby and made our

way to the bank of elevators. A couple of people got on the elevator with us, so I pulled Dare to stand in front of me to make room. The imp subtly pressed his ass against my erection, and I had to bite my lip to keep from groaning out loud. I dug my fingers in his hips, which only encouraged him more. I'd chosen a room with a spectacular view on one of the top floors of the hotel. It seemed like we stopped on every floor for the other passengers to get off the elevator. Then it was finally just the two of us.

Without warning, I spun us around so that Dare was facing the wall of the elevator and I was pressed against his back. One hand still held his hip and the other gripped his hard-on through his jeans. Dare whimpered and pushed back against me. God, I could've taken him right there and not given a fuck about the consequences. That was how wild he made me.

The elevator finally stopped on our floor and the doors opened. I grabbed Dare's hand and eagerly led him to our room. My hands shook so bad it took me a few tries to open the fucking door. Once inside the room, I was on Dare before it even shut. Need, lust, and passion clawed at my guts as my body demanded release.

Dare danced out of my arms and shook his head. "Not yet."

"Darren, get over on this bed so I can fuck you."

"Ohhh, you brought out my full name." Dare's wicked smile said he was enjoying my suffering way too much. "I have something special planned for you."

"I have something special for you too." It was several inches long and ready to fuck.

"Let me have my fun first," Dare said. "I promise that you're going to love it." He grabbed a club chair from the living room setup and moved it so that it faced the wall of windows in our room. "I want to make sure you have a nice backdrop."

"I'm not fucking you for the entire city to see," I told him.

"The windows are tinted. They can't see in, but we can see out."

It wasn't a chance I was willing to take until Dare started to peel his clothes off. When he was down to nothing but a sexy pair of navy blue briefs, he gestured to the chair. "Welcome to the VIP room of Drinks and Twinks. Would you like me to grab you a drink before you enjoy your twink?"

"Jesus," I moaned.

"He's not a dancer here," Dare said seriously. He crooked his finger at me. "This is the best seat in the house."

I started to take off my clothes, but Dare shook his head.

"We don't run that kind of establishment, Mr. Davison. You'll get a dance and nothing more."

"I'm getting a fucking-lot-more than a dance," I growled as I marched toward him and his chair.

"Why, Mr. Davison. I—"

I shut him up with a kiss and felt his resolve starting to fade as our passion ignited even more. A minute ago, I would've taken advantage of the situation and bent him over the chair to fuck him. I still might, but only after I got my fucking dance.

I slapped him on his pert ass then pulled back from him. "Let's see what you got, Sparkles." I tossed my jacket on the sofa then sat in the chair.

Dare's face was flushed with need, but he'd thrown down the gauntlet and there was no turning back. He pulled up a bluesy, slow song with a heavy beat that I'd never heard before. Dare smiled seductively as he walked toward me. He picked up my hands and placed them on the arms of the chair.

"House rules: no touching the dancers." Rules were something I used to strictly adhere to, but not since falling in love with Dare. I was determined to play along to make him happy though.

Dare began to sway to the beat, his ass so close in front of me but still so far away. When he turned around to face me, I saw that pre-cum had soaked his briefs, letting me know he was as hard and horny as me. When I finally got ahold of him, I would take him hard and fast. Later, I could draw it out and make him come many times, but I needed to take the edge off first.

Dare surprised me by straddling my lap.

"I thought you said no touching," I groused.

"Those rules only apply to you. Me… I can do whatever my heart desires."

Apparently, his heart desired that he release my cock and rub our erections together with only the thin layer of his underwear between us while nibbling my neck and tangling his fingers in my hair. The friction was out of this fucking world and his whimpers for more made me crazy. I wanted to play his game, I really did, but I wasn't sure I could take it much longer.

Dare lifted his head and stared into my eyes. "I've been thinking about doing this for so long. The thrill of knowing that *I* can reduce *you* to a quivering mass of need and lust makes me crazy. Seeing your pulse pound in your neck and feeling the way your cock strains to have me makes me feel invincible."

I wanted him to feel invincible and revel in the power he had over me. I gripped the armrest and gave myself over to him, knowing that there would be plenty more times that night to get my way too. I stopped fighting my climax and gave him all my pleasure. When I came all over myself, I shouted his name and reveled in the happiness I saw on his face. I forgot about the rules and lowered the elastic band of his underwear to grip his cock and jerked him to completion.

"That'll be a thousand dollars," Dare said drowsily before he nipped my bottom lip.

"Sparkles, you should've asked for your cash up front."

"I can think of another way you can pay for my services."

"So can I." Bent over the chair in front of the window, in the shower, sixty-nineing in the middle of the king-sized bed. The possibilities were endless, as was the love I felt for him when he fell asleep right there on my lap.

Chapter
Nineteen

Dave

HATED THAT I FELL ASLEEP ON WREN AFTER MY LITTLE lap dance. I'd told him that I wanted to sleep in his arms, but I thought that I'd at least debauch him until the middle of the night before I crashed. Instead, I woke up tucked up next to him in the middle of the night. *Fuck! I crashed hard.* The last thing I remembered was smiling down at his sated face and teasing him about paying me for the lap dance and his happy ending. I slept through Wren carrying me to the bed and cleaning us both off. I didn't even stir when he climbed in bed beside me and missed out on drifting to sleep in his arms. I felt robbed of a beautiful moment.

I wanted to wake him up so that we could fall asleep together, but I suspected I knew what would happen if he woke up. It would be so easy to do too. I could trail my fingers up and down his stomach and dip them beneath the sheet to tease his trimmed pubic hair. I bet he would have me on my back with my legs spread within seconds of touching him. My cock stiffened at thoughts of Wren letting go of his control and releasing his unbridled passion on me. I sensed how close I came the night before, but he still held himself back. Why? Fear of letting me see all of him? Fear of hurting me? There was nothing he could show me that would push me away, and I knew with utmost certainty that he would never hurt me.

Wren was sleeping too peacefully for me to disturb him though, so I lay there and listened to him breathe while relishing the way he held me tucked beneath his chin. A lot of people would've scoffed at our date night or called it lame, because the freedom to eat out and spend the night away from home was something they took for granted. I did not regret moving in with Grandpa and taking care of him, but I worried that it might become a strain on my relationship with Wren. How long would he be willing to keep putting his needs aside? After tonight, would he be okay with sleeping separately? Would I?

It wasn't long before Wren's even breathing lulled me back to sleep. When I woke the second time, it was from Wren's fingers dancing up and down my stomach from my sternum to my dick. The early-morning light was shining through the windows, bathing the stark white bed in orange and yellow light.

"We have a few hours before we have to check out," Wren said huskily, making goose bumps pop up all over my body. I loved the rough, sexy timbre of his voice first thing in the morning. "Any suggestions?"

"Breakfast in bed?" I asked.

I meant that I wanted to eat him for breakfast, but he rolled over and grabbed the room service menu. "Your pout is adorable, Sparkles. I'm sure it will take at least thirty minutes for our food to be delivered. We can do a lot in thirty minutes."

"Is French toast on the menu?" I asked.

"Yep, is that what you want?"

"Mmmmm. Crispy bacon too."

Wren placed the order then yanked the covers off me, exposing my nude body to his eyes. "How many times can you come in thirty minutes?" he asked before he curled his tongue and teased my nipple.

The answer was four.

"I didn't know guys like you existed," Wren said. We'd been on the road for about twenty minutes and had another twenty before we arrived back home.

"Snarky?"

"Well, you are, but that's not what I meant."

"Flexible?" I inquired. Wren glanced over with a quirked brow. "Oh, a screamer."

Wren snorted. "You weren't screaming for mercy, but you were kind of begging loudly. I would've stopped but you kept digging your heels to pull me deeper inside you. I didn't mean anything sexually either, although, your particular talent is very impressive."

"So is your stamina to pull it off."

"This conversation is headed sideways," Wren said.

"What did you mean?" I asked. "What kind of guys like me?"

Wren cleared his throat like he either found it hard to speak or he was too embarrassed to say what he was thinking. "You're kind, loving, devoted to your friends and family, creative, funny, and sexier than one person should ever be. I still expect to wake up at my old apartment and find this has all been a dream."

"Me too," I admitted.

"It's going to be hard sleeping alone in my apartment now that I know what it feels like to sleep beside you." My heart sank because he was echoing my fears. How long was he willing to put up with it?

"Do you really think your grandpa would be okay if I stayed over on occasion?"

Warmth spread through my body. "Grandpa loves you, Wren. He wouldn't mind."

"I'm still going to struggle with it, and I'm not making your mattress squeak while Grandpa sleeps beneath us," Wren said dryly.

"We'll have to get creative then." My brain went into overdrive thinking up quiet ways I can rock Wren's world. "We might need to stop at Kim's Toys for a ball gag."

"Oh fuck!"

I started to tell Wren where to find the place, but my phone rang. My first thought was that it was Maren calling to tell me that something was wrong with Grandpa. "It's my dad," I told Wren. "Hey, Dad. What's up?"

"Dare, are you on your way home?" I could tell by the sound of his voice that something was really wrong.

"We're about fifteen minutes away," I told him. "What's wrong?"

"Grandpa fell and broke his hip. They're about to take him into surgery now."

My heart shattered into a million pieces, and I could barely talk through the tears. "Which hospital? Why didn't Maren call me?"

"He's at the county hospital in Goodville," Dad said. "Maren wasn't there when it happened, Dare. I came over this morning to spend time with Grandpa so Maren could go to church. He got up to get something when I was making breakfast and just fell." My dad's voice wobbled, but he pulled himself together, unlike me who cried like he said Grandpa had died. "I'm just now getting a chance to call you."

"Where to?" Wren asked calmly.

"Goodville," I answered. To my dad, I said, "We'll be there as soon as we can."

"Is Ralph okay?" Wren asked worriedly.

"He fell and broke his hip," I told him then repeated what my father had said.

"Ralph's a tough guy, Dare. He's going to pull through." Wren reached over and squeezed my hand that rested on the console.

I turned my hand and linked our fingers, needing his strength. Neither of us spoke for the rest of the trip to the hospital. I knew where my mind had gone, but I couldn't gauge what was going on with Wren. I wouldn't say he had returned to the distant and aloof guy that I first met, but he did seem more guarded than usual. He politely shook hands with my father, mother, and sister when I formally introduced them. I would've invited Wren to dinners with my family, but he always tried to catch up with Jimmy and Danny every Sunday. I hated that Wren was meeting my family for the first time under these circumstances.

"What are they saying?" I asked.

"He has a femoral neck fracture and needs to have a partial hip replacement," Dad answered. "They're going to replace the ball and femoral neck with a stainless steel prosthesis. He's going to require weeks, maybe months, of physical therapy." I could tell he was bracing himself to deliver sad news to me.

"Dr. Stanley is recommending that Grandpa be moved to a nursing home while he undergoes rehabilitation for his hip."

"Dare, this is nothing personal against you, and I promise that we're not trying to railroad Grandpa into a nursing home," Mom said gently. "He just needs around-the-clock care right now, and he needs to be in the best place for him."

"He'll die," I told them. "Grandpa hates the idea of living in a nursing home."

"Dare, let's approach this as a temporary solution right now. If Grandpa recovers fully then maybe he can move back home with you," Dad said. "We have to put his safety before his feelings, Son."

I nodded because I knew they were right, but it hurt to think of Grandpa being miserable.

"He's going to be too tired and too sore to put up much of a fight the first few days that he's there, but we'll have to keep him focused on his recovery when he becomes more alert," my dad said. "You're going to be key in that effort, Dare. He'll feed off the energy you put out."

"I'll do my best," I said tearfully. "I only want what's best for him."

"And right now the best thing for him is a rehabilitation unit in a nursing home," Mom said. She pulled me into a hug and held me tight. "Grandpa is tough, Dare. He's going to pull through."

"I sure wish we were getting to know each other under better circumstances," I heard my dad say to Wren.

"I do too, Mr. McCoy."

"Please call me Brian," Dad told him.

"And please call me Sara," my mom said. "Mrs. McCoy will always be my beloved mother-in-law."

"The surgery should only take a few hours if everything goes well. Then he'll be in recovery for another hour or two before they wheel him into a private room. We might as well have a seat and try to get comfortable." Dad looked pointedly at me. "Everything will go well, Dare. You need to have faith."

"Are you named Wren because your father goes by Falcon?" Kristy asked. "Your parents should've chosen another bird of prey like Hawk. Wren doesn't sound very fierce."

"Kristy," Mom, Dad, and I all said at the same time.

"What, it's a fair question, or are we supposed to pretend that Dare isn't dating the Rock King's son?"

"It's a rude question, Kristy," I said.

Wren placed his hand at the back of my neck, and I calmed immediately. "I don't mind answering her question," he said to me. "Wren actually means ruler, which is a play on my dad's rocker status rather than his stage name."

"Interesting," Kristy said.

I could tell my mom and dad were all kinds of curious too, but they didn't ask him any questions other than if he wanted coffee. The two hours stretched on for what seemed like two months before the surgeon finally called us into a little room where he went over Grandpa's surgery in detail and gave us Grandpa's prognosis.

"Overall, Mr. McCoy is in exceedingly good health for his age, so he should make a full recovery. How long that takes depends on his cooperation and how willingly he does his physical therapy exercises. With surgery at his age, there's always a chance for complications like pneumonia. He will be closely monitored, and we'll get him up and moving as fast as we safely can to help guard against respiratory issues."

"He'll be a model patient, Dr. Adams," I said. My dad snorted, and I was forced to amend my statement. "Okay, he's going to be a curmudgeon on some days, but he's tough and will fight through it."

"That's probably more realistic," Dr. Adams said in good humor. "It's obvious that Mr. McCoy has a great support system, and that helps a lot. Do you have any questions for me?" We looked at each other then shook our heads. "Okay then. We'll let you know when he's moved to a private room." The surgeon shook our hands again and let himself out of the room.

"Is anyone hungry?" Dad asked when we were back in the waiting room. "The food in the cafeteria is decent."

"I'm not hungry," I said. "Are you, Wren?"

"I'm good."

"I'm not hungry, but I'll go with you," my mom said. "Come on, Kristy. You can come too."

My sister rolled her eyes but followed our parents, leaving me alone with Wren. He looped his arm around my shoulders and pulled me toward him so that I rested my head on his chest. Wren ran his hand up and down my back, and his body heat chased away the chill and fear that permeated my body when I answered Dad's phone call.

"Grandpa is going to be okay," I said with conviction. I had to face the harsh reality that he might not ever move back home, but I was determined that he recover and adjust to his new life.

"Of course, he is," Wren said into my hair. "Do you want me to leave so you can be alone with your family?"

"Of course not," I said quickly then sat up. "Would you prefer to leave though? I don't want you to feel pressured to stay?" Then I remembered it was Sunday. "Are Jimmy and Danny coming over?"

"You're not pressuring me," Wren assured me. "I just don't want to add stress for anyone by being here."

"You're not," I assured him.

"I told Jimmy and Danny that we were going away for the weekend, so they weren't planning on coming over anyway."

"Okay, but if you—" Wren silenced me with a tender kiss.

"I'm right where I want to be...with you."

"Okay." I returned my head back to his chest, and Wren wrapped his arm tighter around me like he was trying to shield me.

My parents and sister returned fifteen or twenty minutes later. No one was in much of a chatty mood, not even Kristy. I suspected that my parents had a harsh word with her about bugging Wren when they were gone. Time seemed to crawl by and it was almost dinnertime before a nurse told us that Grandpa had been moved to his room.

I wanted to rush into his room to assure myself that he was okay, but I also wanted to hide in the hallway. I didn't want to see him hooked up to tubes and looking weak, but I knew he would want to see me. I pushed my fear aside and pasted a smile on my lips before I opened his door.

Grandpa's eyelashes fluttered but didn't fully open. He had an IV in his arm and a thin breathing tube looped around his ears and secured beneath his nose. Grandpa looked pretty good all things considered.

"He's on some pretty strong pain medicine right now, so he'll be a little groggy," his nurse said. "He might seem confused but try not to be alarmed. He'll become more alert once we start dialing back his pain meds. His vitals look really good though."

"That's good to hear," I told the nurse. "Thank you."

"Is that my Dare?" Grandpa asked weakly from the bed. He sounded higher than a kite.

"I'm here, Grandpa." I went around to the side of the bed and covered his hand. *Don't cry and upset him. Don't cry and upset him.*

"Dare, I saw your grandmother." His eyelashes fluttered more, but his bright blue eyes remained hidden.

I looked up at the nurse and she mouthed, "Anesthesia."

"Like in a dream?" I asked him.

"Yes," he replied sleepily. "She looked like an angel."

"That's good, Grandpa."

"Everything is going to be okay, Dare. She said so."

I rubbed his hand gently. "Okay, Grandpa."

"Be sure to take care of the house for me, will you?" His voice trailed off until it was nothing more than a whisper. I would've panicked if his chest hadn't been moving up and down at a steady rhythm.

"I will, Grandpa," I promised even though he didn't hear me. I kissed his forehead. "I'll be back later to see you."

Mom, Dad, and Kristy took turns kissing his forehead too. Then Wren approached the bed and gently patted his hand.

"Get plenty of rest, Ralph. I'll be back to play rummy and you'll need your energy to cheat," Wren said. My dad snickered because we all knew it was true. We just let Grandpa get away with it.

"I know it's difficult, but I'm going to recommend that you all go home and get some rest," the nurse said. "We'll call you if there are any changes in his condition. He's heavily sedated and will sleep throughout the night. Tomorrow morning is when he can use some smiling faces."

"I'll be here," I told her.

I didn't say anything on the ride home until we pulled into the driveway. I sat staring at the house for several seconds after Wren shut off the engine.

"I don't think I'm ready to go in there without him."

"Then don't," Wren said softly. "Come home with me."

There's a saying that home is where your heart is. My heart was conflicted between two places and two people. One represented the foundation that molded me into the man I became, and the other was the one I wanted to build my future on. That night, I chose my future when I accepted Wren's offered hand and followed him up to his apartment.

Chapter
Twenty

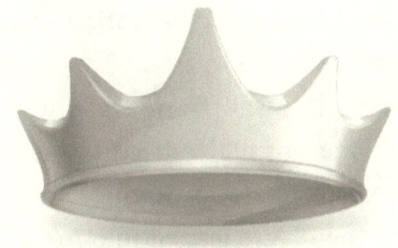

Wren

I HAD RETURNED TO THE PRE-DARE, DARK AND DISMAL place when he had first taken the call from his dad that Ralph had fallen and broken his hip. I knew that, once again, I was the reason for someone else's misery. I was the reason my mom was rejected by her family and a living reminder of the man she lost. I was the reason a young guy nearly lost his family when I couldn't keep my hormones under control as a teenager. I was the one who took Dare away for a weekend getaway and upset the balance in Ralph's life. Maybe if Dare had been there on Sunday morning, he wouldn't have fallen and broken his hip. Dare was convinced that Ralph would die if he was forced to live in a nursing home for an extended period, and I didn't want to think about Dare's devastation if his grandpa died.

Would he blame me? Would he see me as the person who caused the biggest heartache he's ever known instead of the one to give him the greatest pleasure? The thought of Dare turning away from me in disgust stole my breath and nearly induced panic on our drive to the hospital. It was selfish of me, I admit, but all I could think about was losing Dare and the sparkle and joy he brought into my life. Against all odds, and my better judgment, I had lowered the drawbridge and let Dare into my soul. I teased that he stormed the castle and took me by force, but that wasn't true. I wanted him—needed him—in my life. I craved his vibrancy and adoration as strongly as anyone would desire a substance or habit.

I felt myself pulling away from Dare with every mile that brought us closer to the hospital. I tried to maintain that distance even when Brian explained the procedure and the doctor gave a good prognosis, but then Dare leaned into me in the waiting room seeking comfort from me, and I knew that my resistance was futile. I would be his until he told me otherwise. Pulling away to protect myself was an act of selfishness when the person I loved most in the world needed me. I would do, and be, anything Dare needed for as long as he wanted me in his life. Wasn't that the best anyone could do and hope for in return? There were no damn guarantees in life beyond I would be miserable if I didn't give everything I had, physically and emotionally, to Dare.

I felt the tension fade inside me when I came to that realization and put all my energy in to supporting Dare instead of resisting him. Seeing Ralph in that hospital bed was a hard blow. I knew he was nearing ninety years old, but he had seemed so full of life during the many conversations we had. I'd come to love the man like I would a grandfather and it was just fucking painful to see him doped up and confused. I could see how hard Dare fought not to cry in front of him because Dare always put the needs of the people he loved first. Ralph and Dare's bond was a beautiful thing.

When we arrived back home, I saw Dare struggle with the idea of going into his house knowing that Ralph wouldn't be there. I had planned to spend the night with him regardless of which bed he slept in, but I loved the idea of having him in mine all night long. It was big and spacious and… *Down, boy! Not the time.*

Dare wasn't really in the mood for talking or eating, but he did eat a little bit of the soup I warmed up for us and nibbled the crusty edges of his grilled cheese sandwich.

"I admit that I don't like Andy sniffing around you, but he sure does excellent work," I said, looking around the remodeled kitchen. The only things left to do were paint and put on the finishing touches.

The first thing the carpenter did was make sure I had a temporary kitchen set up while the cabinets and countertops were installed. Of course, I made sure Andy knew that I shared my meals with Dare and Ralph. I didn't let Dare cook for us every night either. I treated the guys to diner cuisine or pizza a few nights a week. I even surprised them with a chicken and stuffing casserole I had learned from watching my mom. It was her favorite meal and the McCoy fellas enjoyed it a lot. It felt good making people happy with my mom's recipe.

Dare had looked up from his soup and smiled for the first time since answering the phone call from his dad. Then he shook his head like it was the most ridiculous thing that Andy could find him attractive. "I love you, Wren."

"I love you too, Sparkles." Which was why I was keeping my eye on that wily carpenter. Dare had told me a dozen times that Andy was hung up on Milo, the guy who owned the bookstore and coffee shop with his sister. I wasn't taking any chances.

That night in bed, I held Dare as tight as he wanted while doing my best to ignore my body's urges. The man I loved was naked and pressed against my side, so it was only natural that my dick would be on high alert. Dare had felt my body tense when he lay his hand on my stomach and knew the cause. His body reacted to my arousal, but I was more than willing to grit my teeth and ignore it.

"Why are we pretending we're not horny?" Dare whispered in the dark, pressing his cock against my outer thigh. "I could come from just this."

"I'm trying to be sensitive and caring," I replied through gritted teeth. "You're not just someone I fuck."

Dare threw back the covers and straddled my hips. "You know what makes someone feel special and loved?" Before I could answer him, he said, "An orgasm." Dare made quick work of preparing my cock and stretching his hole before he rode me until we both came hard enough to see stars, but even those didn't shine as bright as him.

The next morning, we went to see Ralph as soon as visiting hours began. He wasn't exactly sitting up and chatting easily like he normally did, but his blue eyes were open, and they lit up when Dare walked into the room.

"There's my boy," Ralph said, sounding weaker than I liked. "Tell me about your weekend."

Dare looked like a huge weight had been lifted from his shoulders. He stood taller and walked confidently to the bed where minutes before he slouched slightly and his steps were more hesitant.

"We had a great night, Grandpa," Dare said, holding Ralph's hand between his.

"Hi, Wren. It's good to see you," he said when I joined Dare beside his bed. His other hand shook when he extended it to me.

I clasped it in both of my hands too and smiled warmly at him. "Can we get you anything, Ralph?"

"I think it's time you call me Grandpa," Ralph said. "You come to mind every time I think of Dare now. I used to wonder what Dare was up to and now its Dare and Wren. You know what that means, don't you?"

"That you're still high on pain meds," Dare teased.

"Yes, but I'm still of sound mind," he whispered. "I remember the days when I went from Ralph to Ralph and Norma Mae. It wasn't long after that before we became Mr. and Mrs. McCoy." His eyes took on a faraway look as he smiled happily.

"Neither of us will ever be a Mrs.," Dare teased.

Ralph cackled softly. "I know that, silly. I'm just really happy that you've found that special someone. I'd always hoped to live long enough to see you settled."

"You will, Grandpa," Dare said. "This is just a bump in the road."

"You'll be back to beating us at rummy in no time, Grandpa," I told him. He smiled when I didn't call him by his first name.

"I was thinking about starting poker nights," Ralph said. "Then I fell." Ralph narrowed his eyes at Dare and added, "Don't you be mad at your father. This wasn't his fault."

"It's no one's fault," Dare said. "I just want you to get better, so we can take you home."

Ralph smiled sadly at Dare. "I think we both know that won't happen, Dare."

"I know nothing of the sort," Dare said boldly. "You'll have to go to the rehabilitation unit at the nursing home, but you can come back home once you're mobile again."

"Dare, it's not fair for you to spend all of your time taking care of me. That should never have been your role in my life. I was selfish and silly."

"No, Grandpa. I wanted to move in and help you."

"I should never have let you though," Ralph countered. "Let me get this out before the next dose of pain medication knocks me out, okay?" Dare nodded. "My Norma Mae came to me in my dream while I was having surgery. She assured me that I was going to be all right and that it still wasn't my time. The love of my life told me I needed to be a little bit more patient and a whole lot less selfish."

"You're not selfish," Dare said, sounding panicked.

"Allowing my grandson to move in with me and assume re-sponsibility for my care at twenty-four years old is the definition of selfish. Don't you argue with me." Ralph's voice got louder with agitation. "This is how it's going to be, Dare. I'm moving to that nursing home and I will stay there until the good Lord calls me home and reunites me with the love of my life."

"But…"

"I'm not going to go in there moping and pouting like Norma Mae said I would either. I'm going to make the best of it and maybe make some new friends my own age," Ralph said proudly. "I only want you to do one thing for me, Dare."

"What's that, Grandpa?"

"I want you to bring me the box of letters from my closet. They're the letters that your grandmother and I exchanged during the Korean War. They are my most precious treasure and define what home means to me."

"I can do that," Dare agreed eagerly.

"But not until I get settled at the nursing home," Ralph clarified. "I shouldn't be here much longer. They can give this bed to someone who will need it."

"That's the spirit," I told Ralph.

"The house is your home, Dare. I want you to feel free to do whatever you want with it. Remodel it to make it feel like your home, or you can even sell it if you want."

"Are your pain meds kicking in?" Dare teased.

"No, smartass," Ralph said with an ornery gleam in his eyes. "I legally signed the house over to you through my attorney on your eighteenth birthday so that I wouldn't be forced to sell it in this situation. The look back period is five years and you've owned it for seven. It's your home and the vultures can't take it from you."

"Why didn't you tell me?"

"It wasn't relevant until now," Ralph said practically. "I'm saving your grandmother's jewelry for Kristy. I know that's what Norma Mae would've wanted."

"Kristy will cherish it, Grandpa."

"I was going to wait until I died, but I'd like to see Kristy's reaction and maybe see her wear a few pieces." Ralph thought about it. "I'll wait just a little bit or your dad will think I'm preparing to die. I think there's a lot of life left in me still."

"I know there is," Dare told him. "You look like you're getting sleepy. Wren and I will step out for a while, but we'll be back. Ask one of the nurses to call me if there's anything you need in the meantime. Dad, Mom, and Kristy will be by a little later in the day. Dad said they were only working a half-day and bringing Kristy for a visit between school and ballet."

"I'll be right here when you get back." Ralph's eyelids fluttered a few times then remained closed.

Once we were back in my truck, Dare said, "I hate to leave him, but I need to get a lot of things done that I would've normally done yesterday. Do you mind if we stop at the grocery store on the way home? I can make it a quick trip now and get the rest of the things I need for the week later."

"Dare, can I share a secret with you?" I asked. "It's something I've never told anyone before, but I think I can trust you." My voice sounded ominous and he looked nervous, but he nodded his head anyway. *That, my friends, is love.* "I like grocery shopping."

Dare gasped loudly, and his eyes bugged out of his head. "No! Who the hell likes to shop for groceries? And you of all people?"

"Why shouldn't me 'of all people' like grocery shopping?" I asked.

"I mean, um, you just kind of look too…" His words trailed off as he tried to find an adjective that wouldn't offend me.

"Uncouth?"

"No!" Dare exclaimed. "I wasn't going to insult you, you big idiot."

"You mean like that?"

"Well, I wasn't going to insult you the first time," he clarified. "You just look too cool or badass to do something as mundane as buy groceries."

"My mom hated grocery shopping," I told Dare. "I tried to find ways to make it fun for her, and later, after she got sick, I took over the job. I got a lot of satisfaction from buying things that made her happy, especially if I found a coupon to save money."

"Coupons?" He sounded like I'd spoken a language he'd never heard.

"Why wouldn't I save fifty cents on something I planned to buy anyway?" I asked. "That's the key to couponing. Only use ones for something you already planned to buy or save money on something you want to try. Otherwise, you're spending money you didn't plan to and buying things you don't really want or need."

Dare had grown silent so I briefly took my eyes off the road to look at him. His mouth hung open in an adorable way. I could only think of a few times when he was speechless. Even when my dick was in his mouth, he made little humming noises that vibrated up my cock and zapped my balls.

"What's the matter with you?" I asked, refocusing my eyes on the road.

"Are you one of those crazy coupon people? Do you go into the store and get three carts of groceries for eleven dollars and forty-nine cents?"

"That's a very specific number, Sparkles."

"It's the first number that came to mind," he said casually. "I need to know before this relationship goes any further, Wren. Will you someday back your truck into the driveway and unload enough toilet paper to wipe our asses for a hundred years." He gasped dramatically again. "Are you a prepper too?"

"Unless you're talking about condoms and lube, the answer is no."

"To which part?"

"I don't do extreme couponing or have a doomsday plan. I do believe in having extra condoms and lube on hand. That's as prepped as I get," I told him.

"I could bust your balls about the extra condoms and lube," Dare told me.

"You just busted my balls this morning."

"Don't split hairs with me, Wren."

"I never have split ends, Sparkles. It would ruin my rep as a stylist." I pulled into the grocery store parking lot and was glad to see it wasn't busy. I might like buying groceries, but I hated crowds.

"You're just full of it today," Dare said when he opened his door. He didn't wait for me to get out before he started walking toward the entrance.

I caught up to him and wrapped my arm around him. "Nah, I'm pretty empty because I already spilled 'it' down your throat this morning."

Dare's steps faltered, but he didn't stop walking. We bought groceries for the week and argued over who was paying for them at the register. I won. I let Dare decide where he wanted to store them—his place or mine. It didn't matter to me because I would go where he went, do what he wanted to do. I wasn't that surprised when he chose his house after having a nice visit with Ralph.

We put away groceries and started laundry—mundane things that shouldn't have made me so happy. Once the washer was started, I took Dare up to his room and showed him that I still had something left in my tank after all.

Chapter
Twenty-One

Dave

GRANDPA WAS MOVED TO A NURSING HOME THAT WAS halfway between Blissville and Goodville by the end of the week. His mood had fluctuated considerably as they weaned him off the pain meds, but his spirits mostly remained high. As promised, I brought him the box of letters that he and Grandma exchanged while he was in Korea, but I didn't stop there. To make his new room feel more like home, I brought framed photographs to set on his dresser and television stand. My favorite photo was the one where Grandma held my dad as a newborn baby. The look of love and adoration on her face was so beautiful. Grandpa's favorite picture was the one someone took the day they eloped. Grandpa had worn his military uniform and Grandma wore a light-colored dress that I assumed was white. It was a black-and-white photo, so I couldn't be sure. I placed that picture on his bedside table closest to him.

I also brought his favorite blanket, flannel bathrobe and his comfy slippers. I only brought enough clothes for ten days since I wasn't sure how big his dresser and closet were. I'd met with the nursing home coordinator and she explained the services that would be provided to him, which included weekly laundry. My favorite thing about the nursing home was the relaxed visiting hours since I worked a lot of evenings. Grandpa was worth getting out of bed early to see, but it was nice to know it wasn't necessary.

Wren kept Grandpa company while Mom, Dad, and I toured the facility and met Grandpa's team of doctors, therapists, and a nutritionist. Since Grandpa didn't have many dietary restrictions, he was able to eat almost everything they served. I knew the food would probably be blander than he preferred, but I was impressed with the first meal they served to him while we were there.

All things considered, life was looking up. Grandpa had a good appetite and his spirits were high. Rumors already started to circulate after his first week that he was a card shark, which Wren thought was hilarious. He even encouraged Grandpa's bad behavior by giving him a fist bump after Grandpa's favorite nurse, Jake, told us about his questionable behavior during activity time.

"Your grandpa is a hoot," Jake told us one afternoon. "I can see that the two of you are a lot alike." Wren, of course, thought the nurse was flirting with me and staked his claim. Luckily for all of us that just meant his hand on my lower back. I must admit to the thrill that snaked its way up my spine when Wren acted a little caveman-ish. I tried not to encourage it, or exploit it, but I didn't exactly discourage him either. I sure as fuck curled my toes and shouted a horny hallelujah each time he drove home the point that I belonged to him when we were alone.

It was hard to say that life returned to normal, because Grandpa wasn't living with me anymore, but we began a new normal that included Sunday family dinners at the nursing home now. I loved watching Wren interact with my family and was grateful my mom no longer ogled him like she did the first time she laid eyes on him.

Things were going great at the salon too. Curl Up and Dye was featured as one of the best salons in the state and Josh won businessman of the year from the local rotary club. He was even approached about opening a second location in Cincinnati, but I suspected he would pass up the offer. He was too hands-on with his salon and couldn't be two places at once. He also had his weekly news segments on Channel Eleven that he filmed every Monday, and of course, his twin toddlers. Maybe he'd begin a Curl Up and Dye franchise, but I suspected that day was way off in the future.

I was happy for Josh's success, but it really made me hungry for my own. As much as I truly enjoyed my job at the salon, it didn't allow me to do what I did best. I had hated working at O'Dell's, but I loved the opportunity to see my designs become reality. Even the most difficult clients who doubted my sanity ended up loving the finished project. I missed that so much more than I could've predicted. I spent a lot of my free time working on various design concepts just to stay connected to my passion.

"There has to be a design company that would love to hire someone as talented as you," Wren said one night after dinner.

"I'd have to drive to Cincinnati each day or move closer," I told him. "Neither of those options appeal to me. I'd really love to be my own boss someday, but I know I have to start small. Hell, I'd be happy to do something like the garage apartment remodel for someone. That turned out beautifully."

"It's stunning," Wren said. "Not that I'm there very often. Andy did an excellent job with your design." I could tell how much he hated saying it, but it was true. "You know, I don't see why you can't set up a small business and work from home. Give yourself a name, create a website and a social media presence, and see what happens. Be sure to post before and after pictures of the garage apartment. I bet you know several clients from O'Dell's that would continue to use you or give you excellent references at the very least."

"You really think it's a good idea?"

"I think it's a great idea," Wren corrected. "It might take a long time for it to take off or you might end up doing this full time before you know it. I know you love Josh and everyone at the salon, but that's not the career you're meant to have, Sparkles."

I gave it some serious thought for the next few weeks but didn't act on it. Out of the blue, Andy knocked on our door one night after working on the vacant house across the street. I didn't ask about the interior, but it must've been in a real mess when he bought the house since it was taking him so long. Then again, he worked on the house in between paying jobs.

"Yeah?" Wren asked when he answered the door.

Andy snorted. "Good to see you too. Is Dare home? I'd like to propose to him. I mean, propose something to him. B-b-business proposal," Andy stammered. I couldn't see Wren's expression from where I sat on the couch, but I could see his body language and understood why Andy sounded so nervous after his blunder.

I walked to the door and placed my hand on Wren's tense shoulder. "Let the man in, babe." Wren took a few begrudging steps to the side and Andy smiled at me in relief. "What's up?"

"As I was telling Wren, I have something *business* related that I'd like to propose to you."

"I'm all ears," I told Andy. "Come in and have a seat."

"That's okay. I won't take long."

"That's nothing to brag about," Wren whispered under his breath just loud enough for me to hear. I elbowed him in the ribs, but not hard enough to do any real damage. Who was I kidding? I might as well have punched a mountain. Wren didn't even grunt to indicate he felt it.

"I'm almost finished renovating the house across the street and will want to list it for sale soon," Andy said. "A realtor friend of mine recommended that I stage the house when I list it. Is that something you're familiar with?"

Excitement blossomed at the idea of working on even the simplest of projects. "Sure! You rent furniture, art, rugs, and décor for as many rooms as you want," I explained. "There are a few stores in Cincinnati that I've worked with dozens of times. I'd be more than happy to help you."

"I'd pay you, of course. I wouldn't ask you to work for free."

"Let's go in the kitchen and discuss what you envision for a design and I can start putting a plan together."

"Are you sure?" Andy asked, but he wasn't looking at me. I cleared my throat and pulled Wren and Andy's attention back to me.

"*I'm* positive," I told him. "Would you like a cup of coffee or something cold to drink?"

"No, but thank you."

I grabbed my laptop off the counter where I had left it and pulled a notebook and pen from a drawer. "I'm going to assume that you want to keep the cost down. Basic furniture, maybe an area rug, but not a lot of décor or artwork. Does that sound right to you?"

"Yeah," Andy said. "I want people to get a feel for the home but not have so much crap in there that they can't imagine their own stuff in the space. I hear that's important."

"Very," I agreed. "The same is true with the design. If you go too strong in one direction, then people can't see any other design for that space."

"Makes sense." Andy nodded. "How many rooms do we stage?"

"That really depends on your budget, but would you like my advice?"

"Of course," Andy said, nodding. "That's why I'm here."

"Let's just focus on the key rooms: kitchen, living room, bathroom, and master bedroom. Can I see the place tomorrow and get a feel for the layout so I can start putting a proposal together for you? I don't charge a consultation fee. Once I know how big the project is, I can put together a fee schedule for you. Does that sound fair?"

"Very." Andy nodded his head some more. "Tomorrow night is good for me. What time?"

"Six-thirty? I'm having dinner with Grandpa since it's my early night at the salon."

"Works fine for me. I'll see you then." Andy stood up, shook my hand, and headed for the door. "Later, Wren," he tossed over his shoulder.

Wren grunted. Once we were alone, he pulled me onto his lap and wrapped his arms around me. "You have your first client."

"Not yet, I don't. It's never a good idea to get my hopes up until a contract is signed."

"Did you have many people reject your designs?" he asked.

"Reject? No. Take my designs to someone else to do them cheaper? Yes."

"That's a dick move," Wren said. "At least Andy won't do that to you."

I raised a brow. "Are you friends with Andy now?"

"No, but I can tell he's a straight shooter."

"Can you now?" I teased.

"Quit busting my balls and start getting serious about making a business plan. You need a snazzy name to play off your nickname," Wren said. He rotated his eyes up to the ceiling as he thought it over.

"Sparkles?" I asked.

"The other one," Wren answered.

"Right There, Baby?"

"Getting warmer," Wren told me.

"Yes! Yes! Yes!"

"Dare!" Wren exclaimed.

"What? Why are you yelling? I'm sitting right here."

"Use Dare in the name of the business, or some form of it. Daring Designs or something."

"Truth or Dare?" I suggested.

"No, but we can play that later if you're lucky."

"All jokes aside, I see what you mean about the name. I'll try to come up with something catchy but not cheesy. I'll need a website, which I can set up myself, and business cards."

"Social media accounts too."

"Got it," I replied.

I thought about it for the rest of the night but couldn't decide on a name. So far, I didn't like any business name that used Dare in the title. I thought it might scare off people with conservative design styles.

The next night I met Andy at his house across the street without Wren. I took pictures of the room layouts and measured the square footage of the spaces we were going to stage.

"Andy, I don't know what it looked like before, but this house is going to be a showstopper when we get through with it. Can I make a suggestion about the furniture choices?"

"Sure."

"Let's just go with a neutral gray palette with small pops of color here and there. Let your craftsmanship be the showpiece here. That rustic mantel is gorgeous up against the white brick fireplace. We want that to be the focal point, not the sofa."

"Sounds good to me."

I gave him a verbal description of the layout I had in mind and the type of furniture I saw in my head. When we stood in the dining room, I happened to glance out the window and saw Wren sitting in Grandpa's recliner. I'd have taken that thing to the nursing home if I could, but they drew the line at furniture. Wren had never sat in that chair before, and I knew it wasn't a coincidence that he was sitting in it now. He kept his eyes aimed at the television but he wasn't fooling me.

I turned away from the window and caught Andy's eye. I realized that he had stayed within view of that window the entire time I'd been there. I just shook my head and continued with the discussion. "I didn't originally mention this to you last night, but I wasn't aware this house had such a lovely dining room." I looked up at the tray ceilings and crown molding. "I think that the dining room has to be high on the list of rooms for staging. We can back off one of the other rooms if..."

"No, it's fine. I really like everything you've said so far. So, what's next?"

"I put together a design proposal and fee schedule for you to approve," I answered. "If you do, then I place the order for furniture and schedule a delivery."

"How long will that take you?"

"I'll have a proposal to you by the end of the week," I told him. "Delivery of furniture can take days or weeks depending on how much you order and if they have our pieces available. I can take you to a few showrooms if you'd like."

"I trust you," Andy said quickly. I figured it had more to do with the hulk of a man across the street, but I let it pass without comment.

"I'll be in touch soon," I told him before I left.

I didn't exactly stomp across the street, but it was close.

"Bad meeting, Sparkles?" Wren asked after I slammed the front door shut.

"It was a great meeting," I replied. "The best I ever had." That earned a raised brow. "I'm pretty sure I got my first paying customer."

"So why do you look so mad?"

"Why are you sitting in that chair, Wren?"

"I wasn't aware that Grandpa's chair was off-limits. I'm pretty sure he'd want me to sit in it and get good use out of it. I bet he stays awake at night worrying that we're neglecting his chair."

"You're so full of shit," I said, trying to hold back the laughter. "You were spying on us."

"I wouldn't do that," he said, shaking his head.

"You would, and more importantly, you did." I shook my head slowly. "This kind of behavior can't go unpunished, Wren."

"Oh, what are you going to do to me?"

"I don't know right now, but it's going to be diabolical." The solution came to me that night just before I fell asleep. It looked like I needed to make another trip to Kim's Toys.

Chapter
Twenty-Two

Wren

BEFORE I KNEW IT, MARCH HAD ARRIVED WITH A whispered promise of pleasant weather that Mother Nature would most likely viciously yank back at any second. A person didn't pack away their winter gear in Southern Ohio in March, or even April for that matter, because that fickle beyotch, Mother Nature, giveth then taketh away. One day it could be a warm, sunny day in the upper fifties and the very next it could be a blizzard. You'd go from windows down and radio blaring, to bunkering down all wrapped up in a burrito of blankets. Now, if that burrito of blankets also included a sexy, naked man who you loved more than your next breath, you find it really hard to be upset when the weather turned cold again.

My life had changed so much since I met Dare that I almost

didn't recognize it, or myself. It got harder every day to plant an indifferent mask on my face when Dare lit me on fire from within. However, it was comical to see the shock on people's faces when I laughed or smiled.

"Did you ever watch *Beauty and the Beast*?" Dare asked me one afternoon at the salon. I quirked a brow and he shook his head in disappointment. "Of course not, but we can change all that now that I've domesticated you."

"Domesticated me?" I wasn't a fucking alley cat or stray dog!

"Mellowed you out," Dare suggested instead. "Don't get stuck on that part of the conversation, love. Pay attention and keep up." Then he aimed a disarming smile at me before continuing with the story about a prince who was changed into a beast and his castle full of servants who were turned into objects like brooms, candelabras, and teapots.

"You and your fairy tales," I muttered under my breath.

"We all want a fairy tale, Wren. The difference is in the type of fairy tale and the outcome. No two people's happily ever after is the same. And that's how it should be." This was said to me in a deadpan, serious voice like you'd expect someone to use while discussing the history of the world. My guy took his fairy tales and happily ever after very serious, but I already knew that.

"Tell me more," I told him.

Dare continued to tell me in fine detail about how Belle was their only hope of breaking the spell. For that to happen, Beast needed her to fall in love with him. "True love fixes everything," Dare said dramatically. "Anyway, there's this one scene in the movie that Beast is trying to look less threatening and he smiles at Belle, but it's all teeth. He looks like he wants to eat her for lunch instead of...."

"Maybe he does. Did you ever stop to think about that?"

"No, Wren! Don't go there with my fairy-tale heroes and heroines!" He wasn't joking either.

"I'm sorry, Sparkles. I didn't mean any offense."

"It's okay," Dare reassured me. "Some things are too precious to sexualize like my Disney characters and Santa Claus."

"*Santa Claus?*"

"There's porn for everything, Wren." He shook his head like he couldn't believe my ignorance. "Back to my story." Dare pinned me with a look that warned me not to interrupt him again. Fuck, I crazy loved him. "Anyway, that's kind of how you're smiling right now at people. You're showing a lot of teeth."

"So, it's not a shock that I know how to smile? I just have big, ugly teeth?"

Dare dropped his head to the kitchenette table and sat there a few seconds. When he raised his head, he was mostly composed. "I never said they looked big and ugly."

"Sharp then?"

"You have perfect fucking teeth, Ruler!" Dare had started calling me that after he learned the significance of my name. He said I ruled both his body and his heart. I fucking liked it a lot. I called the bedroom we shared the Fortress of Fuckery. "They're just not used to seeing them because you usually only give those smiles to me. Maybe I should be hurt that you're sharing them with the world now. Just doling those smiles out all willy-nilly like for just anyone to see."

"I smile for you and because of you."

"Oh," Dare said, covering his heart with his hand. "That's a good one, Ruler."

By this point, I stopped pretending to live anywhere other than Dare's house. I'd spent every night in his bedroom wrapped around him while we slept. More often than not, I woke up with him plastered to my side with his leg thrown over my hip so that I couldn't escape him. I had no intentions of running from him ever again. He was my fairy tale, happily ever after, and whatever else romantic people called it. Moving in together just seemed like a natural progression to me. I didn't see a need for a big discussion, but Dare wasn't on the same page.

He bought this amazing cock ring that had tiny little bullets that vibrated my sac. He too had his very own little remote and loved to torture me by bringing me right to the edge before he let off. The first time he used it was to get even for me spying on him and Andy at the house across the street. I kind of laughed Dare off that he wouldn't get a confession out of me, but I sang like a fucking canary. I would've done anything to come. He used the same tactic to *convince* me that I should move in with him.

"How can you trust that I'm living here for the right reasons after you coerced me?" I asked after I came hard enough to rupture a nut.

"Coerce you?" Dare scoffed. "Baby, this was a promise of good things to come."

"Oh," I'd said seconds before I lapsed into a deep sleep.

The next morning, Dare looked hesitant when he came down for breakfast. "Are those pancakes?" he asked, sniffing the air.

"Blueberry," I told him. "I thought it was an excellent way to commemorate our big moment."

"About that, Wren…"

I slid the last two pancakes on our plates and carried them to the table. "Having second thoughts this morning? Buyer's regret?"

"Not me," Dare said, rolling his eyes. "What about you?"

"Dare, do you seriously think you could convince me to move in with you if I didn't want to be here? You know me better than anyone, or at least I thought you did."

"I do," he rushed to say.

"That's a line best saved for another day," I teased. It was my turn to get nervous when Dare turned pale. I thought he might blush prettily, but the opposite happened.

"Um…" I wasn't sure how to back away from my mistake. "I forgot to get the butter and syrup out of the refrigerator."

"Butter?" Dare asked. "Who eats butter on their pancakes? It ruins the taste of the syrup."

"Um, everybody eats butter on their pancakes *with* the syrup because it *enhances* the taste, not ruins it." I shook my head as I walked away.

"I draw the line if you put ketchup on scrambled eggs, Wren. I mean it," Dare declared. "I can't live with someone who desecrates something as delicious as scrambled eggs."

"Gross," I said. There would be times that I would do something just to get a rise out of him but putting ketchup on scrambled eggs wasn't one of them. "How do you feel about salsa on eggs?"

Dare tipped his head to the side and pondered my question for a few seconds. "I can live with that. I would even try that myself."

"Then I see no reason why this can't work between us. We love each other and are committed to this relationship. We're mature adults who know what we want."

"We are, and we do."

"I want to fall asleep beside you every night and look at your face every morning. I want to be the person you turn to when you want to vent, celebrate, cry, or make love."

"Obviously."

"Speaking of fucking—"

"You said 'make love' not fucking," Dare pointed out.

"Same difference."

"It's not and we both know it."

"When it comes to us it's the same," I countered. "When I fuck you, I do it with love. Therein lies the difference."

"Therein?"

"I know words, Dare. I have depth."

"Mmmm hmmmm," Dare replied. "Eat your breakfast so we can explore your depth."

That was how we confirmed that the discussion we had during sex was still valid and we both wanted the same thing. Neither of us commented again on my "I do" remark, even though I knew that every day I spent with him was one day closer to saying it again. Only the next time, we would be wearing something snazzier than sleep pants and T-shirts, there would be considerably more people to bear witness, and those two words would hold significantly more meaning. Life was uncertain, I'd learned that the hard way, but giving Dare the fairy tale he dreamed of was an absolute certainty.

The first step in securing an amazing future was healing my broken past. I started that process the night I cried in Dare's arms when I talked about my mom and really let myself mourn her loss. I took another baby step forward when I extended a tiny olive twig toward Alaric the night we showed up at the same restaurant on the river. It wasn't enough though, I needed to do more.

On a sunny day in mid-March, Dare and I went to Alaric and Samantha's for dinner. It was a surreal moment when Alaric answered the door barefoot in ratty jeans and a T-shirt. I wasn't looking at the man who broke my mom's heart, or the Rock King, I was looking at my dad. Alaric held my infant brother, Tobias, in his arms who smiled and shook his fists in the air.

"Toby says hello," Alaric said.

"Oh my gosh, you are so cute," Dare said, using a voice a person reserves for babies and animals.

"Do you want to hold him?" Alaric asked.

"Sure," Dare replied, holding out his arms. "I love babies."

"Come on in and let's have a drink. Sam is in the kitchen putting together some appetizers before the main course is finished."

"We didn't want her to go to any trouble," I told Alaric as we followed him through the large house. Mansion wasn't the right word because the house wasn't pretentious, but it was grander than anything I'd ever seen up close and personal. "We would be happy with pizza."

"Nonsense," Alaric responded. "We're happy to do it. Besides, I'm the one making the main course. I have a pork roast in the smoker as we speak. Sam handled the appetizers."

"We brought dessert," Dare added, and I held up the cake carrier. He had insisted, and my dad reluctantly agreed. "It's my grandmother's carrot cake recipe. Trust me when I say that you'll never eat cake as good as this."

"Sounds delicious."

Samantha was working at a massive kitchen island. It had a sink in the middle and high-back stools that lined the opposite side.

"Hey, guys," she said happily when she looked up and saw our approach. "Tobias, did you make a new friend already?"

"I'm not sure he likes my hairstyle," Dare said. I looked over and saw that Tobias had two fists full of Dare's hair. "He thinks I need a new stylist."

"Everyone's a critic," I teased. I reached over and patted Tobias's back, and he jerked his head around to look at me. I would swear that the kid was sizing my hair up too.

"You better tie that back if you want to have any left when you leave here," Alaric said, gesturing to his ponytail.

"Are you guys hungry?" Samantha asked. "I have ham, cream cheese, and jalapeño roll-ups, shrimp cocktail, and a fruit and cheese plate."

"It sounds delicious," I told her. "We haven't eaten since early this morning and the salon was a zoo today. Rather than ruin our appetite for dinner, we decided to grind it out."

"Oh, I can't do that," Samantha said, shaking her head. "If my blood sugar gets low then you better watch out."

"I have the scars to prove it," Alaric said, kissing her on the cheek.

"More where those came from if you don't watch it." Alaric nuzzled her neck then with his beard and made her giggle. Samantha kept giggling and elbowing to get him to stop. When he finally did, she looked over at me. I could tell she was unsure what my reaction would be to the obvious affection between them.

"If he's like me, the back of his thighs are particularly ticklish spots. You can probably get him to agree to anything if you use it to your advantage," I suggested to her.

Samantha's relief was swift and palpable. "I know all about that one already." She winked and gave me one of her genuine smiles. "I like you."

"I like you too." Just like that, the tension was gone, and it was like it had never existed.

After appetizers, Samantha took us on the tour of their new house. "We've only been in here a few weeks, so we're still adjusting to where everything is. It still doesn't feel like home yet. I don't know why that it is."

"Can I be blunt, Samantha?" Dare asked.

"Sure," she said.

"As beautiful as this house is, it doesn't feel like you and Alaric." He held up his hand. "Granted, I don't really know either of you that well, but the home lacks the warmth I associate with you."

"That's what I said to Alaric, but he pointed out that we'd hired an interior decorator who put this together after meeting with us. To be fair, I did approve the designs."

"Not all designers are created equally," Dare said. "It's the same with any profession. You really need to get to know your client's likes and dislikes. Take these for example." He gestured to some beige-looking throw pillow. "I would've added a teal or jade pillow in there for contrast. Maybe even a deep purple."

"Wait, are you a designer?" Samantha asked.

"That's what I went to college for, but I haven't engaged in the business as much as I had hoped."

"He started his own business though," I told Samantha. "Charming Designs." I nudged Dare because this was a huge opportunity for him. "Tell her your tagline. It's adorable and Dare is a very talented guy."

"Wren," Dare said under his breath like he was embarrassed by my compliments.

"Creating castles one room at a time," I told Samantha.

"That is cute," she said. "Everybody has a fairy tale."

"So I've heard," I replied, but I only had eyes for Dare who was still holding a sleepy Tobias. I knew I was looking at my future and it made me deliriously happy.

"Dinner!" Alaric bellowed from the kitchen. "This meal is to die for."

"I hope he doesn't mean literally," I whispered to Dare as we followed Samantha to the kitchen. Dare elbowed me in the ribs and shushed me.

Alaric's smoked pork was as epic as he promised, better even. I couldn't remember the last time I had anything so good. I looked at Dare and said, "Babe, we need a smoker for the house."

"Have you two officially moved in together?" Alaric asked. A few months ago, I would've looked for a hidden slight in every word. I was doing much better at taking his words at face value.

"We have," I told him. "It seemed silly to pretend that I wanted to be anywhere else."

"That's so sweet," Samantha said then turned to my dad. "You're the songwriter, but you never say sweet things like that."

"I put them in the songs that I write for you," Alaric said.

"True," she conceded. "You do have a way with words." To me, she said, "Keep up the good work, Wren."

After dinner, Dare and I offered to do the dishes. Of course, they declined, but we didn't listen. We just started gathering dishes and carrying them to the kitchen anyway.

"The brussels sprouts were a thing of beauty," Dare said mournfully looking at the empty dish. "I need to get that recipe. I could pick out some of the herbs, but not all."

Samantha entered the kitchen and winked at Dare. "I'll get you the recipe if you let me do the dishes with Wren. I'd really like a few minutes alone with him, if that's okay."

Dare looked at me, and I nodded. He stood on his tiptoes and kissed me before he left.

Samantha didn't say anything right away, and I figured she was choosing her words. Intelligent people didn't rush in with both guns blazing, they took their time picking the best thing to say.

"I don't think Alaric will appreciate me telling you this, but I think you have a right to know what happened between your parents back in the day." She reached over and placed her hand over mine when I stiffened. "Honey, I'm not about to run your mama down or anything. I know a side to the story that you don't, and I truly hope it helps heal the rift between you and your dad once and for all."

I dried my hands on the towel and turned my full attention to her.

"You know by now that your dad left Cincinnati and pretty much never looked back. He stopped here on tours, but that's it. Do you know why?"

"I thought it was to escape my mom."

"He never intended to leave her behind for good, but Alaric was surrounded by people who only cared for themselves, not what was best for him."

"Tony Durano," I said between gritted teeth.

"Your mother called Alaric many times, but Tony always intercepted the messages at the hotels or the recording studio. When she finally put her foot down and told Tony that she was pregnant with you, it triggered a series of horrible events." Samantha closed her eyes and shook her head slowly, like she wasn't sure she could finish the story.

"It's okay, Sam," I said using the nickname my father used.

"Tony told your father that he'd hired an investigator to check up on Terry because Alaric was worried that he hadn't heard from her. Tony told him that your mom had gotten tired of being alone and found a new guy. He even told him that Terry was pregnant, but he lied about how far along she was so that Alaric wouldn't leave the band. What he did to your mom was so much worse though. He sent her a telegram and money that was supposedly from your dad to pay for an abortion. Wren, he never did that. He truly loved your mom." Her chin wobbled and said. "If you only knew how much that man loves you and wants to be a part of your life."

"Don't cry, Sam." I gave her a hug to comfort her. "When did he find this out?"

"Your mom told him after she got sick. We weren't dating at the time, but he told me about it when we started getting serious. He said, 'Samantha, I have a son. He's a beautiful, angry young man filled with resentment toward me, but I hope someday that will turn around. I need you to know that I'll never choose another person, or my career, over him again.' He meant it too."

"Why didn't my parents tell me the truth after they pieced together what happened?" I asked. Why let me spend more than a decade angry at Alaric for something that wasn't his fault?

"I don't think they wanted to compound your hurt and misery. What could have been is a terrible thing to live with, especially for a boy who just lost his mom."

"Thank you for telling me now," I told Sam. "I guess Alaric fired Tony, huh?"

"He destroyed that rat bastard's career." Sam smiled softly and said, "I didn't tell you this to add any more pressure, but I knew that Alaric wouldn't do it. He would rather you hate him the rest of his life than hurt another minute over things neither of you could control. He still took most of the blame because fame had gone to his head and he lost sight of who he was and did let your mom down."

"Thanks, Sam."

"You're welcome," she replied. "I'm going to speak to Dare about some design ideas. I know he's going to argue with me about paying him, but I'm not taking advantage of his kindness because he's family."

"You're going to have a fight on your hands," I assured her.

"I'm a lawyer, sweetheart. I can talk around him in circles." She stopped suddenly and said, "Did you know that Alaric wrote a song about you? It's called If You Only Knew."

"I'll give it a listen. Thank you."

When it was time to leave, I skipped the handshake and hugged Alaric. He stiffened in surprise but loosened up and hugged me back, lingering like maybe he might not get another chance. "Can we do lunch next week?" I asked

"I'd really like that, Wren."

"I'll call you… Dad."

Alaric's eyes widened in surprise, but he smiled like I'd given him the greatest gift in the world. And I had: forgiveness.

Dare stayed up late working on designs for Sam while I watched television. It wasn't until he fell asleep that I downloaded If You Only Knew and listened to it. The song was about regret and yearning for a second chance. Most people would've assumed that it was written for a woman, but I heard the truth in the lyrics. Plus, the first letter in the four versus spelled my name. When I went to sleep that night, I knew I'd found the peace with my past that would allow me to have an amazing future.

Chapter
Twenty-Three

Dave

THE FOLLOWING WEEK, WREN ANNOUNCED THAT I WAS going to be redesigning the interior of his dad and stepmom's new house during dinner with my family at Grandpa's nursing home.

"You're going to be the interior designer for Falcon's new house?" my mom said, covering her chest. "That's amazing."

"Congratulations, Son," my father said proudly. "Nice work."

"Cool. Does he have an indoor pool or bowling alley?" Kristy asked.

"When do you start?" Grandpa wanted to know.

"Wait a minute," I said, holding up my hand. "Nothing has been decided yet. I sent some preliminary proposals to Samantha to look over, and we're meeting later in the week to look at my 3D renderings."

"Babe, you've got this job," Wren said calmly. "You let me read the email she sent you in response to the proposals. What part of 'OMG! You are simply amazing!' gives you the impression that she's thinking about going a different direction?"

"You know my philosophy, Wren. I don't consider them a client until they sign a contract."

"It's a good plan, Dare," my dad said. "You're pretty damn practical for a creative person."

I snorted. My dad believed people were either A- or B-type personalities, when a lot of people had tendencies from both, even if they leaned stronger in one direction over the other.

"I understand, Sparkles, but my gut tells me that you'll be designing that house. I think this could open a lot of possibilities for you. I think you're one design away from seeing your dreams become a reality."

There were so many things that I loved about Wren, but his commitment to seeing my dreams come true was near the top of the list. Of course, I teased him about wanting to get a break from me. Working together and living together was bound to take its toll eventually. I suggested that perhaps I was wearing on his nerves and he was getting sick of me. Wren blew it off, or blew me, to prove that wasn't the case at all.

"Thanks, babe." I only called him Ruler in private. I didn't want people getting the wrong impression about our relationship. Of course, he didn't hesitate to call me Sparkles in front of anyone.

Sparkles and Ruler, two very different nicknames for two very different men. We didn't just mesh though; we gelled. Like all successful couples, we pulled from each other's strengths and learned from our weaknesses. In Wren, I found a man who surpassed any fairy-tale knight I'd ever dreamt of, who put my dreams and concerns above his own, and showed me in the most beautiful ways how much I meant to him. With me, Wren knew his fears and sorrows were as sacred to me as his heart, his smiles, and his laughter.

He recognized that no one and nothing would get in the way of my love for him.

"Wow, Falcon's house," my mom said, earning a glare from my dad. He didn't mind her crush when the rock star idol from her youth was nothing more than a fantasy she would never meet, but it was different when I started dating his son and could get her access to the legend.

"He lives there with his wife and infant son," my dad reminded her.

Grandpa cackled, and I smiled at him. It did my heart good to see him smile and laugh. He caught me staring at him and winked at me. "Say, Dare, do you want to be my euchre partner on Wednesday night in the tournament?"

"Sure, Grandpa. I'd be honored."

"Good, we need to work on silent signals to communicate. I hear that Bob and Teddy win every single year. They're a bit too cocky for my taste, and I'd like to put them in their place."

"Wouldn't you rather do that by winning fair and square?" I asked.

"Not really," he said, dismissing the idea.

"Sure, we can work on silent signals."

Wren and I stuck around for a while after Mom, Dad, and Kristy left. Grandpa instructed me to wear a ballcap and sunglasses when I showed up for the tournament.

"This isn't poker, Grandpa."

"Don't sass me, boy. My reputation is on the line."

"Yes, sir." I bit my lip to keep from laughing and Wren coughed to cover up the laugh that escaped him.

We rolled through some signs, but nothing too obvious, and Grandpa found ways to change them up so that the other players didn't catch on to us. The signs were touching my earlobe, the bill of my cap, or bringing my hand to my chin while I pretended to ponder my hand. After Grandpa assigned the meaning of each gesture, he gave me strict instructions to follow.

"Listen, we need to throw in some fake signals to confuse them. Like looking over your glasses at your cards or something. We need to have a sequence of signs like a baseball coach, so only you and I know what we're saying. I need you to look natural when you throw out a few fake signals. Two fake, the real deal, then a final fake one. If we make it to the semi-final and final rounds, we'll change the order around for the real signal," he said seriously. "Let's practice."

"I understand, Grandpa," I told him.

"I still want to practice a few times," he insisted. "Just to be sure." It didn't take him long to realize that I had well and truly caught on. "Okay, get on home so I can get some rest," he said shooing me out. "And, Dare," he said after I kissed him and headed to the door. "Congratulations on landing your first big client."

"Grandpa, I—"

"I know," he said ruefully. "You don't like to count your chickens before they hatch, but I have a really good feeling about this."

"Thank you."

"I'm so proud of you, Dare. I couldn't ask for a finer grandson."

I felt myself tearing up beneath his praise. "I'm proud of you too, Grandpa. We're going to kick some serious euchre ass on Wednesday."

"You damn betcha!"

Wren slipped his arm around my shoulders as we headed for his truck. "I know it's still hard to leave him here, but surely you see how happy he is, Sparkles. There's no faking that kind of fighting spirit. It's something you're born with and life brings it to the surface."

"I know he's doing really well, but yeah, I miss him."

"I'm sure he misses you too. When the weather warms up, we can pick Grandpa up and take him someplace for the day."

"Okay, but can we pretend like we're busting him out of there?"

"You got it," Wren told me. "Have I ever told you how special you are?"

"For loving my grandpa?"

"What you do for him goes beyond love," Wren said. "Trust me, all those nurses talk about how special you are."

"All of them or just one?" I asked.

Wren narrowed his eyes at me. "Is there one nurse in particular that you're most concerned about? One that wears his scrubs two sizes too small so everyone can notice his *assets*?"

"You've obviously been paying a lot of attention to Jake." Jealousy didn't sound good on me.

"I've noticed *him* noticing *you*."

"Not that again," I said, rolling my eyes. I was about to say more, but my phone rang. "Hey, Andy," I said into my phone. "What's up?"

"We sold the house!"

"What? Already? You've only showed it one time."

"They gave me full asking price too. Becker told them the house would go fast when he showed it. He said they should hurry if they wanted to make an offer, and so they did."

"Wow! Congratulations, Andy."

"I couldn't have done it so fast without you, Dare. Since this flip was so successful, I'm thinking about trying it again soon. Are you interested in doing the interior design if I do?"

"I'd love to," I replied. Wren narrowed his eyes, although I have no idea what he thought I was agreeing to with him standing right there. "Let me know the next time you buy a house to flip."

"I will. Say, are you interested in advertising your business on my website. I'm thinking about adding a section for my business partners to make it easier for people to find quality work and services."

"Andy, that would be amazing. I would like to do the same for you on my site. Wren and I are so thrilled with the work you did at our garage apartment. We have a potential tenant looking at the space on Tuesday."

"It's a great apartment, and you'll have it rented out in no time."

"I hope so," I told him. We chatted for a few more minutes before I said goodbye to Andy and pocketed my phone. "Andy sold the house," I told Wren, looking at him across the bed of his truck.

"I guessed as much from hearing your side of the conversation," Wren replied wryly. "Get in the truck, Sparkles. The faster we get home the quicker we can celebrate."

"Oh, wow. This apartment is much bigger than I would've guessed," our potential tenant, Julius Shepherd, said. "Especially for the rent you're charging. I paid three times as much in my hometown and my apartment would fit in the bathroom of this one."

"Where's your hometown again?" Wren asked. He was going for casual, but I saw through him. He was sizing the guy up to see if he could be competition. Okay, the guy lit up a bit when I answered the door, but he dialed it down when he saw Prince Chest Thumper join us on the porch.

"Philly born and raised," Julius said proudly.

"Blissville is a far cry different than Philly," Wren said.

"It was time for a new beginning," Julius explained. "Plus, the science program at Blissville High School is ranked in the top five percent in the entire country. I couldn't pass up an opportunity to teach there." He had that nerdy science guy thing down to an art, but it was adorable on him. "I'm ready to fill out the application and get the ball rolling."

Julius followed us back to the house and filled out the application. After he left, I ran credit and background reports while Wren called his references. An hour later, I called Julius and let him know that the apartment was his.

"First and last month's rent up front," I told him.

"No problem," he said. "I'm staying in a hotel in Goodville. Do you mind if I come by tomorrow to sign the lease and pay you?"

"That sounds great, but can you do it before five? I'm in a euchre tournament with my grandpa at his nursing home."

Julius chuckled. "Sure thing."

He ended up stopping by the salon at noon. Julius was all smiles and happiness until he saw the client sitting in Wren's chair. When the new superintendent, Romeo Bradley, looked over and caught the young science teacher staring at him, Julius looked away quickly and turned a pretty shade of pink.

"Um, I'll just sign this so I can be on my way."

Did I just let it go? Do you even know me? "Hey, isn't that the new superintendent of Blissville schools?" I asked.

"Um, yeah," Julius said casually, staring at the form he had read the day before. "That's him."

"Silver fox," I said, practically purring.

Julius shrugged, but his face turned a brighter shade of pink. I glanced over at the silver fox in question and saw that he seemed pretty taken with the teacher also. Only after Wren asked him a question did he return his focus back to my guy. I wondered if Wren saw the exchange too. If so, we could place bets on how long it would take before Julius started staying away at night or we caught Superintendent Silver Fox sneaking away from Julius's apartment. I was suddenly glad we had ringside seats for this little romance.

I might've chalked it up to my wild imagination, but I caught Julius checking out the older man from the corner of his eye a few times. He stiffened when Romeo Bradley stood up and headed in our direction. Julius picked up the pen to sign the leasing agreement, but it was out of ink.

"Oh dear," I said. "Try this one." I handed him another. It didn't work either. "What the heck is going on? These pens were working just fine." I knew fate was at play, but I kept my mouth shut and kept looking for a pen that would work.

"Here, use mine," the older man said smoothly as he stepped up to my desk. "Hello again, Julius. It's good to see you."

"Hello, Mr. Bradley."

"It's Romeo or Rome," the older man told him.

Julius signed the lease and handed it to me along with the envelope containing cash for the first and last month's rent. Then he returned the pen to Romeo and said, "Thank you, Mr. Bradley. See you in a few weeks."

"Safe travel back to Philly, Julius." Romeo had no difficulty addressing the teacher by his first name. He stared after the younger man a few seconds after he left then turned his attention back to me. "Can I schedule my next appointment with Wren before I leave?"

"Sure can. Let me pull up his schedule. Does this day of the week and time slot work okay for your next appointment, or would you like a different time?"

"I would prefer something around four so that I don't worry about taking too long on my lunch hour."

"Does four thirty on April fourteenth work?" Romeo checked his schedule and confirmed the time and date. "We also have an app where you can book appointments around the clock. Are you interested?"

"Sure, where do I go?"

I told Romeo where to find the app and gave him a tutorial on my phone before I collected his payment and Wren's tip. After he left, I walked Wren's tip over to him. Had we been alone, I would've shoved that ten-dollar bill in the waistband of his ass-hugging jeans. Maybe asked him to dance for it, but Wren wouldn't find my antics funny at work.

"Ten dolla to make you holla," Wren whispered suggestively in my ear. *Or maybe he would.*

"After the salon closes," I told him.

"No good, we have the euchre tournament at the home."

"Stop calling it that."

"That's what Grandpa calls it," Wren replied.

"He's allowed because he lives there."

"Oh." Wren hooked his finger in my belt loop before I could walk away. "Raincheck on that mixing room after-hours action?"

"Definitely."

Wren and I left the salon at four o'clock so we could eat dinner with Grandpa before the tournament. I was a nervous wreck, but Grandpa looked as cool as one of those professional poker players.

"Did you give him extra meds?" I asked Jake. "He seems extra mellow."

"He's in the zone," Jake explained. "He's determined to win at all costs, so he started getting in the mindset after his nap."

"I think he's still asleep," Wren suggested. "It's hard to tell with those ridiculous aviator sunglasses on."

"Hey, he borrowed those from me," Jake said. "I think he looks badass."

I walked over to where Grandpa sat in his chair. "Ready to whip some ass, Goose?"

"No way," Grandpa said, shaking his head. "I'm Maverick, and you're Goose."

"If you say so, Grandpa."

"I do," he said. "I could've easily been mistaken for Tom Cruise in my day."

I looked just like my grandpa and no one ever told me I looked like a young Tom Cruise. I believed in letting him think what he wanted as long as he was happy and healthy.

"We'll call Wren Iceman," Grandpa said.

"Great," Wren said dryly.

"Just don't chew gum like him, or I'll slap you out of your chair."

"Yes, sir," Wren told Grandpa. "We better get to the dining room if we want to fuel our bodies for the big fight."

Grandpa was getting around so much better, but he grew tired at the end of the day and needed the assistance of a wheelchair. Wren always pushed him, and I always got a rush of love from how gentle my giant could be.

Grandpa ate his meatloaf and mashed potatoes like it was any other day of the week while I was too nervous to eat more than a few bites. "Get it together," Grandpa said when we headed toward the rec room. "Those two card sharks will eat you alive, Dare."

"Yes, sir."

"I'm counting on you."

"I won't let you down, Grandpa."

We played Irv and Gilmore the first round, and we didn't need to deploy many tricks to beat them. We played Betty and Millie the second round and had to step up our game quite a bit to make it to the semi-finals where we played Mo and Jessica, a husband and wife team that had been playing cards together for sixty years. I figured it would be hard to beat a team so in sync with each other, but we did it. I would've felt guilty, but I saw Jessica giving her husband a few signals and they weren't *I can't wait to get you alone* signs either unless Mo had an earlobe-tugging fetish.

"Look at them preening about," Grandpa said about Bob and Teddy as we neared the table set up for the finals. "Wren, make sure there are no mirrors or windows the old geezers can use to look at our cards."

It was all Wren could do to keep from losing it. Grandpa acted like they had pink slips to their race cars on the line.

"This shouldn't take long," Bob said to Teddy. "We'll be back in our rooms in time to watch *Jeopardy*."

I lowered my voice so only Grandpa could hear. "Let's rip these arrogant bastards to shreds."

"You're my favorite person on earth, Dare," Grandpa said emotionally. To our rivals, he said, "Quit your yapping and let's deal."

The match stretched out three times as long as the others, but it had more to do with the four of us trying to out-cheat one another than any real skill. In the end, only two men took home trophies.

"Congratulations, Ralph and Darren," Tiffany, the events coordinator, proudly said. "You've fought a hard battle and you get these beautiful trophies and an extra chocolate pudding to celebrate."

"Yippee!" Grandpa said when they handed him his small trophy. "Dare, spending this evening with you means more to me than this trophy. I'll have you know that."

"Aw, thank you, Grandpa. I feel the same way." I leaned down again so only he could hear me. "I love you so much that you can have my pudding too."

"Yes!" he said, waving his trophy in the air as Wren wheeled him back toward his room.

We did end up winning in enough time to watch *Jeopardy* and eat dessert. For the first time since he fell, I wasn't sad when I said goodbye to Grandpa. I finally accepted that he was happy in his surroundings and where he needed to be.

"What do you think about remodeling our house and putting our stamp on it?" I asked Wren on the way home.

"Can I choose the carpenter?" he asked.

"Yes, because I know that you're going to choose Andy too." I reached across the console and patted his knee. "I want to build a life with you in a home that feels like ours. Right now, it's still my grandparents' house."

"I think it's a great idea, and yes, I agree that Andy is the man for the job." He glanced at me in annoyance when I giggled. "Man for the construction job."

"Oh, I thought you were finally tired of me and calling in a pinch hitter."

"Not a fucking chance."

"Good, because I need victory sex after the battle I fought and won tonight."

"It was euchre in a nursing home with ninety-year-old men," Wren countered.

"Hey, Bob and Teddy are in their seventies and are wily as hell. I had to be on my game tonight, or I would've tarnished the family name."

"You're right, Sparkles. I apologize."

"Oh, good. An apology fuck," I said.

"Five," Wren said.

"Five minutes?" I asked.

"You know what number I'm talking about, Sparkles. Don't play coy with me."

My ass puckered, and blood rushed to my cock. "There's no way."

"Yeah, and people probably thought we'd never fall in love either," Wren countered. "We did, and you will."

"Everyone knew you were my prince. Now take me home and give me my happily ever after."

"Yes, dear."

Epilogue

Wren

ONCE UPON A TIME, ON A WARM JUNE DAY, A PRINCE RODE his trusted steed to a castle to ask for his lover's hand in marriage. It went a little something like this...

I was nervous as fuck when I parked the Harley and got off. It didn't help that people stared at me as I walked by them.

"I didn't know they had period actors at Chateau Laroche," one person said.

"Me either," their companion replied. "He's clearly dressed like a prince though. Let's follow and see what happens."

I cringed internally, but I had to shove all of that aside to focus on my main objective. Find my own prince and make him mine for good. I had a lot of help setting up my surprise, and I couldn't let other people's opinions count.

I looked at my watch and noted that it was almost four, which meant that I was cutting it close. I walked faster and got in position to wait for the love of my life to step onto the balcony that overlooked the castle grounds in Loveland, Ohio. It was a gorgeous stone castle built along the banks of the Little Miami River. People were milling all around enjoying the beautiful day. Some of them eyed me curiously while others grinned knowingly.

Finally, Dare stepped onto the balcony holding Tobias. My dad and Samantha stepped out after him followed by Dare's family. I don't know how they managed it, but they found a way to get Ralph up those castle steps because there was no way I was letting him miss out on the big moment. Grandpa smiled and waved from his wheelchair.

Dare looked down and saw me standing there. His eyes widened, and a smile spread across his face. He knew that I would be joining them, but he didn't expect me to be wearing a red, crushed velvet jacket, black leather pants, and biker boots. The best part of the costume by far was the ridiculous crown. I had strapped it to my motorcycle so that I could wear a helmet on my way there.

"Where's your horse, my prince?" Dare asked.

"I rode a Hog instead of a steed," I answered.

"A modern-day prince."

I dropped to one knee and looked up at my love beseechingly. "Will you do me the great honor of—" My words died when Dare handed Tobias to my dad then disappeared from the balcony.

It wasn't long before he came running across the grass. "Okay," he said, sounding a little winded after running down several flights of steps. "Now you can ask me."

"Will you—"

"Yes!" Dare launched himself at me, knocking me to my back. "I will marry you."

"I love you so much, Sparkles."

"Hey, Wren? How about we sneak up to one of the rooms they

roped off?"

"As much as I'd love to hear your cries echo off the castle walls when I make you come, I think we better pass."

"Did you say yes, Dare?" Grandpa asked.

"Yes, Grandpa." He looked down at me with tears of happiness in his eyes. "And we'll live happily ever after."

The End!

Want to be the first to know about my book releases and have access to extra content? You can sign up for my newsletter here: http://eepurl.com/dlhPYj

My favorite place to hang out and chat with my readers is my Facebook group. Would you like to be a member of Aimee's Dye Hards? We'd love to have you! Click here: www.facebook.com/groups/AimeesDyeHards

Other Books by
Aimee Nicole Walker

Only You

The Fated Hearts Series

Chasing Mr. Wright, Book 1
Rhythm of Us, Book 2
Surrender Your Heart, Book 3
Perfect Fit, Book 4
Return to Me, Book 5
Always You, Book 6
Any Means Necessary, Book 7

Curl Up and Dye Mysteries

Dyeing to be Loved
Something to Dye For
Dyed and Gone to Heaven
I Do, or Dye Trying
A Dye Hard Holiday

Road to Blissville Series

Unscripted Love
Someone to Call My Own

**The Lady is M
ine Series**

The Lady is a Thief

Coauthored with Nicholas Bella

Undisputed
Circle of Darkness (Genesis Circle, Book 1)

Standalone Novels
Second Wind

Acknowledgments

First, I need to thank my husband and children for their constant support and encouragement. It's not easy living with a writer who often disappears into a fictional world for long periods of time. They do so many things to help me out so that I can realize my dream. I love you guys more than words can ever express.

To my creative dream team, thanks seem hardly enough for all that you do. Miranda Vescio of V8 Editing and Proofreading, thank you for your tireless work, feedback, and many laughs while editing. Jay Aheer of Simply Defined art is an incredible artist, and I love how she brings my words to life. Stacey Blake of Champagne Formats is also an amazing artist who does incredible interior formatting, illustrating, and designing for e-books and paperbacks. Let's not forget Judy Zweifel of Judy's' Proofreading. She does an amazing job of finding the tiniest details that make a book shine.

To my lovely PA, Michelle Slagan. I'm not sure how I ever did this without you. I love you to the moon and back!

Lastly, I am so grateful for my beta readers and the honest feedback they provide me. Thank you for all that you do, Racheal, Kim, Laurel, Michael, Brittany, and Jodie.

About
Aimee Nicole Walker

Ever since she was a little girl, Aimee Nicole Walker entertained herself with stories that popped into her head. Now she gets paid to tell those stories to other people. She wears many titles—wife, mom, and animal lover are just a few of them. Her absolute favorite title is champion of the happily ever after. Love inspires everything she does, music keeps her sane, and coffee is the magic elixir that fuels her day.

I'd love to hear from you.

You can reach me at:

Twitter—twitter.com/AimeeNWalker

Facebook—www.facebook.com/aimeenicole.walker

Blog—AimeeNicoleWalker.blogspot.com

Sign up for my newsletter here: http://eepurl.com/dlhPYj